Don't Look at Me

J.P. Grider

Published by J.P. Grider, 2018.

Don't Look at Me
Published by
Fated Hearts Publishing
Cover design by Indie Solutions by Murphy Rae
Cover Photography by Brian Scully
Cover Model Katie Della Terza

I dedicate this book twice:

Once...

To my beautiful **mother**, Leanne, who is *nothing* like the mother portrayed in this story.

Mom, thank you for loving me unconditionally...warts and all.

And Twice...

To my **Children** and **Grandchildren**.

May you always see the inner beauty in yourselves and others.

Gauge your beauty by the reflection in the eyes of those who love you. They are the best mirrors.

– Mike Naundorff

DON'T LOOK AT ME

1.

HAVEN

If a mother's love is truly unconditional, I wouldn't be sitting behind this second-rate news desk at the ungodly hour of two a.m. striving to attain "the most sought-after newscaster" title on television just to impress her. Sometimes, when I'm alone in my car, or under the shower's hot stream of water, I can almost taste the idea of living a life where Hannah Quinn's appraisal is of no consequence to me. It's overwhelmingly satisfying. Incredibly sweet.

"Wrap it up," Eric says, circling his two fingers from his floor-manager's spot in the center of the small studio and plummeting me back to reality.

I close the segment the same way I have for the past two weeks. "Please be safe out there, Stratford. Our slasher is still roaming the streets, so buddy up. Especially at night. From my lips to your ears, this is Haven Quinn giving you your red-eye news. Thanks for staying the course."

"It's a wrap," Eric announces to the crew. To me, he says, "Wanna get a drink?" right before Devin barrels into him and says, "I'll come, too."

"Watch it, Randolph," Eric tells him, addressing him by his last name. "And you're not coming. You're not invited."

"Let me get my purse," I say to Eric, who became my friend when his girlfriend came into the studio, saw me, and insisted on meeting me. Eric was so embarrassed by her impertinence that he'd bought me a cupcake from the local bakery as an apology. All three of us have since become great friends.

"Great job, Haven," Devin says, aiming a middle finger at Eric. "You get more comfortable in front of the camera every night." Devin, our one and only cameraman compliments me nightly. We've gone on two random dates, but I think he's trying to charm his way into something more.

"I don't think I'll ever be comfortable in front of the camera, but thanks for saying so."

He tips his wool flat cap, which promptly replaces his headset, and straps on his backpack. Dark circles are evident on his sculpted face, but he's still generous with his smiles, even after pushing around the camera for the past several hours; he also serves as cameraman for the station's cooking show and two automotive segments.

Eric follows me to my makeshift research desk—two rolling metal carts and an old talk-show stool I found in props. "What the hell is this?" He holds a picture of Deanna Emerson, an actress whose rocker husband sliced her from ear to ear.

"It's my next big story. I'm trying to draw in a bigger audience."

"We're on in the middle of the night. No one's watching us, they're watching Netflix."

Taking the picture from him, I place it back on top of my pile. "I'm researching stories about women who've suffered facial disfigurement at the hands of an assailant."

"Why would you wanna do that?"

"It's apropos, don't you think? Besides, I'd like to understand why these men do it." I sling my purse over my chest and take out my keys.

"Why us *men* do it?" Eric riffles through my pile and pulls out another picture.

"*She* was a model back in the Eighties whose landlord slashed her because she wouldn't go out with him," I say of the picture in his hand. "And I didn't mean you specifically, but you have to admit, it's usually a man who does the attacking."

"Yeah, well, those are the sick bastards. We're not all like that," he says, tossing the picture back on my desk.

I put the photo back in its place in the pile, but Eric is already heading into the control room.

"Eric, you can't leave." WSES's production director is yanking on his collar and speaking on the phone while signaling for Eric to get into the editing room.

"Dammit, Bert, I'd like to go home." Besides being our floor manager, Eric is also editor, assistant director, and everything else that falls under "all other related duties of the studio."

"Sorry," he tells him, holding the phone away from his ear, "but I need you in editing."

Eric frowns. "Can you wait, Haven? I don't want you walking out alone?"

"I can walk her." Devin says, walking up behind me.

"Only if you're headed out. I'll be fine by myself." Patting my crossbody bag at my hip, I say, "Got my pepper spray."

"It helps if you actually take it *out* of your purse." He opens the door, bends at the waist, and waves a hand dramatically to guide me out.

"Did your parents send you to charm school?"

He winks and lets the door close behind us.

About two blocks from SES, Devin says, "Why do you always park this far away?"

"I didn't ask you to walk with me. Please don't feel obliga—"

"I want to walk with you. I just wish you wouldn't park so far. What if one night, you *are* alone?"

"I park near the Brew House." I point to the coffee house two buildings up. "I get my tea before work and then walk. It's my only exercise."

"Ever heard of a gym?"

When we reach my new teal CR-Z, Devin says, "Here you are."

"Thank you for keeping me safe," I say, cringing at such flirtatious words. "And walking me to my car," I add, hoping to make clear my intent.

"Can I take you to breakfast in the morning?" With his knuckle, he brushes my forearm.

Guilt sinks to the bottom of my stomach. Devin is *so* great. My first day at SES, he caught me wincing at the proffered coffee Bert gave me, so during a break later that night, Devin handed me a cup of tea, saying, "There are two types of people in this world: coffee drinkers and tea drinkers." He's become a friend ever since. But I work with him, and this job is still new to me. It may only be breakfast he's asking, but last Saturday, it was drinks. Before that, ice cream. I take care *not* to make insouciant decisions, especially with people I need to see every day. I should have refused the first time.

"Thank you for asking, but tomorrow's payday." My chest warms at the thought. "I spend all my allowance at the Dingman's Corner Book Shop."

"You spend all your money on *books*?" I must admit, Devin's even handsome when he looks like he's been sucking on a lemon.

"Maybe another time?" I suggest, even though I want to say no.

"I'm gonna hold you to that," he says with wink and a tip of his hat.

AS PROMISED, ON PAYDAY, I visit my favorite bookstore owner.

"Mia bella. Beautiful flaxen-haired Haven," he says, kissing the tips of his chubby fingers to the yellowed ceiling tiles. "So lovely to see you today." His thick Italian accent is warm and inviting. "It's always a pleasure seeing you walk through my doors.

"Good afternoon, Mr. Vescovi." I make my way carefully between the oversized desk and piles of boxes filled with newly shipped books. "It's always a pleasure to be here."

"Your face is still as youthful as when you first visited the store as a small girl."

"Thank you, but I hope I aged a little since I was nine."

He winks at me and changes the subject. "I have some new books back there you might like."

"Some *new* books?"

"New to me. You know all of my books are used, bella."

"Of course I do, that's why Dingman's Corner Book Shop is my favorite place to be." I've been coming here since my mom heard about the store fifteen years ago—a recommendation from a fellow librarian when Mom was looking for a specific copy of *A Wrinkle in Time* by Madeleine L'Engle. At nine years old, walking inside that store felt magical. My heart soared with excitement at the thought of all that was happening on the pages inside those books. If I could have lived inside that store, I would have. "You have a unique collection."

"Si. Si. I do indeed. I worked very hard for my collection, bella."

"And your customers appreciate it." I nod in gratitude before heading back to the shelves that support Mr. Vescovi's unparalleled selections of gently used, hard-to-find books. From nonfiction to the classics, paperbacks to leather-bound, the smell of his store is as intoxicating as the characters that live inside his written treasures.

I crouch down to start at the bottom shelf, not wanting to miss one new addition to his collection, and skim each binding with my fingertips.

"Third shelf up, bella, the lovely Ernest Hemingway. 'But man is not made for defeat, he said. A man can be destroyed but not defeated.'" I recognize the quote from Hemingway's *The Old Man and the Sea*.

Rising to my feet, my eyes go directly to the third shelf up. Mr. Vescovi is already at my side pulling out the book. "The Old Man and the Sea. Hardcover." I take the book into my hands and stroke the cover.

"A first edition," Mr. Vescovi adds.

An Ernest Hemingway collector's edition. Mr. Vescovi knows my weakness—classic books...from romance to science fiction. I treasure them all.

"I...put it aside for you if you'd like?"

"Oh, I don't know, Mr. Vescovi, I really shouldn't..." Turning the book in my hand, my mind scrolls through my monthly expenses. The numbers conveniently balance, and I think, why not? "You know what? I think I *will* purchase this one now."

"Molto bene, bella."

At the register, while Mr. Vescovi carefully wraps my book in brown tissue paper, a book sitting on a back credenza catches my eye. "Is that a first edition of *in our time*?" I ask in awe, noticing the lowercase title.

"Ah. Si. The Paris printing. My most expensive Hemingway. I just had it appraised."

"It's exquisite. How much?"

"Ah." He picks up the plastic encased book and holds it close to his chest. "Worth very, very much, bella. But I cannot sell it. Even for much more than it's value." With longing in his eyes, he says, "It is not mine to sell. It belongs to—no, I cannot sell it, but would you like to see it?"

My eyes widen. Does he even have to ask?

Holding it in my hand is like holding the key to Heaven. Hemingway's first collection of short stories printed by

Three Mountains Press in 1924. "My goodness, isn't this a jewel?" I had to refrain from saying he was lucky. Praise could easily display my desperation, and I do not want to make him feel bad that he can't sell it to me.

Mr. Vescovi hands me my lesser valued but equally coveted purchase, and I hand him back his book. "Enjoy, bella."

"Thank you, Mr. Vescovi. I will see you next pay day."

BUT I DON'T SEE MR. Vescovi next pay day.

He died of a heart attack that following week. I am devastated. Mr. Vescovi meant so much to me that I find it difficult to even hold my recent Hemingway purchase. The strong scent of his Old Spice cologne still lingers on its leather cover. I find out that he held equal regard for me when I receive a certified letter from Hart and Foster law firm informing me that I am a recipient in his will. A signed first edition hardcover of *Green Hills of Africa* inscribed by Ernest Hemingway himself. The executor to the will must hear the disbelief in my voice when I phone to verify the details of the letter. He listens quietly while I blather on that I don't deserve such a gift. I am not family, just a regular customer. In a tone that is running out of patience, he instructs me to pick up the book at the bookstore before the end of the week, when Mr. Vescovi's grandson would be returning to California.

I drive to the bookstore, wishing I'd see Mr. Vescovi behind the desk, with his silver-white hair, stark against his olive skin. His big smile greeting me in his slightly broken English. "Mia bella, how lovely to see you today." My heart is heavy with the longing to hear his voice one more time.

Parked out front, my stomach uneasy, the dark store adds to my grief. Undeterred, I step onto the pavement and walk up to the window. Peeking in through the glass door to see if anyone is inside, a cold chill runs up the back of my sundress. The store is dark, lifeless.

I walk to the corner of the building and take a peek through Mr. Vescovi's display of Little Golden Books mixed in with classic children's books such as *Charlotte's Web*, *Where the Wild Things Are*, and *The Complete Tales of Winnie the Pooh* in the large window. A light is on in the back storage room, so I figure someone is probably here after all.

"Hello, hello," I say in vain, as if anyone can hear me through the glass. Instead, I ball up my fist and knock hard on the window. "Hello. Is someone in there?"

A dark shadow appears in the storage room doorway, so I rap the glass again and wave. "Hello. Hello."

The tall image with broad shoulders and large torso raises his hand and waves me away.

I find myself suddenly pounding the glass, going from using my knuckles to my whole fist.

I see him, rather than hear him, say something as his hand flies at me in another go-away gesture.

I don't relent and continue rapping on the glass until the figure moves forward, revealing himself to be even larger than I'd first thought. The dark tee-shirt pulling across his chest exhibits the muscles that help contribute to his size.

"We're closed," he shouts loud enough for the man standing on the corner, taking a drag off his cigarette, to look in our direction.

My adrenaline high, I flap a finger toward the door, signaling for him to open it and let me in. Again, he shouts, "We're closed."

At this point, a pride of lions couldn't stop me from entering Mr. Vescovi's store, so I continue knocking until he finally unlocks the door and pushes it open an inch or two. How generous. "I said, we're closed." This is not the warm and cheerful Mr. Vescovi. This man may be tall, handsome, and twenty-something, with eyes the color of a Van Gogh sky and hair as black as midnight, but he is the complete opposite of his gentle-hearted predecessor.

"What do you want?" he growls, his voice is deep, charred from either years of tobacco use or a lifetime of yelling at people.

"I'm Haven Quinn."

"I don't care if you're Angelina Jolie. We're closed. Indefinitely."

"But. I'm Haven—"

"Yes. You've stated that," he interrupts.

"Your grandfather named me in his will."

If I think that piece of information will bring out his warmer side, I am mistaken. Pushing open the door a few more inches, so he can scrutinize me from head to toe, he lets spill his assumption. "You're a little young for my grandfather, aren't you?"

"Excuse me?"

"Why else would he leave you a collection worth five hundred and forty thousand dollars?"

"Five hundred and forty thousand!" I blurt out childishly. "I think you have the wrong person. Your grandfather left me an Ernest Hemingway book. One." I doubt it's worth five hundred and forty thousand dollars.

"No," he sneers. "It's you. Besides that *one* book, he also left you my *entire* collection of signed first edition Ernest Hemingway books. Totaling about five hundred and forty thousand dollars. Those books are the most expensive collection he had," he continues through gritted teeth and fluttering nostrils. "I hope you were a good lay, and it was worth it for him."

"You don't even know me to make that kind of assumption."

"I know your type, gorgeous. You get by on that long golden hair, those deep brown eyes—" He eyes my body top to bottom again. "—those long lean legs. You expect the world to cater to you, and you don't care what you have to do to get what you want. Including getting old guys off in exchange for their fortunes."

"Who the hell do you think you are?" My two inch heel grinds the cement step. A stinging warmth of perspiration collides with the salty tears forming on the rim of my burning eyes. Reality hits me in an instant. Forever gone is my kind, old friend, mentor and nurturer who shared my love of books. I fling open the door and hold my hand flat against it so he can't pull it shut. "Your grandfather is probably looking down on you shaking his head in disgust. I don't need the Hemingway book. I'm just here out of respect for a dear friend." I turn on my heel and walk away, heartbroken for a man I'll never have the pleasure of talking with again and maddened by a man I hope never to see again.

Not ten feet from the door, my hopes are already dashed.

"Wait." Not even a please.

"What?" I say with just as much contempt when I turn around.

"Sorry I was rude, but a half-million dollars is a lot of money."

He expects me to respond, but I turn back around and take a step toward my car.

"Maybe—" he shouts so I stop walking. "—we can discuss this pathetic stipulation further. When I get back from California."

Once again, I turn to face him and sigh. "I don't even know what you're talking about. I received a phone call from a Mr. Samuel Hart saying that I was to pick up the *Green Hills of Africa* book that Mr. Vescovi left me. He never mentioned anything about a five hun—"

"Right. Well, there's a bit more to it. I don't have time to get into it right now, I gotta be to the airport in an hour, but can we meet in two weeks? I'll bring a copy of his will."

"Fine." Aside from being a regular customer, it doesn't make sense that Mr. Vescovi would leave me anything, but I can't just ignore his grandson, rude as he may be.

"Is there somewhere we can meet around here?"

"Oh. We're confirming plans *now*?"

"Unless you want me to *guess* where you're gonna be."

Jackass. "I can give you my phone number."

He holds up his hands. "No pen."

"Cellphone?"

"Not on me."

What. An. Ass. "Fine...There's a diner on route 206 in Branchville. Jumboland."

The guy snorts. An *immature* ass.

"So I just need a day and time," I say.

"Monday the twenty-sixth. 7 p.m."

"I work in the evenings."

"Doing what?"

"None of your business." My voice cracks. Betrayer.

"I can find out on the internet if I really want to."

"Be my guest."

"Does noon work?"

"Noon works." It goes against my nature to leave a discussion without a proper farewell, but that's exactly what I do when I turn on my heel and leave Quest Vescovi once and for all.

2.

Q^{uest}

"I'm not gonna apologize, Ma."

My mother, the woman who has teetered between walking on eggshells around me and hitting me in the ass with her wooden spoon for the past three years, kept hammering for me to call Haven Quinn and apologize for being so rude to her the day she came into the store. As if I don't have reason for being so—she would be the beneficiary of over a half a million dollars worth of signed copies of Ernest Hemingway books if I don't hold up my end of the bargain, according to my grandfather's Last Will and Testament.

"It was the right thing to do," my mother tells me, from atop the kitchen counter as she dusts her eclectic cookie canister collection. "From what you've told me, you weren't very nice to her."

One Sunday when I was about eight years old, I was standing outside of church upset that I had to wait for my parents to get finished talking with the other parishioners like they did every Sunday after twelve o'clock Mass, when Mrs. Fink came over and squeezed my cheeks. "Oh, Quest, your chubby face is so adorable." Not only did the woman smell like perfume and body odor, but I was already pissed-off at my parents for making me wait to go out skateboarding with my friends. My impatience, combined with the ninety-degree weather, made me yell, "Geez, lady, take a bath," to which my father, grabbing me by my earlobe, shoved me into the backseat of his Ford Crown Victoria, and punished me from skateboarding for the rest of that summer. No matter what the circumstances, I was expected to be kind and polite. So when I told my mother that I barely opened the door to talk to the woman my grandfather evidently thought so highly of, she was not exactly happy with me. To tell the truth, I was disappointed in myself. I know better. But once I'm having a bad day, once anger sets in, it doesn't disappear without consequence. At twenty-five years old, I'm still trying to work on that part of myself.

"I don't get why he's making me do this. It's crazy, having to uproot my life like this. I don't get it. And why the *hell* would he give away *my* money if I don't?"

"I don't either, dear, but he has his reasons, I suppose. Maybe he'd always wished you were a part of his life. Maybe this was the only way he could do it."

"That wasn't my fault."

"No. Your father took you away from him, but we should have ended that falling-out after your dad died. We could have made the effort, you know?"

"How? Was I going to travel from San Diego all the way to New Jersey on my own? Would you have come? Besides, right after high school, I joined the Army. I wasn't even around."

"What about calling him?"

"Did you have his number, Mom? Because if you did, you never gave it to me?"

"It got lost with your father's stuff, I suppose. I don't remember coming across it, but I'm sure we could have called information." My mother drops her shoulders and sighs. "I could have made sure we kept in contact. I'm sorry."

"Right. So don't go and blame me."

"I'm not blaming you. I already said I could have made more of an effort myself." After a pause, she says, "Listen. What's done is done. Your father walked away from his father when you were just a boy, and you lost out on a grandfather. We can't do anything to change that, but we can respect his wishes now and take care of his store."

"But I don't want the store. And wouldn't it be disrespecting my *own* father by running it?"

"Your father held grudges too long." She's right. Franco Vescovi was not a man you ever wanted to cross. Not if you wanted to keep him in your life. One time, his softball buddy blamed my father for losing a game. His friend told him that had he put a little fire in his feet, he would have beaten the first baseman to the base, and wouldn't have gotten the last out of the game. His buddy later apologized, stating he was just pissed that they lost, but my father never spoke to his friend again. My father went as far as not signing up for softball the following year. What was that saying my mother loved to say? "He cut his nose to spite his face." Well, that he did, because he never got to play again. My father was killed in a car accident the following year. I won't let my thoughts linger there for too long, though. Not if I want to remain upright.

"Well, maybe I do too. Whatever his father did to him to make him move across the country, should be good enough for me to continue this grudge." I knew the words were wrong the minute they left my mouth, but my quick temper tended to spew words that my otherwise rational brain would never say.

"You can't continue being so angry, Quest. Ever since you got discharged from the Army, you've been so—"

With the side of my fist, I punch the table to interrupt my mother. I push back from the table so hard, I knock over my chair. My mother's eyes close; she knows she's wrong. I don't talk about my discharge. *Ever*.

The madman has taken over my body once again, and I'm filled with the red-hot rage of a lion mid-roar. In order to deflect the fury before it unleashes itself in violent form, I two-step the dark wooden steps leading to my weight room in the basement, and seek immediate relief. The red weighted bag, hanging from the ceiling by a thick silver link chain, takes my fisting like the champ it proclaims to be. But after several beatings, even it's not enough. Turning to my smaller, yet quicker opponent, its platform also hanging from the ceiling, I hit my speed bag with a force not as heavy, but with my fists working at a much faster pace, it is much more satisfying. Sometimes, in order to release the rage quickly enough, I need to work double-time. Soon, I'm afraid the bags and the weights won't be enough, and some innocent bystander will end up the casualty. Which pretty much makes running a small used bookstore a bad idea. Innocent people frequent bookstores. And me? Around people? No longer a good match.

I'm back at the red bag throwing slow, powerful punches when my mother comes down holding out a bottle of water already coated in condensation.

"Thanks." Knocking back the water, I let the icy coldness coat my tongue and chill my throat.

"Sorry I brought it up, Quest. I just hate seeing you like this."

Crushing the now empty plastic bottle in my hand, I turn my back to my mother. "I can't forget it, Ma. I see it over and over. Whether I'm sleeping or awake." *I'd just drawn the Jack of Spades, the card I'd needed to complete the set that'd end my hand when I heard the squeal. Throwing down our cards, Joe and I grabbed the Glocks from our holsters and ran toward the scream...an instinct we never learned to ignore despite knowing the backlash of going against Army rules—written or otherwise.*

My mother walks up behind me and places a firm grip on my shoulder. I feel her chunky fingers through my sweaty t-shirt and I'm suddenly prodded back to my father's funeral—my mother and me, saying goodbye for the last time...she, trying to keep it together, me, already falling apart. "I know, baby. That's why I think relocating to Jersey would be good for you. Change of scenery."

I turn back to face her. "I can't just run away from my thoughts. They come *with* me. Remember?" They never disappear. Ever.

She sighs, sitting back on the bench against the wall. Her hands on her knees, her chin tucked into her chest, she cries, "I just want my son back."

Her son. The boy who loved nothing more than to help her roll balls of ground beef, bread crumbs, and egg every Sunday after twelve o'clock Mass, while Dad settled down in front of the television to watch a ballgame. The boy who, when his father died, did everything he could to make it up to her—mowing the lawn, fixing the railing, balancing the goddamn checkbook. "Well...he's gone, Ma," I say, thinking back to who I used to be. "Dead." I throw the crushed water bottle into the wastebasket and return to the speed bag again; hitting it harder and faster, in attempt to drown out my mother's crying. I can't stand to hear her cry. Because of my actions. Because of the man I've become. Because of the good son I can no longer be.

"CORPORAL VESCOVI, HALT. Now. This is a command." After another couple of thrusts to the commander's throat with my fist, my commanding officer demands again, "I said stop, now, Corporal, or I'll shoot."

But I don't halt. I can't. I don't want to stop until this man beneath me is dead and his brains are splayed out across the ground he's lying on.

"Quest."

My eyes are closed. My breathing ragged.

"Quest," Ginny, my therapist, says again.

I let go, temporarily, the visions that plague my mind every time I close my eyes. "What?" I rasp.

"When the visions bombard your thoughts, take a few breaths and count to ten. Let yourself cool—."

"No. That doesn't work for me anymore."

"Have you thought about seeing your psychiatrist again, going back on your medication?"

"No. It's too expensive. I don't have insurance, I told you that."

"Yes, you did. We do have to control this anger, though. It's not healthy for you to act out." She's right. Last week, while I was tuning up my car, I spilled oil on the garage floor, so instead of getting annoyed like a normal person would and say a few curse words as I went about cleaning up the spill, I took the can of oil and tossed it at the wall, effectively splaying oil all over the garage. Including on my 1969 Chevy Camaro, which I'd spent the last three years restoring to mint condition.

Leaning my head back against the couch, I remark, "I don't know how to change it. Seeing it over and over again just makes me want to kill the mother..." I stop myself from cursing in front of the woman.

"We've talked about this before, Quest. If the techniques we've gone over aren't effective, then we can try support groups. Do you still have the contact list I gave you?"

"I told you. I'm not sitting in a circle with a bunch of other loser guys and whining about my woes. I'm not that guy."

"You're not happy with *this* guy, either," she says, nudging her chin at me.

"I thought I paid you to be nice to me."

"You pay me to listen. And all I hear are your excuses." She's right; every time she offers a suggestion, I have a reason against it. She'd told me a yoga class might be fun. My response? "A colonoscopy sounds better."

I fist the pillow next to me then stand from the couch. "I believe my time is up."

"Your choice, Quest." Ginny follows me to the door, and reaches her arm out in front of me, grabbing the doorknob before I get to it. "Give the support groups a chance. You don't have to join in on the conversations. Just listen. Someone else's story may end up helping you."

I stare at her hand, willing her to turn the knob.

"See you next week, Quest."

"No. I'll be in New Jersey next week."

She moves her body in front of the door, now blocking me completely from leaving. "Come see me Thursday at four then. We can talk about your grandfather's bookstore. Your options."

"Yeah. Fine."

Ginny moves from the door, and I leave.

A support group. She's crazy if she thinks that'll do me any good.

3.

HAVEN
    I'm prompt for my lunch date with Mom, but she still taps the crystal face of her wristwatch.

"Hello, Mom." I greet her with a kiss to both cheeks, just like she expects, even though she is clearly annoyed that I'm late.

"Darling."

I order a blood orange tea and a cucumber dill sandwich. Mom's tea is already in front of her, and seeing as she only has an hour for lunch before needing to go to her biweekly Saturday afternoon mani-pedi appointment, she's already ordered.

"So, how is work, sweetheart?"

"It's good. The hours suck, but—"

"Language, Haven. It's not attractive."

Rolling my eyes, I apologize to my mother for my unladylike language.

"And don't roll your eyes at me, Haven. *Children* roll their eyes."

"Right, Mother." In my thoughts, I roll my eyes again. In my thoughts, I also flip her the proverbial bird.

"I take it you're not enjoying the middle of the night newscast?"

"I enjoy it very much so. I'm just having trouble adjusting to the hours. I don't sleep in the afternoons like I should."

"Stop playing with your pearls, dear. I didn't buy them for you to use as a fidget toy."

I roll my fingers one last time around a pearl on the strand around my neck, then drop my hand.

"You could have gotten a job in Manhattan, Haven. I don't understand why you took a job at an unheard of local television station. You might as well have taken a job in cable."

"Mother. The jobs in the city were production assistant jobs. I'm on the air up in Pennsylvania. I like being in front of the camera."

"But there isn't any chance of moving up. In New York, you would have had hundreds of opportunities."

"Thank you for your concern, Mother, but I'm happy with the decision I made. So, can we change the subject?"

"You know, you should be grateful that I let you live your life the way you want to. *My* mother would have never allowed me to make such decisions."

Yeah, okay, Mother.

"Do you have a man in your life yet?"

"You know I don't."

"Pearls, dear...In the city there are plenty of—"

"Yes, Mother. In the city there are plenty of men. I'm not interested right now in meeting one. How's Daddy?"

"Busy. There are way too many crimes in this state, but if there weren't, we couldn't live a comfortable life, right?"

Daddy is a criminal defense lawyer in Morristown, and he's one of the best, whether I believe he is doing the city a service or not. He made a name for himself when, as a young lawyer on his first case, he'd defended an officer facing a twenty year prison sentence for paying an FBI informant in drugs, and he was found not guilty.

Mom is a librarian at the Morristown library. A respectable position, despite her air of superiority.

"So, you know that bookstore we go to up in Layton?"

"Mr. Vescovi's place. Yes. I haven't been there in years. What about it?"

"Mr. Vescovi passed away, Mom. He had a heart attack."

"Oh, that's too bad." Mom doesn't sound like it's too bad. She signals for the waitress and demands her teacup be filled. For someone whose nose is always in books, she certainly lacks the empathy that comes from reading a lot.

"It is, Mom. He was a nice man. I'm gonna miss him."

"You're going to miss him?"

"Yes, Mother, I'm going to miss him. Very much."

The waitress brings our lunch, and I can't help but feel envious when I notice the effortless way her braids fall, and the tiny hairs that stick out randomly. It makes me wonder if *her* mother ever cautioned her about the importance of perfection.

I wait to continue speaking until after my mother's had a few spoonfuls of her soup. My stomach is suddenly too upset to touch my sandwich. I love my mother, but boy does Hannah Quinn's smugness affect me in the same way it does when someone dog-ears a new book.

"So, anyway, Mother, he named me in his will."

Lowering her tea cup to the table, she raises her brow. "You? Why on earth would he do that?"

"Thanks for the vote of confidence, *Mom*. He left me a rare signed first edition of *Green Hills of Africa*."

"Ernest Hemingway? Hardcover?"

"Yes. And he may or may not have left me a whole collection of signed first edition Hemingway books."

"May or may not have?"

"I'm meeting with his grandson to discuss it. There's some type of stipulation, I'm not sure what it's about.

"An entire signed, first edition collection? My friend Bernadette's granddaughter is an Associate Specialist at Sotheby's. She's engaged to a Harvard Law graduate; your father's rival school. Anyhow, I'm sure she can help you get the collection appraised."

Shaking my head in disgust, I remain silent and allow her to continue on.

"Bernadette said he isn't exactly a young Robert Redford, but we all know that money shadows flaws. It is a shame that your money will be the earnings from a gift instead of a husband, but you can invest in stocks, real estate. Get a nose job!"

"Mother."

"I'm just saying, darling, you're the one who chose television as a career. Your nose should be *screen*-worthy."

Matthew Schmidt had the whole sixth-grade lunchroom laughing when he'd told them that I made my nostrils so large because I stuck markers up my nose every night before I went to bed. Hannah was of no comfort when I'd come home in tears, "Haven, you need to grow a backbone and not cry every time someone on the playground teases you," she had said.

"Oh my goodness, Mother, you are so cruel," I say in response to her screen-worthy comment. "There is nothing wrong with my nose." Swinging my hair forward, tickling my nose in the process, I unintentionally contradict my declaration. I shrug it off and add, "And I'm not selling the book *or* the collection if I get it. If Mr. Vescovi thought enough of me that he wanted *me* to have his collection, then I am certainly not getting rid of them." I reach for my pearls, but decide otherwise.

"I value a good book as much as you do, honey, but I know you're not making a lot at that tiny television station. You really should supplement your income with it."

"Stop it, Mom. I'm twenty-four. I can live my own life without your input."

"I was the top corporate and legal research librarian for Wannamaker Oil Company by the time I was your age, Haven. *And* I was married and taking care of our finances by then. I certainly know a thing or two about saving for the future and giving you advice."

"Yes, and I appreciate your advice, but I'm not selling anything I receive from Mr. Vescovi."

My mother holds up her impeccably manicured hands. "It's your decision, Haven."

I motion to the waitress to wrap up my sandwich as I take a last sip of my tea. "I have to get going." I could sit here and finish my sandwich, but I can only take so much of my mother's condescension.

"Haven, don't act like a child. I only have your best interests at heart, you know that."

"Yes, Mother, I know that. But you don't make me feel very good about myself."

"Haven, there you go feeling sorry for yourself again. No one likes a martyr."

"I'm not being a martyr, Mother. Just—" I stand up and grab my bag. "Just stop, okay? I have to go."

I get in my CR-Z and drive home, understanding why my father spends most of his time at his office working. Twenty-minute intervals is more than enough time with my mother. I turn on Keith Urban and sing away thoughts of my mother and her pretensions.

About three Keith songs later, I find myself at Marisela's house instead of my own home. My best friend since first grade, she and I are joined at the best-friends' necklaces we used to wear around our necks in elementary school. Mine still hangs in my jewelry armoire in my bedroom. Ten-year-old Marisela had just returned from Puerto Rico when she gave it to me. She was already wearing her half.

"Havey baby, what are you doing here?" Marisela hugs me, her long arms squeezing me so hard I won't be surprised if she leaves a bruise. When she lets me go, she squeals again. "I can't believe you're here. It's been, like, a month."

"Sorry about that, Mari. Working so late has really screwed up my days."

I follow her into the new bungalow she's renting on Lake Hopatcong. "I'm just so happy to see you, Haven. I've missed you."

"I've missed you. You have any wine?" I ask, plopping on her oversized leather sectional, her first purchase after she signed her lease.

"At two-thirty in the afternoon?" She laughs. "Have lunch with your mother again?"

"You know me so well." I knock my head back against the couch. "Why do I let her get to me?" I ask while she pours me a glass of wine.

"'Cause she's your mother. We all let them get to us. Here." I sit forward as she hands me a red-wine filled goblet and keeps one for herself. "It's my homemade Sangria."

"Ooh, I love when you make this. You must have known I was coming."

"You know our minds are always in sync."

I nod. She's right. There have been times she would call me to tell me about a book she'd read, and I had just finished reading the same book, or I'd get a phone call in the middle of the night from her telling me she'd been craving a Monte Cristo sandwich at the same time I'd woken up dreaming of one. And the moment I'd found out my grandfather died, she'd called me five minutes later, sensing that something was wrong. That is how connected we are. I may be an only child, but I never feel that way. Not with Marisela as my best friend, non-blood sister, confidant.

"So," she starts. "How's the job? I see you on YouTube. You're doing great. From my lips to your ears," she mimics.

"Corny."

"Not at all. Perfectly you."

"So how's your job going?"

"Been working my ass off."

"Your ass? Doesn't your job require only your fingers and your brain?"

A half-moon indent forms on Marisela's right cheek. "Information Technology work isn't as easy as you think."

I laugh. "I know that. I'm just teasing ya. This Sangria is awesome, girl."

"Thanks. My mom's recipe never fails." Marisela grabs a piece of fruit from her half-empty glass with her finger, and I tell her to get a fork. What would Hannah Quinn think?

In the spirit of catching up with each other, I mention the whole Mr. Vescovi/Hemingway business and surprisingly, my best friend's response is not too different from my mother's. "Just imagine, Haven...a half million dollars worth of books. You can sell them and put a down payment on your own TV station." Again, doesn't anyone place value on the emotional aspect of a book anymore?

I don't speak my mind, but I do say, "Right. I'd rather buy the book store."

4.

H AVEN
About five minutes before the close of my segment, Eric slams a piece of paper on my news desk—big black letters announce that the Stratford Slasher has claimed two more victims within the last hour.

"Oh my God," I mutter, momentarily forgetting I'm live on the air. Inhaling a breath of calm, I compose myself before speaking. "I'm sorry to report that the Stratford Slasher has attacked two more women tonight, brutally assaulting them with his knife." It's times like these that I'm glad I'm not some big news channel newscaster reporting hardcore news. This is bad enough.

Continuing, I report, "We are unable to name the victims, out of respect for family members who have not yet been notified, but please...heed caution out there, Stratford. He is still out there, and until he's caught, we here at Stratford Red-Eye News urge you not to walk outside alone. Buddy up. From my lips to your ears, this is Haven Quinn giving you your red-eye news. Thanks for staying the course."

"Aaand we're out. Hey, Haven," Eric walks up to me before taking off his mic. "You okay? You look pretty shaken up."

"I'm all right. This is scary though."

"Wish they'd just catch the guy already."

"Me too."

Taking off his headset and laying it on the anchor desk in front of me, he says, "Why don't you wait with me tonight? It's not worth going out there alone. And Katie would kill me if I ever let anything happen to you." He chuckles.

"I know, but it's been a long day. I have my Mace, and I'll run to my car instead of walk."

"No. Don't. I only have to stay an hour, and aren't you the one that just told all of Stratford to buddy up?"

"You're right." I agree and decide to use the extra time to do some more research on this Stratford Slasher. I need to figure out his motive, if he has a specific type; I feel useless reporting about him without having some insight. The more I can enlighten my audience, the more in control of this situation we all can feel.

I decide I need to give our police department a visit. So before leaving for the night with Eric, I ask Devin if he'd come with me to the police station tomorrow...with his camera. Of course, he says he will.

AT THE POLICE STATION, I'm met with overly friendly, barely helpful police officers—eager to talk to me but averse to giving me any solid information. Even when I resort to begging. "You do realize," I say to one of them, "the more people know, the less likely the slasher will attack. We empower the public with knowledge, we take away his leverage. I just want to know certain facts. Does he have a 'type'?"

The officer, and the one behind him, double over in laughter "You're kidding, right? We can't hand over information on an open case for you to put out there. It's confidential."

"I'm trying to compile facts. I don't want anything confidential."

"He strikes in the dark," the first officer says.

Really?

The second officer cracks his neck and tries to smile. "Look, I realize you're with the media. I can only give you so much though. No one was arrested yet. The victims' names are public record. We don't have any suspects yet. I'm sorry."

I'm about to ask for the list of victims when the first officer, who's a little too creepy, in my opinion, to be a police officer, says, "Yeah, sorry we couldn't help you here, but maybe I can buy you a drink at Rudy's when I get off duty. You know, as a *peace* offering?" Then he has the gall to wink.

Just as I'm about to chide this guy about his lack of ethics, Devin blurts, "What kind of woman do you think Haven Quinn is? She's a well-respected reporter. You should be ashamed of yourself."

The obnoxious officer bursts out laughing, but before I drag Devin out by his arm, I turn back, deciding I want the names of the victims.

When we do finally leave the police station, Devin's face is as red as the blood coloring the faces of the victims in the photographs we were shown with the list of names.

"You okay?" I ask him.

When he parts his pursed lips, he says, "What the hell kind of police officer makes a pass at a woman while he's on

the job? Who the hell does that?" Shades of red go from
deep to deeper as Devin's jaw tightens.

"Devin," I say, resting my palm on his arm. "It's okay, I
can handle it. I'm not easily offended."

His jaw still firm, he says, "Well I am."

With a pat to his arm, I tell him to calm down. He takes
off his black framed eyeglasses and rubs his head with the
back of his wrist. His eyes closed, he expels a deep sigh. "I'm
good," he says, returning his frames to his nose. "I'm good,"
he repeats, reassuring himself.

"Good. Now let's go visit our first victim."

Susanna Washington peeks through the two-inch crack
of her latched red door. "Can I help you?" she asks in a voice
that says she'd rather not.

"Miss Washington?" I say, holding up my station ID
badge so she can read my name while I tell her. "I'm Haven
Quinn, and I work for Red-Eye News on WSES."

"Again, can I help you?" She's annoyed, and I feel bad.

I contemplate backing down her wooden porch and
pretend this never happened, but I stand firm. Pocketing my
ID, I say, "I'd like to do a story about the victims of the
slashings so we can alert our viewers. Knowledge is power,"
I say, regretting it as soon as the sentence is out. I shrug and
continue with, "Maybe we can help other women with your
story."

Miss Washington takes a few seconds, but she nods and
closes the door to open it and let Devin and me in. Two
jagged parallel purple lines brand her right cheek. Her eyes
avert ours, but she welcomes us in. If it were me who'd been
assaulted, I wouldn't let *any*one I didn't know into my house

ever again. "What would you like to know?" she asks, after leading us into her parlor.

"Is filming you or your house out of the question?" Devin asks.

"No, that's fine," I say right away. "We don't need to get anything—"

"I'd rather you not film me. And I'd rather the man who did this not know where I live."

"Fair enough," I say, though my instincts tell me to apologize for bothering her and leave right now. My mission to become the next Erin Andrews or Megan Kelly...or dare I say Diane Sawyer, prevents me from listening to them. "May I ask if this was a sexual assault?"

"It was not, thank God."

"Was he wearing anything to cover his face? Did he say anything to you? Did he—"

Shaking her head, she says, "As I told the police—"

Devin interrupts. "That police department is a joke."

"I'm sorry, Miss Washington," I say, apologizing for my rude cameraman. "Please continue."

"He wears a ski mask," she begins. "A black one. And the only thing he said was, 'shut up and stay still, unless you want me to kill you.' So I shut up and stayed still."

"Gosh." Feeling her fear, I clutch my necklace. "I'm so sorry."

"And he just left me there, bloodied and crying. I literally crawled to where I'd dropped my purse to get my phone and call 911."

I hesitate to question her further, because it feels so insincere to be doing this interview. "Did he steal anything? What was his purpose? Not that you would know, really."

Shaking her head, she says, "He took the twenty dollars I had in cash, but that's all. It's as if his soul purpose was to leave these two gashes," she points to her right cheek, "on my face. I heard he'd done the same with the others as well."

Susanna Washington is right. The three more victims I interviewed said the same thing, almost word for word. The masked man etched two parallel lines on the right side of their faces, and quickly fled the scene afterward. Those who had cash, had it taken. Otherwise, the assailant took nothing.

"Ready for the next one?" Devin asks when we step off the porch of the fourth victim.

"We're done," I tell him, feeling guilty for intruding on these already frightened women. "We have enough information. I don't feel right invading on their privacy anymore. Four interviews is plenty." I unlock my car door and get in.

When Devin gets inside, he strokes a finger down my bare arm and says, "You gotta harden your heart if you're gonna succeed in this business."

Maybe I don't want to succeed in this business. Not if it means violating someone's privacy and exploiting their fears.

5.

Q^{uest}

I don't want my grandfather's bookstore, but Sam Hart made it clear—Haven Quinn needs to know what she'll be awarded if I don't keep the store open for at least five years. Am I willing to give up my half million dollar Hemingway collection? Hemingway—his favorite author. He talked about his stories as if they were his own. As a young boy, I'd listen to my grandfather read me stories about Nick Adams, Jake Barnes, and Robert Jordan. He'd later reference them throughout our days. I had no idea why he'd talk about these people well after the story was over. After later reading some works of Hemingway in high school, it clicked. My grandfather lived inside his books. He lived vicariously through Ernest Hemingway's fictional characters. When I'd come to realize what Nick, Jake, and Robert had meant to my grandfather—they were his *friends*—my grandfather had long since been out of my life. I have no real inkling why. The reason died when my father did. Now I need to know. Why were we ostracized from my grandfather's life? Why would he leave me his most prized possessions, but under a condition? Why is he willing to give to me his friends, his past, but only if I keep his store open for five years?

Noon on Monday comes quickly.

When I pull up to Jumboland in my Ford rental, the blonde I'd met at the bookstore is already standing near the front. Haven Quinn. Tall, slim, and quite beautiful. Her beauty is something I'd only noticed on the surface that first day—just enough to note her attractiveness as something to be used—a weapon, for instance. But she's not just attractive. She's stunning. Though the flowing pink sundress hints at cleavage and offers a glimpse of slender legs, Haven possesses an elegance that only a *natural* beauty would possess, regardless of the fabric that covers her.

"Quest?" she asks, perhaps not sure if I am the same man she'd met a couple weeks ago.

"Yes." I hold out my hand to shake hers as I say, "Haven. Thank you for meeting with me."

"Sure." She nods and holds open the door for me, but I place my hand above hers, and motion for her to go first. If I'd ever walked through a door and let my mother walk in behind me, you better believe my father was taking away my video games that night.

Haven, however, stands there holding the door for me, *insisting* that I go first.

With a small groan, I drop my hand from the door and walk into the diner ahead of her.

When the hostess asks if we are a party of two or if there'd be others joining us, Haven speaks up before I have the chance. "Yes, it'll just be the two of us."

"Right this way." We follow the hostess to a small booth in the center of the restaurant.

"So," Haven begins before we even open our menus. "As I said to you over the phone, I'm only interested in the book your grandfather originally intended for me. I have no idea what the whole collection has to do with me, but if they are yours, I don't want to take them from you. So...really, you didn't have to meet with me, I would have—"

"Whoa," I say, holding up my hand, already irritated that she's jumping ahead of me in conversation. "Let me explain. By law, I have no choice. And, I haven't been to the store yet, so I don't have *Green Hills of Africa* with me. "

"Okay. That's fine. Please go on." She's formal in her manner, but I haven't yet decided if that's her nature, or if I've just managed to piss her off by interrupting her.

"I need to eat first," I say quickly. "I got in late last night and there's no food at my grandfather's house." I think about the rudeness of my behavior and my mother's hand whacking me in the back of the head if she were here. I change tactics. "Would you like something as well?" I ask, hoping my tone is more courteous. "It's on me."

"Yes. I could go for a burger," she says confidently, but strokes the pearls around her neck.

After we place our lunch orders with the waiter—a light-haired youthful man who looks like he'd rather be surfing the next big wave than wearing a black bow-tie and taking food orders—I slide a copy of my grandfather's will across the table. "This doesn't take the place of a formal meeting with the lawyer, but I thought if we could discuss this beforehand, we could come to some kind of agreement."

As she slowly flips through the first few pages, I want to stop her, to send her to the right section, but I can't pull my eyes off of her. Not only is she stunningly beautiful, but the deep dimples in her cheeks and her slightly wide, button nose, make her out-of-this world adorable as well. When she finally looks up at me and says, "This is all quite personal. I shouldn't be—," I interrupt her and say, "Page four. Second paragraph," effectively breaking my trance.

She turns to the section and her brown eyes grow wide when she reads it. "Wait." She starts talking while still reading the page. "You don't want to keep the store open?" Finally, she looks up at me, her face contorted in surprise. Page four, paragraph two states that if I choose to walk away from the store now, or before the end of fifty-ninth months, I must hand over Raniero Vescovi's rare Ernest Hemingway collection to Haven Quinn.

"*That's* what you're concerned about?"

"Well, yes. It's a great store."

Shaking my head, I say, "No. I don't want to keep the store open."

"That's a real shame."

"Maybe, but that's not the issue here."

"It should be. May I ask *why* you don't want the store?"

"Not my thing. However, as you've read, if I don't keep the store open for five years, I lose the Hemingway collection. A collection, according to my grandfather's will, worth a half million dollars."

"Yes, I see that. A half million dollars is a lot of money." She's still eyeing the document while her fingers return to her strand of pearls.

"It's probably more than what the whole stocked store would sell for without them. My grandfather's been collecting those books since he was a boy. His imagination, much of his livelihood, came from those stories. They were his friends, his brothers. When I was young, he used to read them to me. *In Our Time.* You're probably familiar with the short stories."

"Of course."

"Well, I used to sit with him on his front porch, or in his store, while he'd read them out loud—" I pause, enjoying the memory that I'd forgotten for so long. "It felt like I was right there alongside them crossing that lake to the Indian camp." I surprise myself for remembering the scene from the book. "Anyway, when I was ten, he and my father had a falling out, and my father moved us three thousand miles away from him. I never saw my grandfather again."

"Oh that's sad. What was so bad that they ended their relationship like that?"

"Don't know. My father never talked about it. I wasn't even allowed to *talk* about my grandfather. I guess, being ten, I didn't know much how to get in contact with him. I'd never called him on the phone, so I never had a number, then...years went by, and I never thought about it anymore. When I got the call that he'd died, I was filled with—" I swallow back the sour taste in my mouth. "—a lot of guilt. I never made the attempt to contact him."

Haven stares at me, speechless.

"I've been feeling guilty ever since."

"I'm sorry. He was a wonderful man."

Wondering why I even shared all that with this woman, I shake it off, remember where I am, and ask, "What *was* your relationship with my grandfather anyway?"

"I was a customer who visited his store. It was nothing more than that."

"Then why would he even suggest you have this collection? Even the one book? There was no mention of any other customers in his will."

The waiter brings our food, momentarily interrupting our conversation, which by the appalled look on Haven's face, is probably a good thing for me, considering it was me who put it there.

"Don't even suggest there was anything illicit in my relationship with your grandfather. That would be a disgrace to such a wonderful man. Not to mention rude."

"Yes, you made your point last time I made that assumption."

After taking several bites of our burgers, we get back on topic. "Anyway, I don't want the store, but obviously, I also don't want to give away the whole collection. Maybe I can make an offer?."

"An offer?"

"I don't know. A few of the books? Preferably, not the most valuable one...especially since the most valuable book is the original publication of—"

"*in our time*," she says at the same time I do. "Your grandfather showed it to me just a few days before he passed. He just had it appraised."

"So you know how much it's worth."

"Not really. He never told me. Its monetary worth is not what makes it so valuable."

"Agreed. For me, it's much more than that."

"I held it in my hands," she sighs, her shoulders squeezing inward, her eyes closing for just a moment. "It was like holding the Holy Grail. But you're right, I'm sure to you it means a lot more than it does to me."

"I will give you *some*thing from the collection. There are doubles, some worth more than its duplicates, but—."

"Quest," she interrupts then dips her fry in ketchup, takes a bite, and points the other half of the fry at me. Right after swallowing, she says, "I'm not interested in your collection, whether you keep the store or not."

"Really?"

"I don't deserve it. Not even part of it. It wouldn't be right."

Sitting back in my booth, I wonder what Haven Quinn is all about. Who would give up half a million dollars that easily? "So, you're saying you don't want any of the books? Except for the one that has no stipulation attached to it, of course."

"I would treasure them with all I have, but I'd *never* take what is rightfully yours."

"Even to sell them?" I sit up and lean forward, attempting to get a glimpse into her eyes. Maybe if I look close enough, I can tell if she's playing me or not.

"Sell them?" She puts down the ketchup-covered fry she was about to eat. "Sell something that had obviously meant so much to Mr. Vescovi that he'd keep them instead of selling them for the amount of money they are worth?"

"Couldn't have meant *that* much to him if he was so quick to give them to one of his customers instead of his grandson. Unless it was me who hadn't meant that much to him."

She picks up the fry and, like before, takes a bite and waves the other half at me. "See, I don't think it's all that simple. I think your grandfather really wanted you to take over the store." The rest of the fry disappears inside her mouth, and she doesn't speak again until it's finished. But I know she has more to say, so I don't interject. "I think he probably knew that collection meant enough to you to keep the store open in order to keep the collection. And he must have had a reason for wanting you to take it over."

"And what possible reason could that be?"

"To get close to him, for one." Her eyes pop, as if the light bulb has just come on. "Quest. His soul. It's connected to that store. He's still there. Maybe this is his way of bringing the two of you back together."

I run my hand down my face. His soul is still there? Isn't that just some kind of guru propaganda to get people to believe that a person's life doesn't end when their body dies? "Then why bring you into it?" I ask, skeptical of her reasoning.

Shaking her head while she bites her burger, she shrugs.

I finish my lunch and push away my plate. When she's done, she does the same and sits back against the booth.

"You know, Quest," she sits forward, elbows flat on the table, "*in our time*. He'd just had it appraised, as I said." She sighs, looking thoughtful, a smile playing on her lips. "I'd asked him how much it was worth, and he, thinking I guess that I wanted to buy it, told me, 'oh, this is not mine to sell,' or something like that. He was about to tell me who it belonged to, but then he'd changed his mind. But the look on his face," she palmed the table with both hands. "He was thinking about you. I know that now. There was this light inside of him. A smile in his eyes. And longing. I remember that well." Haven shakes her head and leans back again. "He probably chose me because I was there that day, and that's all. I was probably the closest thing on his mind when he was writing his will. He'd just had it appraised. Don't you think it could have been for the will?"

She's said so much in the past sixty seconds, I have to absorb it all before I can speak. After I've considered her words, I say, "That sounds feasible."

Haven is proud of her epiphany. The huge smile on her face and the satisfaction in her eyes tells me so.

"You think you're pretty smart right now, don't you?"

She nods. "Pretty much." Her smile is infectious, because I suddenly feel one creep across my own face, and I haven't felt the urge to smile since before my father died.

"Anything else I can get you?" the waiter asks with a smile that doesn't extend to his eyes.

"Oh no, I'm good." Haven says before looking at me and saying, "I need to get going. I have some errands to run before work."

"Just the bill, please," I tell the waiter. To Haven, I say, "So, in the meeting with the lawyer, what is our stance?"

"That I don't want the collection. Just *Green Hills of Africa*. I'd like it as a remembrance of what a generous man your grandfather was."

"You'll sign away your right to them?"

"Of course."

"Thank you, Haven. I appreciate it."

"If you don't mind my input some more..." She doesn't even wait for me to respond. "I'd rethink the store. I don't know what you have going on in your life, but I think this is a way to erase your guilt, and maybe get to know your grandfather again. Through his business. Through his books."

I leave the waiter a larger than usual tip—maybe he can use it toward a trip to the beach—then I thank Haven for her time and tell her I'll see her soon.

Haven has given me a lot to think about.

I don't know whether to take what she says to heart or with a grain of salt. *Do* I have anything going on in my life right now that would make keeping the store open not an option? No. Not now, nor in the foreseeable future. My discharge from the Army has taken care of that.

Still, do I really want to move across the country to run an old used bookstore? My first impulse is to say no, but then I think about it and wonder—what do I have to lose? Not very much. Mom is happy at home with her new boyfriend; she certainly doesn't need me around to worry about. I have no job. No life, aside from punching my bags and working out. I have no money left to buy another car to restore. Do I have the energy to run a store, though? Physically, yes. Mentally, I don't think so. My mind has been so out of focus lately that I don't know if I could concentrate long enough to put books on the shelves, never mind getting to know the authors and placing orders. I know nothing about running a business. Nor do I know anything about books, other than those introduced by my grandfather when I was young. How would I possibly run a successful business with that little experience?

Still...Haven makes a good point when she says I'd get to know my grandfather again. Maybe she's right in assuming his soul is still tied to that bookstore. Who am I to say whether a person's soul lingers or not? All I do know right now is that my grandfather is dead, and I know very little about him. Do I want to make the effort to change that...or not?

6.

H AVEN
    "Good show," Eric says after calling it a wrap. "Even though no one's even watching, 'cause they're at the fireworks."

"I'm sure they're home by now," I tell him, as I push back my chair.

"Still. We could have just run a repeat of the auto show like Bert's doing on Friday nights now."

"No sense complaining after the fact. At least we have tomorrow off." I tidy up the news desk and grab my purse from my research cart. "You leaving?" I ask Eric on my way out.

"Not right now. Got stuff in editing. Why don't you wait?"

"I'm falling asleep as we talk. I think I'll just head out now."

"I really wish you'd wait."

"I'll be fine, I promise. I'll run."

"Oh," he says as an afterthought. "We're meeting at four tomorrow at our place. Katie's cousin Justin is looking forward to meeting you."

Halting, my hand already poised on the exit door, I groan. "Eric, please don't tell me you told him I'm interested." I adjust my purse strap on my shoulder.

He holds up his hands. "Whoa, Katie's idea, not mine," he says before walking into editing and shutting the door.

I return my hand to the door handle and Devin's hand covers mine.

"Oh my gosh, I'm sorry. I didn't see you there," I tell him.

"Be careful out there," he says and proceeds to open the door and hold it for me.

"You're not leaving?"

"Editing."

"Bert's a slave driver, isn't he?"

"You bet. Be careful, Haven."

I pat my bag and reassure him. "Pepper spray."

7.

H AVEN
    Even the moon is afraid to show her face. Without her companionship, I am forced to rely on the scattering of buzzing street lamps and flickering neon *CLOSED* signs to provide illumination as I labor past padlocked businesses and unoccupied parking meters. My silk camisole feels like wet cling wrap against my ribcage as I make my way through the thick black night. A sole intruder in a slumbering city, I am quickly regretting my decision to leave work unaccompanied.

Haven, you deliver the warning every night. Stratford, Pennsylvania is no joke right now. There is a serial slasher on the loose. Women are being left on sidewalks and in alleyways lacerated and bloodied. Why are you out here? It's three o'clock in the damn morning. You shouldn't be alone. A belated thought urges me to pluck the pepper spray from my sling bag just in case.

As my navy and black Chanel ballerinas gain pavement beneath me, a sprinkle of fireflies emerges before me. Their waltzing glow reflecting in the window of the Stratford Bar and Grill delivers a message. Slowing to take a look, I squint into the dark glass and notice the streetlight across the road standing vigilant behind me.

I am not alone.

I really should have waited for Eric.

Fingernails dig into my padded palm as my grip tightens around the slim pink can of Mace. The shadow of the man in the glass moves, and I'm intensely aware that he is closing in on me. My gut yells, "Run, goddammit!" but I'm knocked to my chest before my flats leave the ground. My hands are yanked behind me, the useless self-defense spray still in my grasp, the bitter taste of concrete now on my lips. Pulling away is futile, because he's bound my wrists. Spitting gravel as I attempt to scream, I'm silenced when the stranger straddling my waist jerks my head back, my strand of pearls scoring my throat as he clenches them to still me, and ties a piece of fabric around my mouth. When the task's complete, he releases my neck and my face smashes back against the pavement, tiny pearls scatter beneath me to make their getaway. Lucky pearls. I'm then wrenched off the ground and carried face-down, a curtain of gold dangling from my temples, into the alley next door. The stench of garbage has me heaving just as my attacker drives me back down to the ground, face first, my vomit seeping through the gag cloth. When he flips me over, my conjoined hands stab into the hollow of my back, and I get my second glimpse of the devil who's taken hold of me. His ski mask covers everything but his God-given darkly-lined eyes, his irises the color of the knife blade he suddenly wields in front of me. Swallowing back the bitter particles left in my mouth, I try to rock myself free of his control, but he's mounted on top of my thighs, both his denim-covered knees at my hips, and all I manage to do is gather guck underneath my nails. The rate of my heartbeats has now surpassed a safe speed, and I'm sure my heart is about to stop.

The tip of his knife gains size the closer it gets. Not the face. Please not the face. But my wishes go unheard when the blade penetrates my cheek. Mom, I'm sorry. I didn't mean to put myself in danger. I didn't—my thoughts are interrupted when the knife makes contact a second time. My eyes widen as this man with the steel eyes drags the edge across my nose, and twists it when he's found the other cheek. Like a lion's teeth clamping into my flesh, the pain is not like anything I've ever known. Even the sting of my mother's criticisms doesn't hurt this much.

When the blade again pierces my skin, my body shivers from the cold. The orange glow of a lone firefly hovers overhead as I gasp for air. The surrounding buildings begin to twirl as the glimmering fly pirouettes. The beast above me sinks his tool into the side of my nose, and I once again disgorge the contents of my stomach. Choking on my own vomit, I pray for my last breath to expel, but that doesn't happen, because lucky me, my assailant is a compassionate one. He swings me to my side to allow the chunks to spill out over my gag. I let a sluggish laugh slip from my lungs when I envisage how dignified I must look. Would you mind taking a minute to snap a shot for my mother?

8.

Quest

The papers crinkle within my grasp. "What do you mean I have no choice?"

Sam Hart rises behind his desk. "Calm down, Quest. Why don't I get you a glass of water, you're looking a little flushed."

"I don't need water, I need to get out of this damn contract!" Despite my refusing a glass of water, I pull on my collar to cool off.

"The only way to get the collection without keeping the store open is to contest it. And that can end you up in court, maybe up to a year from now, maybe more. It's also not a guarantee you will win."

"Goddammit." I stand from my chair and toss the crumpled documents onto Sam's desk. "What a clusterfu—"

"Quest." Sam gestures to his secretary who just entered the room.

Nodding, I apologize to the woman for my outburst and tell Sam I'll be getting back to him.

I guess I don't have a choice in keeping open Dingman's Corner Book Shop if I want to keep the books. Sam Hart won't draw up papers to have Haven sign away her rights. My grandfather said under no circumstances do I get his collection unless I keep the store open in my name for five years, and his lawyer made it clear—unless I contest the will, this is how it stands. So, now I'm forced to decide between running a small bookstore in a smaller country-town in the mountains of northern New Jersey, *not* running the store and giving up a rare eclectic collection of Hemingway books worth a ton of money, or bringing the Last Will and Testament of Raniero Vescovi to court.

I leave Sam's office confused as to what to do, and pissed because Haven never showed up. Sam called her the afternoon I'd met her for lunch, and according to him, she was able to make it. Today, she not only missed the meeting, but she hadn't even called to inform us. The only conclusion I can come to is that she has reconsidered her option. Most likely, she spoke with friends or family about the situation, and they told her how crazy she'd be to walk away from such a valuable collection. Can I say that I blame her? No. Most people *would* be crazy walking away from that much money. But I am disappointed, because something about her made me think she was refreshingly different from most. It pisses me off that I'd misread her so significantly.

9.

H^{AVEN}

"THERE HAS TO BE SOMEONE who can fix her face. Look at her. She's hideous."

"Ma'am. She needs time to heal. She'll look much better after a few months. After that, if she chooses, we can perform plastic surgery to perfect her face. We won't know what she'll need, though, for several months. Even a year or two may—"

"Years!? She'll be too old to start her career then. No. Unacceptable. We need to find a surgeon who will work on her *now*. Immediately."

"I'm sorry, ma'am, but that will be impossible. Her wounds are severe. To repair the deepest lesion, she needed two-hundred and thirteen stitches...five layers deep in one section. She needs a tremendous amount of time to heal from the surgeries. It will take many—"

"Then I want to take her somewhere else."

"You're in New York City, Mrs. Quinn. You won't find a more capable team."

"Oh. I will."

Oh, shut-up, Mother. She's been carrying on about how repulsive I look since they unraveled my bandages for the first time yesterday. I haven't looked in a mirror yet, but according to my mother, I'd probably break it if I did. I wish she would just leave the hospital already—my mother *and* her false sympathy. "Oh, dear, I feel so bad for you." "Oh, my baby, how could anyone hurt you like this?" "Oh, my love, it pains me to see my daughter hurting so." Yeah, right. More like it pains her to see me so hideously ugly.

The minute she thinks I'm out of earshot, or sleeping, it's more like, "There is no way my daughter is leaving this hospital looking like that." "There has to be someone who can do a better job at fixing that hole in her face; she looks like the goddamned Grand Canyon." "She'll never have a broadcasting career now. Who'll want to look at *that* on their television screen?" Mother of the Year. That's my mom.

"Don't you worry, Haven," my mother says after vociferating the woes of having a beastly daughter to my doctor. The very tip of her finger, the tippy-top of her nail, grazes beneath the knife-slash on my face. Though she scarcely touches me, I'm acutely aware of the pain it causes. If the look of revulsion on my mother's face is any indication, I imagine it's equally painful for her, only for different reasons—she now has Erik, *The Phantom* as a daughter. Holding her stomach with her free hand, she says, "We'll have you looking like new in no time. I don't care what they say, I *will* find a surgeon who will fix this, this," she points to my cheek, just barely touching near my ear, "this *monstrosity*," she emphasizes.

"No." I barely make a sound, but it's the first word I say since the night I walked by myself to my car after work and got slashed by the very man I'd been warning my viewers about. My mother has been doing enough talking for the both of us.

"No? What do you mean, no?" The day my mother found out I accepted a position as news anchor, for a news program that aired at two o'clock in the morning for a television station she'd never heard of in a Pennsylvania town she'd never heard of, she nearly fell forward, her jaw leading the way. That's the exact response I'm getting right now.

"I don't want any more surgeries. It hurts too much." My voice is strained and sounds weak, even to my ears. My face is on fire, and talking only exacerbates it. Since the moment I was flown from Pocono Medical Center to New York Presbyterian Hospital, the slow drip of morphine that feeds my veins has tried relentlessly to lessen the burning agony, but even *it* has failed. Trying to concentrate on the sterile smell of bleach, or the pleasant chatter of the nurses, even the merciless blathering my mother so needlessly feels she must spew, has done nothing to get my mind off the biting wounds on my face. If I could rip it right off, I would in an instant.

"You cannot go out looking like that, Haven. There was a golf-ball sized hole in your cheek and it looks like they just stuffed it with cotton it's so swollen, and I don't want to even mention the long gash across your face."

She doesn't want to mention? I should be so lucky.

TWO WEEKS LATER, I'M back at my home in Bushkill, Pennsylvania. Out of danger of any more infection—that's what the doctors say. Morphine in the form of pills instead of a drip sit on my side table next to my couch. And I am out of sight of gaping onlookers.

Mother Dearest wants to stay with me after she brings me home, but I can't stand to hear her unsolicited advice any longer. Yes, I'll most likely need more surgery. Yes, I look hideous. Yes, I'm embarrassed to go out looking like some kid carved out his science project on my face. But I can't go through the pain of another surgery. Not right now.

"Please go home, Mom. If you're here, it's just going to keep me from sleeping. All I want to do is sleep. Okay?"

She eyes the length of my body backwards—from my thick sweat socks and ratty pajamas to my forever ruined face. A disgrace in the eyes of Mrs. Leighton Quinn. "Fine. Call me if you need me to help with your laundry." Reading *between* the words of Hannah Quinn, "I'm sure if you had something clean to wear, you wouldn't be wearing that atrocity."

The door closes, my mother at long last on the other side, and reality sets in. My new life. The beast in my very own horror tale. Not even a floor-to-ceiling library to dispel the loneliness. A state I'd better get used to, since I'll not be venturing out into the public anytime soon.

I sag into the couch and cry. I wish the man who did this to me just killed me then and there. Maybe I wanted to survive *that* night, wanting desperately to break free and get away. Put it behind me, a cautionary tale to tell my grandchildren, but those feelings flew out the castle window when the doctor explained that in about three years, after several focused surgeries, my scars will barely be visible from a few feet away. Years...and three feet away. How ugly must someone be to require years of plastic surgery and still come out looking like a female *Chucky* doll? Besides, Hannah Quinn would certainly agree that a one-way trip to Heaven is more desirable than existing permanently flawed.

The first few days in my house are spent sleeping and barely eating, so the fact that I have nothing but sour milk, stale bread, and a quarter jar of peanut butter in the house isn't a problem.

Until today.

What feels like acid is eating its way through the walls of my stomach. There is no way I'm going to the grocery store though; I haven't even looked in a mirror yet—I had my mom cover them with sheets before I came home. "—sitting shiva over the loss of my beauty," as she so kindly put it. Because asking my mother to bring me food is the equivalent to inviting in the devil, I take out my laptop to find a store that delivers.

Forgetting that a powered-down black laptop screen would reflect my image back to me, I catch a glimpse of my face when I open it. Thank goodness the white square bandage covers the worst part, but the red, swollen, horizontal gash across my face is enough to make me vomit the stale peanut butter sandwich I ate when I woke up.

Getting over myself after several minutes, I search supermarkets that deliver and find there's a ShopRite in Brodheadsville that will deliver to my address. I order the basics, but add a few—like, twenty—pints of Ben & Jerry's ice cream. When I've placed my order, for delivery two days from now, I dial up the local pizza place and order a chicken parmigiana pie and a two-liter bottle of soda before I go on Amazon and download about a dozen Kindle books. I have a feeling I'm going to be reading a lot in the coming months. At least until my leave of absence is over—at which point, I have no idea what I'll be doing to earn a living, since I'm pretty sure my mother's correct in her assumption that my appearance is no longer suitable for television...even if it is just a small local station.

10.

Q^{uest}

I return from California one last time, at least for the foreseeable future. I'm here to make a home in the northern mountains of New Jersey. My decision to reopen my grandfather's store under my management came at the urging of my mother, who wanted me to get involved in something that would take me away from my three-year-long pity-party. The first thing I do when I get there? Buy an inexpensive canvas punching bag and a speed bag at the local sporting goods store and clear out a corner of my grandfather's garage to hang them. My two fists the designated beneficiaries to my anger, I need something close by to console them unless I want my grandfather's cabin to take the brunt of my outbursts. Building a new weight room can come later.

After I'm done hanging the bags, I begin rummaging through the old garage—a garage bigger than the cabin out front where he'd lived.

There are boxes everywhere.

Books. That's what I find in the first three boxes I open. Mostly old paperbacks. I flip through *The Grapes of Wrath* then move on to the boxes lined up on the other side of the garage.

My grandmother's old china sits in several of the boxes on the shelf in the corner. With a careful hand, I skim a plate, recalling the macaroni and meatballs we'd eat on them every Sunday after twelve o'clock Mass. "Wash your hands, Piccolo. You cannot help Nonna make the meatballs with dirty hands." Nonna and Nonno. I'd forgotten the names I used to call them. Back then, they lived in a large house on the top of a hill. My parents and I lived in a smaller Craftsman at the bottom of the mountain. I loved being at their house. My friends did too. After school, Derek, Henry, and I would ride our bikes up that mountain to visit my grandmother. Usually because she had a Sicilian pizza just out of the oven when we got there, but mostly because my grandparents' place was warm and welcoming. Nonna had both a Playstation *and* a Nintendo system for us to play with, as well as a never-ending supply of baked-goods and iced-tea. Afternoons in California, on the other hand, were spent in after-school care until I'd taken up baseball and football in eighth grade, when practices took up the rest of my after-school hours. Gone were my carefree bicycle days and time spent in my grandmother and grandfather's home. A piece of me died during that move across the country, because never again would I know the jovial boy I'd left behind. I'd buried him so deep I didn't know how to resuscitate him.

When I've had enough of the garage, I go into the house, pour myself a scotch, and open my laptop to see if Ginny emailed me the list of support groups in the northern New Jersey area. I still don't want to go, but now that I'll be in Jersey for a while, I need somewhere to go to get out of my own mind. True to her word, Ginny forwarded a list of groups that meet in the surrounding areas. I jot a few of the addresses and phone numbers down and look them up online. The closest group meets fifteen miles away, but I circle the name on my notepad and resolve to making a phone call after I take a shower. It's not something I want to do, but it is something I *need* to do.

THE STENCH OF BURNT coffee lingers in the air of the recreation room at Calvary Lutheran Church. Seven members sit on slate folding chairs at the opposite end of the entrance. Not the huge support group I was hoping for to keep me well-hidden and out of the line of fire. Just the thought of sharing my inner emotions has me pulling on the non-existent collar of my Henley. Mrs. Conklin tried my junior year in high school to get me to talk about how my father's death was affecting me. It sucked, that's how it was affecting me.

A tall slender woman with reddish hair welcomes me into the room, her long fingers directing me to an empty chair within the semicircle of participants. With each step I take across the scuffed porcelain floor, it feels like I'm nearing the end of the plank. I take the seat between a portly man whose beefy fingers clutch a Seven-Eleven Big Gulp and his polar opposite—a petite girl, not yet a woman, hugging some hot coffee-house beverage with both hands.

I soon realize standard practice at the beginning of every meeting includes each member being asked to talk about the events of his or her week. Since I'd been a couple minutes late because I'd parked in the lot closer to the church than to the building where the group meets, the girl next to me seems to be picking up mid-discussion. Alyssa has finally had a few tear-free days for the first time since the loss of her mother two months ago. Warren, the dude on my other side, jokes about almost punching the daylights out of his roommate for eating his leftover barbecue ribs. Cheryl's husband of twenty-three years, who's been cheating on her with a younger woman, finally got his ass a new apartment so she doesn't have to look at his lying ugly mug anymore. And Michele got her purging down to two times a day instead of four—a real breakthrough in her fourteen-year battle with bulimia.

"Quest?" Mary lifts her chin. "Would you like to discuss *your* reasons for being here and the type of week you may have had?"

Straightening my back, I say, "If you don't mind, can I just listen this week?"

"Sure. That's your prerogative. However, to be fair to everyone, it evens the playing field, so to speak, if we all share a little something. Next week maybe?"

"Sure," I agree reluctantly, wishing I'd never walked into the room in the first place.

Mary nods and turns her attention to the man sitting all the way to the right of the semicircle. "John? How were things with your daughter this week?"

John worries his hands together, rubbing his palms back and forth against each other. "The same. The only communication from her was either, 'What's for dinner?' or 'I hate you, and I wish I was never born.'"

"What was your reaction to her?" Mary asks.

"You'd have been proud of me. I kept from correcting her grammar." John lets out a mirthless laugh and says, "Mostly, though, I kept from reacting at all, except for telling her what dinner was for the evening."

"You didn't get mad at her for saying I hate you to you?" Warren asks, setting his Big-Gulp down on the floor while he speaks.

"What's the point? Getting mad at her for expressing her feelings seems pointless to me."

"Getting mad at her will let her know you don't like it when she talks like that." Warren shakes his head and sits back, his frown inviting us to his frustrations with John's response.

"How would you have handled his daughter, Warren?" Mary asks.

"I would have sent her to her room."

"For speaking her mind?" Cheryl asks, her arms crossed in front of her chest, what looks like a perpetual scowl pasted to her face. "All you men are the same. If you don't like what you see or hear, you hide it away so you don't have to look at it."

"That's not what I meant at all," Warren says. "I'd punish her. When my son talks like that, he knows there's going to be consequences."

"Cheryl," Mary says quietly, "let's refrain from insulting whole genders, please."

After the group is finished sharing stories and advice with one another, Mary invites us to finish off the coffee and donuts that hadn't been consumed prior, but I decline and tell her I'll see her in the coming weeks. She thanks me for giving the group a chance, and I thank her for welcoming me, pleased with myself for having the fortitude to actually attend a group where my vulnerability is at a high.

At home, I give my Ma a call.

"Hey, Quest."

"The phone didn't even ring, Ma."

"I've been waiting for you to call."

"I told ya I would." I kick off my sneakers and open a beer from the six-pack I picked up after the meeting.

"Are you okay, honey? I've been so worried. Are you staying calm?"

"I'm fine, Ma. And yes, I'm staying calm. I bought new punching bags and already hung 'em up."

"That's my Rocky," she says, but I can hear the worry in her voice.

"Really, Ma, don't worry. I even went to my first support group."

There's silence. She's probably in shock.

"So really, you don't have to worry. I'm fine." Somehow, I almost believe the lie.

11.

H AVEN

When I ordered my food two days ago, I hadn't exactly thought things through. Now I have a delivery guy standing outside my front door waiting for me to open it. He's been standing there for three whole minutes. He knows I'm home, because when he knocked, my instincts kicked in and I yelled, "Be right there." As my hand skims the door knob, it occurs to me that I have to now *open* the door. And that requires me to come face to face with someone. When I'd ordered the pizza the other night, I'd paid online using my credit card. Then I'd asked the delivery boy to leave my order in front of the door. That won't work with the groceries, since ShopRite requires payment on delivery.

Staring at the inside of my door, I suck in a breath, but the air can't travel deep enough. I try again, but even less gets in. I bring a trembling hand to my neck and gasp. It's too hot. Before I fall down in the suddenly spinning room, I stagger to the kitchen chair, sit down, and bring my face to my head. Wetness. I can't sweat. Sweat will burn my open wounds. Then they can get infected. They *can't* get infected. The scarring will be worse.

"Ma'am," the man calls from the other side. "Did you forget I'm still out here?"

Oh my gosh, no, I did not forget you are out there. How could I forget you are out there when that's all I'm thinking about?

"Ma'am? I have other deliveries and your frozen food is out here melting. It's pretty damn hot out here."

It's pretty damn hot in here too. I try again to catch my breath and speak, but I can't. Oh God, please help. Please help me answer this door.

"Ma'am? If you're inappropriate or something, you don't have to get dressed, just pay me through the door. You don't have to open it all the way."

What? "What?" I choke out, the air thinning, easier to catch.

"Ma'am?"

I draw in another breath and exhale. "What did you say?"

I don't know if it's possible, but I swear, I could hear the guy sigh in relief. "I said if you're in a towel or something, you can just open the door a little and pay me. I won't look. Then you can come out and get your groceries after I leave. I just, I really have to get going."

The forming sweat now feels like ice cubes on my skin. "Okay. Okay. I wrote a check. I wrote a check," I say in a rush, grateful we've settled this. "I can slide it under the door. And a tip." I run back to my table where I have the already signed check and a ten dollar bill. Going back to the door, I try to slide the check beneath it, but there isn't any space. Shit. Just open the door a little. Okay. Okay, I can do that. "Um, can you stand back a bit, I'm going to open the door, but—"

"I'm back, ma'am. I won't be able to see you."

Slowly, I unlock my door and turn the knob. "Here you go. Thank you," I say, sticking out my arm while the rest of me stays hidden behind the door.

"Thank you, ma'am. Have a nice day."

I peek out the opening and watch the boy run down my steps and get into his truck. When he's pulled out of my driveway and down the street, I sag against the wall to ease the spinning. Not until I'm completely stable do I open the door all the way and retrieve my melted food.

The next day, I'm met with an equally frightening situation.

Rain pelts on the steep roof above me as a faint knock sounds at the front door downstairs. Who would come visit me without calling first? Ignoring it, I continue to study the jumbled words on my Kindle—words that don't make sense because my focus is on whomever's lurking on the other side of my door.

The rapping persists, and with each pound, the sound gets louder. Fear keeps me from going downstairs and answering the door, but curiosity insists I find out who it is. Dropping to my knees, I peer out my five feet high triangular shaped window and see an unfamiliar blue-green Jeep Renegade parked up on the rocks to the left of my house. Scooching lower so I can't be seen, I keep my eyes on the gravel walk in front of my house to see if my visitor leaves.

He doesn't. The knocking continues. The sound is loud, measured, and persistent, and my fear has worsened. Feeling panic set in again, I crawl away from the window and sit at the top step, wishing I'd brought my cell phone upstairs with me. Slowly, and trying really hard to be steady, I descend the stairs—half on my butt, half crouched-down like a tiger stalking his prey. Though the irony is not lost on me; I know *I'm* the one being pursued.

Once again, I am on my hands and knees crawling across the floor on the hunt for my phone. It's as I'm reaching for it on my end table that I catch sight of the man at my door. Hooded sweatshirt pulled forward enough to cover his face, he is large and intimidating. My stomach trembles, as do my limbs, and suddenly I am thrusted back into the memory of that night. The screaming. The Pain. The Dark. The evil steel eyes. It's him. He came back to finish the job. The Stratford Slasher has returned to finish me off.

Yes, five days ago I said I wished he'd have completed his mission, but that doesn't mean I want him to take his knife to my face again. The thought alone raises my blood pressure and makes me break into a sweat.

Attempting with all my might to hang on to my phone steadily enough to call 911, I fail. I am shivering so violently that the phone slips from my hand and onto the floor. Please go away. Please don't hurt me again. Please please please. I pick up the phone again and struggle to dial 911, but just as I'm connected to an operator, the hooded man drops his hand, ducks down, then stands up and turns away from me so that I cannot see his face. He's racing toward the Jeep when I hear the operator's voice from the other end of the phone. Paying no attention to the operator, I narrow my eyes on the man getting into the Jeep. But either because of the rain, or because it's intentional, his head is held downward, and I can't make out who he is.

"Hello? Is anyone there?" I hear the soft male voice again.

"Oh. Oh, yes. Um. I, uh..." I trail off, unable to form the words.

"Ma'am. Are you in danger?"

"Um, no. No, not any...I don't think so."

The operator continues to ask me questions, while I try to formulate my thoughts into coherent sentences, but I fail to, and several minutes later, a blaring police car speeds up my block and turns into my drive. Dammit. Now what do I do? I scurry to my bedroom and rummage through my closet with a quick hand, but I don't see anything that would function as a makeshift mask to cover my face. Shit.

The doorbell rings, and it's too soon. I'll have to face the officers with my bare face, and I can't do that.

For the second time today, there's a pounding at my door. "Ma'am, step aside. We're busting down the door."

Damn. I can't find it in me to run to the door and open it, so I run back to my room and let them charge through my front door. It crashes with a heavy thump. Why didn't I listen when Daddy told me to replace the old wooden door with a steel one?

"Ma'am?"

Bringing a hand to the side of my face, I keep my head down and step out from my bedroom into the hallway.

"Miss?" The officer smells like rain—clean, earthy. "Are you hurt?"

No, I'm not, I want to say, but instead I signal with my head, the taste of vomit close to my throat.

"Miss, you called emergency. Is someone else in the house? Did someone hurt you?"

Again, I shake my head, but barely parting my lips, I whisper, "No. No one's here. No one hurt me."

"Your phone call said someone was here."

"Yes," I say, elevating my voice to a more moderate level, but still studying the chestnut carpet beneath me. "There was someone pounding on my door. For about ten minutes."

"Can we sit?" The officer asks, pointing toward the living room.

I nod and lead him to the kitchen table, which is poised between the kitchenette and the living area. My chalet has one large great room, one bedroom, one bathroom, and one loft—a good fit for a single person, but suddenly way too small. I let the officer sit first so that I can sit in the seat to his left. My face is slashed across its whole width, but my right side doesn't have the hole, and it's only covered with a small bandage as opposed to the large white one on my left side. Resting my cheek in my palm, I repeat telling the officer that a man in a black hood was banging on my door.

Before the officer responds, another one, holding a dripping wet black garbage bag, walks through my busted doorway. "We found no one on the grounds," he says, wiping his muddy feet on my now soaked and dirty welcome mat.

Finding it difficult to keep my hand over my face and look at both officers, I give up and drop it before I say, "He took off in a bluish-green Jeep Renegade."

"Did you get the license plate?" the officer at the table asks.

My fingers find my face again while I say, "It was raining too hard to see."

The officer at the door speaks. "Did he have a gun, a weapon, anything to make you think he was dangerous?"

Now feeling stupid and overdramatic, I twist my head in my hand.

"This was on your stoop," the drenched officer at the door holds up the garbage bag. "I took it across the road away from any houses and looked into it. It was only a book. I opened the pages, made sure it wasn't a decoy...it was just a book."

A book?

He holds out the bag, I guess assuming I'd get up to take it, and says, "Ernest Hemingway."

Hemingway. Oh my gosh. His refrigerator size should have been a dead giveaway.

The officer sitting next to me says, "By the look on your face, I'm going to assume you know the man that was at your door."

The rock-solid man with the unkempt curls and eyes so blue the sky is jealous? Yes, I know the man that was at my door.

He drops his hand and sets the bag against the wall.

"Yes, I know who it was. I'm sorry," I say into both of my hands, feeling like the biggest loser in the world. Peering out from the top of my fingers, I apologize again. "I didn't mean to upset your day. I was just scared. I'm really sorry."

"Does your fear have anything to do with what happened to you..." he breaks off and points to my face. "I, mean, assuming someone did this to you?"

Now my fingers work to stop some tears from falling out of my eyes. Yes, someone did this to me. Yes, my fear has something to do with what happened to me. It has *every*thing to do with it. "Yes," is all I say.

"Do you have an abusive boyfriend, miss?"

"No." I pause and say it again. "No. It was that...that..." I've said the name a thousand times from the safety of my news desk, but to say it out loud now...now that I've become one of his victims? It's more difficult than I'd have thought.

"That? You're not talking about the Stratford Slasher, are you?" he says, scrutinizing my face.

My breathing hitches and my body tenses, but I jerk my head forward.

"Oh, dear, I'm so sorry." He clicks his pen, and says, "What's your name?"

"Haven Quinn," I say, dropping my hand to the table.

"Haven Qu...the newscaster? The one on channel three?"

"Yes." I feel my lip tremble as I continue to fight the tears.

"Wow. I'm surprised we hadn't heard about you. When did it happen?"

"About three, three and a half weeks ago." Under my breath, I mumble, "I don't even know what day it is today."

The officer covers my hand with his. "I hope you're getting counseling."

The officer at the door clears his throat. "I'm going to get something to put this door back up temporarily and take measurements so that I can send someone tomorrow to replace it."

"Yeah, sorry about that," Officer Kitchen-Table says. "We didn't know if someone—"

"I get it. It's my fault. I was looking for something to cover my face."

The officer pats his palms on the table and stands up. "I should go help Vic with that door."

When I'm alone again in the kitchen, I fight the urge to cry, knowing the police officers will be back soon, and instead, I put the kettle on for a cup of tea. The house has gotten quite cold since I lost my door. While the water is heating up, I pick up the garbage bag against the wall and pull out the yellow padded envelope. Shoving the wet plastic bag into the garbage can, I take the envelope and sit on the couch. My name is scrawled in sloppy script across the front of it, and the sight makes me sad. I should have just answered the door. If I hadn't been so afraid and thinking so unclearly, I would have realized that if someone was coming to hurt me, they probably wouldn't have come to my front door in broad daylight—and parked their very distinguishable Jeep where all could see.

But I *was* afraid, and I *wasn't* thinking clearly.

And I missed what Quest Vescovi may have wanted to say.

So...in addition to my parents, Marisela, Eric, Katie, and Devin, I can now add a missed call from Quest to my list. Unlike the others, though, Quest's calls stopped about a week ago. If he left me messages, I wouldn't know, because I haven't checked them. The difference with Quest's calls is that his are unrelated to the incident, because he doesn't know that I've been chiseled into some botched up three-dimensional piece of art some man with a vengeance decided to sculpt. He doesn't know that I am a dead woman still able to breathe.

I'm sitting on my chair in the loft, my tea on the table beside me, in the middle of reading Ernest Hemingway's real-life chronicle of his safari across the Serengeti plains, when I hear another car pull up my drive. Why can't I just be left alone to "ring my church bells" in peace?

When I peek out the window, I recognize Marisela's car right away. This brings me both comfort and unease. I love Marisela. I want to jump inside her arms and let her hug all my pain and ugliness away. But I'm embarrassed to have her look at me. I don't want her to see what I've become.

From my triangle window, I follow Mari's hike up my steep driveway until I can no longer see her. As soon as she disappears from sight, I hear the knocking. Light steady cracks against my broken wooden door. The knocking continues as I make my way downstairs—one slow step at a time.

"Haven?" I hear her voice once I'm closer to the door. "Haven, it's Mari. Please let me in."

I shuffle toward the door and place my hand on the door knob. But instead of turning the knob, I squeeze it and press my forehead against the door.

"Haven, please. I miss you."

I miss you too.

"I'm worried about you, Haven," she says louder. "And why the hell is your door broken? Haven, now I'm really concerned. Come on already." Marisela is now banging on the door, an urgent request for her to be let in.

I'm not sure when I started to cry, but when a tear falls onto my finger and slides onto the doorknob, I slowly turn the knob and open the door.

"Oh, thank God," she says as she barrels inside and hugs me hard. "Haven. I just had to hold you."

That's when I break down on Marisela's shoulder. She lets me cry until my well of tears is dry. And then, she backs up and hands me a small gift bag. "Thought you could use these," she says, before walking over to my couch and setting her purse down.

Following her to the couch, I sit and so does she.

"You look like you're in so much pain, Havey."

"You have no idea. It hurts so much." Now, I don't know if Marisela was talking about the physical pain or the emotional pain, but telling her how much I hurt satisfies both types, regardless.

She positions herself on the couch so that she's facing me, and I do the same so that I'm facing her. "I know you haven't been answering my calls, and I know your mother said you didn't want any company, but I know that's not true. They wouldn't let me in the hospital when you were in ICU. I listened to your mom and gave you space, but you've been home now. And I'm not taking no for an answer. You can't go through this alone? I know you need me, Haven. Whether you want to admit it or not."

She's right. She's so right. Of course I need my best friend; I just don't want her to *look* at me. My hands keep naturally moving to my face to cover it, but I know it doesn't keep her from seeing the marks and the bandages.

"Havey, stop. Please don't cover yourself from me. I don't care what you look like, I just care that someone did this to you in the first place." She's reaches forward and rubs my leg. "I love ya, honey. Don't be ashamed in front of me." Mari pulls back and says, "Look in the bag."

"You didn't have to buy me any—"

"Just look."

I reach into the bag, and pull out a huge wad of tissue paper.

"It's inside the paper."

I unwrap the huge bundle of tissue paper, to find a red eyeglass case in the center. Inside the case is a big black pair of sunglasses. "Oh my God," I say, chuckling.

"I figured you'd be a little self conscious, so I got you the biggest pair I could find. They rival Jackie O's."

"Oh my God, Mari. Thank you. Thank you so much." I take the glasses out of the case and put them on. In an instant, I relish my new security blanket.

Marisela sits back, tucks her knees beneath her, and gets comfortable. "What happened, Haven? Why were you walking out there alone?"

I fold my arms over my chest. Chills fill my spine. "I was just so tired, Mari. I thought...if I could just get into my bed." I wipe the wet under my eyes. "I'm so stupid. I knew..." I hiccup and say, "I knew it was dangerous."

"Oh, honey," she says, scooching over to hug me. "You're human. Sometimes we don't think things through."

"It was so scary, Mar. I thought I was gonna die."

Her arms comfort as her hands soothe my back.

"I didn't even fight back," I say between more hiccups. "When he pulled me into that...oh my god." I sob, unable to get the words out. I didn't even fight back. Once he got me into that alley, I let him hurt me. Why didn't I save myself?

Marisela doesn't even need me to say the words; her heart already knows. "We can't predict how we're going to react when we're frightened. Sometimes we're just so shocked that something's happening, that we don't even know we're *not* fighting to get away. Next time, you'll be prepared."

"*Next* time? God forbid."

"Oh my God, Havey. I didn't mean that. That was just a figure of speech. No, there will not be a next time. Things like that don't happen to the same person twice in one lifetime."

I make a conscious effort to believe that last statement.

12.

Q uest

I've spent the last two months going through my grandfather's belongings, both in his home and at his store. Though I've thoroughly examined his bookkeeping and done a physical inventory of his store, I am still not ready for the grand re-opening of his bookstore. I've never owned my own business, and I don't know much about books, but I know keeping the store open is the right thing to do, and not because I want to keep the Hemingway collection. As much as I'm pissed at her right now, I have to admit that Haven Quinn was right when she'd said I'd get to know my grandfather by spending time in his store. Through the index cards of quotes he'd hung on the shelves beneath his favorite books, I have learned that my grandfather was not only a strong man and a hard worker, but his soul was wrapped in goodness and his heart was made of gold. He was a dreamer and a doer, a lover of people and a lover of life. Beneath each chosen edition, my grandfather wrote a little blurb of how that book related to his life. Three of those index cards have introduced me to the essence of what made my grandfather who he was. From *The Alchemist* written by Paulo Coelho, my grandfather had handwritten, "A personal legend is your life's spiritual purpose. My wife and my bookstore are mine." The second quote to give me glimpse of my grandfather was the card beneath J.D. Salinger's *the Catcher in the Rye*. My grandfather wrote, "Holden Caulfield needs to protect himself from the painful emotions that may come from getting too close to a person, but I would rather endure the pain of his loss than to have missed the joy of his love." Underneath the quote, in a tiny scrawl were the initials QRV. My initials. Grief overwhelms me as I let its meaning sink in.

The third index card that cements my respect for my grandfather, despite my father's disdain for him, contains a quote by Leo Tolstoy in *Anna Karenina*, *"It's much better to do good in a way that no one knows anything about it."* Beneath Tolstoy's quote, my grandfather simply added, "Do not let your left hand know what your right hand is doing." If I'm not mistaken, it's a passage from the Bible, and gives hint of my grandfather's altruism.

Through his store, I am learning that my grandfather was filled with kindness and love, and whatever came between he and my father would not dampen my renewed admiration for him.

Tomorrow at ten in the morning, I will reopen the doors to Dingman's Corner Book Shop and continue my grandfather's legacy, whether I am ready to or not.

Tonight, however, I am hanging back with a six-pack of beer, a large chicken parm pizza, and *Pride and Prejudice*, the BBC mini-series, DVD number two. I watched number one last night, and figured I'd already invested the time, I may as well finish it. And no, I am not a Jane Austen fanatic—I've never read her books—but another one of my grandfather's index cards quoted this particular novel. *"I cannot fix on the hour, or the spot, or the look or the words, which laid the foundation. It is too long ago. I was in the middle before I knew that I had begun."* When I'd read the quote, I couldn't fathom its meaning—and his own note, relating to his love of books, was too vague for me to understand— so I decided to get to know the meaning of Jane Austen's words within the context she'd intended. However, being the impatient man that I am, I'd rather watch the five hour movie than read the three-hundred-and-something page book.

When *Pride and Prejudice* is over, and the pungent aroma of pizza long gone, I shut off the TV, and go to bed. My new life begins when I wake—a life my grandfather built for himself, but has now become mine.

AFTER AN EARLY MORNING jog along the lake, and a quick shower, I'm at the store trying to remain calm. James Meadows, the local young adult author I have lined up for a reading is already here and watching me with a knowing smirk. "It'll be fine, bro. Your grandfather's regulars are some of the nicest people you'll ever want to meet," he says. "And they're loyal. They'll be here, don't worry."

I turn the key and then turn around. "It's not them I'm worried about. It's me. I'm not going to be able to answer their questions about these books. I know nothing about them. I barely read."

"Don't worry. They know enough *for* you. His clientele are die-hard readers. As long as you know your inventory, they'll be telling *you* about the books. And what they're looking for if you don't have it."

"Thanks, man."

There are already two customers waiting at the door. "Hello, Mr. Vescovi," the middle-aged woman says. "We're so sorry about your grandfather. He was a wonderful man."

"Thank you."

"Mrs. Gannon," James says. "It's nice to see you."

"Nice to see you too, James. It's always wonderful to see my former students succeed."

"Franky," Mrs. Gannon says. "This is James Meadows. He used to be one of my students. Now he's a famous author."

"Hello, Mr. Meadows," the teenage girl says.

"I'm so glad you all could come today. I kept everything where my grandfather had it, so I'm sure you'll know your way around. James will be doing his first reading at eleven o'clock, but I'm sure he's free to talk now." I look at James who is already nodding and pulling Franky aside.

"You look nervous, honey," Mrs. Gannon says.

"A little," I lie, as beads of sweat pool at the back of my neck.

"Take a deep breath and enjoy it. This is our favorite place to visit. May I call you Quest? That's how your grandfather referred to you."

"Oh, yes, of course. Quest. My grandfather spoke of me?" The sudden rise in pitch in my own voice surprises me.

"Oh, yes. He worried for you when you came home from the war. He was concerned with how you'd deal with being back."

All the energy leaves my body, and the backs of my knees feel soft. Reaching back for the desk I'm standing in front of, I rest against it to keep from falling.

"I'm sorry, Quest. I'm being insensitive. I only meant that he always talked about you, and always worried about your well-being. I'm sorry if I brought up anything painful."

"It's fine," I whisper, but then the bells on the door ring and three more people come in. I shake off the words Mrs. Gannon shared with me and introduce myself to the new customers. After that, the next few hours fly by. The customers couldn't wait to tell me how sad they were for my grandfather, but how happy they were to find out I was keeping his store open. "This place is our home away from home," one or all of them had told me through the course of the day.

While a crowd of about a dozen mingle with each other over the refreshments, a customer I hadn't noticed walk in catches my attention. A tangled blond mess hangs long beneath a purple baseball cap as the unkempt woman browses the Classics section. I walk up behind her to introduce myself, "Hello, I'm Quest Vescovi, the owner—" but I stop when the customer turns sideways and yelps. Instinctively, I grab her shoulder, but she yanks away, adjusting her cap and hair forward so that, with the huge black sunglasses perched low on her nose, all I can see is her jawline.

But it's not enough to hide her identity.

"Haven?"

She shakes her head, turns, and bolts out of the store. Since I'm not as thin and agile as she is, I can't maneuver myself out of the store as quickly. By the time I get outside, she's nowhere in sight. I don't understand why she'd run. And why she's hiding beneath such a large sweatsuit and sunglasses. This, coupled with the fact that she hasn't answered any of my or my lawyer's phone calls, nor did she come to the door the day I dropped off *Green Hills of Africa*—even though I saw her CR-Z parked outside and there were lights on in her house—confirms my suspicions that she's going to fight me for that collection. And now, the building elation that was following me throughout the day, the feeling that I made the right decision by saving my grandfather's bookstore, has been bulldozed in a matter of thirty seconds. Not that it matters...she can fight me all she wants, I just know now that it was definitely the right decision in keeping this store open. Even if it means I have to stay here for five years. She just pissed me off, and there's no way I'll give in now.

And was that a scar I saw on her face?

13.

H AVEN
I should not have ventured out. Showing up at Quest's opening was stupid.

I just want to bring normalcy back into my life. Foolishly, I thought Mr. Vescovi's bookstore could do that.

Wrong.

When I'd first walked into the store, the scent of the books mixed with the dusty carpet and the old cedar walls had me almost believing I'd gone back in time. The absence of my favorite little Italian man certainly kept me rooted in the truth, but when I'd closed my eyes...just for a moment...and inhaled the musty odor I'd come to love *so* much, I could almost taste my former life on the tip of my tongue. I could feel it at my fingertips when I skimmed the leather bindings of Jane Austen's social observations or Jules' Verne's adventures. I could hear it in the excited chattering of some of Mr. Vescovi's regular customers—people I had once considered friends. And upon opening my eyes and keeping them averted from the new store's owner, I could almost see my old life within the narrow aisles that sustained my favorite shelves.

It was when Quest's deep voice interrupted my momentary detachment from reality that I regretted leaving my house. I'd no idea what to say. I hadn't planned on talking to him...hadn't considered that my ridiculous get-up would mask me so ineffectively. I'm sure he saw my face.

What the hell was I thinking?

What must Quest be thinking?

And what the hell would my mother think if she saw me right now?

Sitting at my kitchen table, I bring my palms to the sides of my head and squeeze, attempting to keep the crazy thoughts from escaping. I've become everything my mother despises—a rumpled, neglected mess. I wish the slasher had just finished the job. I don't know how to move on from this. I don't know how to live looking like I do. Not when my own mother can't even stand to look at me.

I want to scream.

Loudly.

But no one will hear.

And what good would screaming do if no one's there to hear me? Where is the relief in that? How do I let go of this anger I have toward this man I don't even know? How do I let him know that he ruined my life? How do I let him know that he took out my soul when he carved out my face? How do I do the same to him?

TODAY IS THE DAY. THE unveiling of Haven Quinn.

Doctor Begley, my plastic surgeon, is set to remove my bandages, and my father is with me, holding my hand, as the doctor uncovers my scars.

He tells me I'm healing nicely as he says, "Let's take a look," and hands me a mirror that looks like a ping-pong paddle.

Reluctant to take the mirror, I close my eyes and hold out my hand.

"You're going to have to open your eyes, Haven. I'd rather you see yourself for the first time here with me, than alone at home."

Slowly, I open my eyes and lift the paddle toward my face. It only takes a brief second to see, I don't want to look any longer. Shoving the mirror at Doctor Begley, I leap off the bed and reach for my purse on the chair.

"Haven. This is going to take a little while," he says, taking my purse out of my hand, and walking me back to the bed. "I promise, though, you will not always hate how you look." He waits for me to sit back up on the bed and hands the mirror to me again. "There is still a lot of swelling that needs to go down, and the redness won't always be there." Touching his finger to the left side of my face, he continues with, "The scar on your left cheek may need another graphing, but I still want to wait and see before I decide. Also, if you're interested, you'll probably be ready for some scar revision on the lesser scars in a little over three months." He cups his hand around my hand and guides the mirror up so that I look into it. I look, but then quickly turn my eyes toward Doctor Begley. "I'd say just after the start of the new year. I'd love to do those surgeries, regardless if you need more graphing on this one," he says, moving my face back and forth with his fingers on my chin. "I think you'll be much happier about your appearance, and it will help you to regain your self-esteem."

Setting the mirror down on the bed, I talk. "I don't want to go through all that pain again," I tell him honestly. "It was...it was just too much. It's not worth it."

He pats my hand. "It will *be* worth it, I promise. Besides, it is not going to be nearly as painful as what you've already gone through. You had just been hurt...very badly. Most of your pain was from the beating you took, not the surgery." He turns around and fetches a few pamphlets from the stand by the door. "Here," he says, turning back and handing them to me. "Read them. There are some links to sites that may help you determine your decision. Don't say no just yet."

I let out a small sigh on top of a smaller smile. "Thank you," I tell him, hopping off the bed.

"Are you sure you don't want to take one more look. A longer look. It's harder to do when you're alone."

"No. I'm not ready."

"Okay," he says, sounding disappointed. "Make your follow-up appointment for a month from now. You can let me know then."

Out in the waiting room, my father asks, "Did it go okay?"

"It went." I'm really not in the mood to talk about it right now, and God bless my daddy, he lets the conversation end there.

On the way back to the parking garage, I stay a step behind my father, hoping to hide behind his large frame. We stop at a Starbucks for vanilla chai lattes, and I make sure to pose my sunglasses low on my nose so as not to let anyone see my newly unbandaged face.

It takes us two and a half hours to get to my development, and when my father pulls up my driveway, he asks if I want him to come in.

"You know, Daddy, I appreciate it, but all I really want to do is go to sleep."

"Pumpkin," he says, alternating his gaze between just over my shoulder and my eyes. It must be hard seeing the scars on his once beautiful daughter's face. "I know we don't have the closest of relationships. I blame that on myself."

I open my mouth to disagree, even though I *do* agree—how can we have formed a bond when he was always at the office?—but he holds up a beefy hand.

"I want to change that. When your mother called to tell me..." He swallows, and a sheen coats his eyes. My father never cries. "I was so afraid you'd..." Another gulp, and tears descend his face. "Haven, I was so afraid you were going to die."

"Oh, Daddy."

"It scared me, pumpkin. I've always taken for granted that you and your mother would always be there." I hand him a tissue from my purse. "I'll never do that again."

"Thanks, Daddy."

"My point is...don't shut me out. You can talk to me."

"Thank you. I really do just want to go to sleep, though. It's not an excuse."

My father reaches out his hand and tucks a strand of hair behind my ear. "You're beautiful no matter what, pumpkin. Remember that...call me if you need me, okay?"

Choking back tears, I go to my room to grab my sweats so that I can change into my comfortable clothes and lay down on the couch—so that I may cry.

It's in the bathroom when I'm putting my sweatpants back on that I take a look at the sheet covering the mirror and wonder if I'm ready to see what I look like. Prior to today, I'd changed my bandaging and put the ointment on without looking. It'd become second nature by now anyway. But as I told Doctor Begley in his office, I'm not ready to see myself just yet. I'm afraid. What if I'm ugly? What if I'm so ugly I decide to deal with the pain and get more surgery? Then will I be too impatient to wait three whole months?

Can I handle seeing my new face? According to my mother, my nose already made me imperfect; how grotesque must I look now? Oh, Hannah, I'm sure I'm a real embarrassment to you now.

Digging my neglected fingernails into my palms, I pace the floor and try talking myself into it. You can do this, Haven. You've withstood your mother's belittling all your life; if you can handle that, you can handle anything.

It's well after the sun goes down that I finally step in front of the covered mirror. With only the moonlight shining in through the bathroom window, I use just two fingers to pull down the dark-gray sheet. There behind the broken light streaming through the blinds is the shadow of a girl I barely recognize. Even my outline has changed—like a drunk man drew a picture of me and couldn't keep a straight line. My nose is different too—wider. There are scars on top of scars on top of scars. A dot-to-dot picture gone terribly wrong.

Reaching out to touch the mirror, I trace my distorted form—familiar fingers on an unfamiliar face—until I can no longer stare at this stranger that holds me hostage. Dropping my fingers and my head simultaneously, I pick up the hairbrush off the back of the toilet and wail it at the mirror. It bounces off the edge of the sink and falls to the floor. Not feeling relieved at all, I pick up the brush again and bang it repeatedly on the sink. Thrashing, thrashing, thrashing. Vibrations tingling through my hand, traveling up my arm. Yet I hammer some more...until lack of energy becomes stronger than anger, and the brush cracks in half. I, then, drag myself into bed, pulling the covers up over my entire body, and lie on my side motionless and emotionless, staring at the silver sky beyond my window until sleep gifts me with a short-lived reprieve.

Sometime during my self-induced coma, the nightmares begin. In each, I don't fight back. Not even a scream. I let him slice my left cheek, then turn my head to give him access to the right. When did I become such a martyr?

When I reemerge from my bed two and a half days later...hungry and done feeling sorry for myself. The first thing I do is grab a rotting banana and stuff it in my mouth. Then, I go into the bathroom, avoiding the mirror, and turn on the shower. The hot water penetrates my grimy hair and skin while it washes away my torment. Sleeping for days had one effect—it opened my eyes to just how compliant I've become. No more. It may take a while to find my bearings, but I will adjust to my new life one day, and I will not take my beatings lying down any longer.

14.

Quest

I wake from a dream—shuddering, sweating, cursing. Haven Quinn takes the place of young Anisa in the nightmare that hasn't varied since leaving the Army.

Why the hell was Haven in my nightmare? Why the hell was Haven chained to the bed instead of Anisa? Why the *hell* was I seeing Haven violated over and over and over? As if watching it happen to that little girl every damn night in my dreams isn't hard enough.

I know what prompted this dream though...I almost slipped at Group tonight. Almost told them about my discharge. Almost told them how absorbed in thought I've become with Haven. But I didn't. My throbbing throat stopped the words from coming out. The only thing I did disclose was that my father died and took me away from my grandfather, who years later left me his world.

Because I can't get back to sleep, I go for my run now, instead of waiting until morning. It's the middle of the night, but I'm hoping it will quiet my mind. The air is brisk and windy, and though I'm not dressed for this weather at all, I embrace the blustery cold, because it helps soothe my mind. I run in the direction of the store, because that's the only direction I'm familiar with; I'd hate to get lost out here in the black night and not know how to get home. The mini flashlight I have with me is not enough to help me navigate through unfamiliar territory. It's even less effective than the flashlight app I have on the phone I left on the table by my front door.

When I get to my store, someone is standing outside, peering in the window. As I get closer, I recognize the purple baseball cap, specifically the blond hair beneath it. "Haven?"

Because I catch her off guard, she spins around, nearly clipping my head with the backpack she has clutched in her hand.

I stop her mid-swing, "Whoa there, missy, put your backpack down. It's just me."

She drops the bag back down to her side, sighs, and turns away, heading for the car that I hadn't noticed a second ago parked at the curb to the left of my store.

"Haven, stop. Please," I beg. "Please." I turn off my flashlight and tuck it in my pocket.

Her footsteps stop, and her shoulders drop.

I walk up beside her, and she turns away.

"Haven? Look at me."

"Say what you need to say, Quest. It's cold and I need to get home."

When I move to stand in front of her, she turns again, and I see her fumbling in her jacket pocket with one hand, as she struggles to keep the wind from blowing off her hat.

"Fine," I say, referring to her refusal to look at me. "Why are you doing this? Why are you fighting me on my grandfather's will?"

Her head drops lower, if that's possible, and I hear a soft whimper escape from her lips. She shakes her head, and I hear her mumble, "I'm not fighting you."

"You damn well are, Haven," I say, resting my hand on her shoulder.

She flinches and steps away.

"Haven," I say, touching her arm.

"Don't *touch* me, Quest," she shouts, and when I see the side of her face, I notice she's wearing those big, dark sunglasses again.

"It's midnight, Haven, why are you wearing these?" I ask as I grasp the side of her glasses and pull them off.

"Boundaries," she yells again, grabbing the glasses from me and hanging on to her hat as she takes off to the side of her car.

There's only one streetlight illuminating the sidewalk that we're standing on, but it's enough to allow me to see that it *was* a scar I saw on her face the other day. More than one. Something terrible has happened to her. "Haven, stop."

She opens her door to get inside, but because she's tossing the backpack into her car, I'm there holding the door open before she can close it.

"Who hurt you?"

Haven turns her head away from me and slides her glasses back on. "None of your business, now let go of my door." She reaches for the handle, but I block her. I'm an ass, I know, but I need to know who hurt her.

"What the heck, Haven? Who the hell did this to you?"

"Just drop it, Quest. I'm not fighting you on the books, so have your lawyer mail me the papers. I'll sign them. Now get away from me."

I don't.

"Move the hell away," she shouts from the driver's seat.

"No. Not until you tell me who the hell screwed up your face."

"Ugh," she yells, punching my balls with her fist and bringing me down. Then she takes advantage of my vulnerable position, pushes at my shoulders and knocks me on my ass. "Get. Away from me." Her command is garbled; I've brought her to tears.

She closes her door, whacking me in the head with the corner of it, and starts her car, peeling away before I can even lift myself off the ground.

Who the hell hurt Haven Quinn and made her so violent? And who sucked the goddamned happy soul right out of her?

I don't even bother running home.

I shuffle.

Seeing Haven hurt like that depresses me. It's not even that I know her very well, but I do remember her smile and the glimmer in her eye that radiated from her soul. Similar to the yellow glow of a firefly, her light shone from the energy inside her. To realize someone stole that light hits me in a way I hadn't expected. Her face is not the only thing that's changed since the last time I saw her. Her heart has too.

15.

H AVEN
Because the power has gone out and has been out all day, I'm grateful that my Kindle's battery has a long life. I can't say the same for my laptop and cell though, and because I don't want to use up what's left of my phone's battery in case of emergency, I have no way of communicating with the outside world unless I see them face to face. My courage is increasing some, because I have ventured outside a little more—I just don't do it during the day, and I only go out for a ride in my car so that I don't run into anyone. Although...last night, *that* worked out as well as New Year's resolution efforts come February. Why the hell was Quest Vescovi out for a walk on a night like last night? It was bitter cold and the wind was howling. Did he actually think it was a nice night to go out for a stroll? At midnight?

I'm sitting in my loft reading, and glancing out the window at the rain that began sometime after sunrise, when I hear my cell ringing on the kitchen table.

It's my mother. I don't bother answering. I'm sure there's nothing she has to say that's any different from the last several messages she's left me— *"Haven, you really need to make an appointment for the scar revision surgery." "Haven, you really need to start looking for another job; don't think they're going to welcome you back to the station. You need to be flawless to be on television...even local TV, Haven." "Haven, look at it this way...if you have the surgery done, you can finally get that nose of yours fixed."* Shut up, Mother.

A few minutes after my mother calls, Eric's number lights up my screen. I really shouldn't have turned on my phone. Though I'm not in the mood for conversation, I don't want to worry Eric, so I answer. "Hi, Eric."

"Hey, Hayv...did you lose power?"

I take my phone and head back upstairs. "I did. You?"

"Of course, but the station has a generator, so business as usual."

"Was this an expected storm? I wasn't paying attention," I say, as I sit on the window seat in front of my rocker. Feeling the cushion beneath my fingertips, I decide I don't like the vintage rose design anymore. It's too cheery.

"Yeah. It was. Listen, Haven, I didn't call to talk about the weather."

"Well, not much to talk about on my end." I run a fingernail through the ice forming on my window. I really should put plastic over this. "Is it going to snow?"

"It's kind of an icy-rain right now. Haven, Bert says you haven't returned any of his calls or answered any of his emails. He's wondering if he should be looking for someone permanently to take your place."

"Tell him why not. He'll never keep me once he sees me anyway."

"Haven, stop. If you just call him back, he's not gonna let you go."

"First of all, he *can't* let me go, because I'm on disability. Second of all, who cares?"

"You started getting your disability checks?"

"No. I haven't gotten around to filling out the online forms."

"Haven. Did you fill out the LOA forms at work."

"No."

"Then you gave him reason to think you quit. I mean, he knows about the attack, so he knows you didn't actually quit, but come on, you're not helping out the situation."

"Eric, if you're calling to chastise me, then don't bother. I'll just stop answering your calls like I do my mother. I really don't give a crap if I have a job or not. He's not going to keep me on once he sees what I look like."

"I'm not chastising you, Haven. I'm worried about you. Do you have enough money to survive?"

I don't respond to that, because no, I do not have enough money to survive. I don't even have enough to pay this month's rent.

"Haven, call him. Please. Tell him you want to stay on at the station. Even if you don't want to go back on camera, tell him you'll stay on to gather the news or do some editing. You know you're qualified for that. At the very least, apply for your disability. What are you going to do? Wait 'til you get evicted and have nowhere to live? You know you don't want to move back home with your mom and dad."

"Too bad they weren't divorced. I'd move in with my dad."

"Haven, you're not listening to me."

"No, I'm not."

"Why don't you come stay with me and Katie? We have a pull-out couch, and I know Katie wouldn't mind."

"That's sweet, but I'm fine. Really. Thanks for the invite, but I can't let my battery die. Can I talk to you when the power comes back on?"

"Sure. At least think about staying with us?"

"We'll see."

Since I haven't had any heat since last night, the temperature inside my house has plummeted, and it's almost dark outside. The only light I'll have in the house, in about thirty minutes, is one vanilla cookie scented Yankee candle. I have a fireplace, but no wood.

Before it gets too dark, I leave my loft to search my closets for anything I can use as a blanket. It may be early October, but it's freaking cold in this house, and I'm pretty sure it's only going to get colder.

After I've shed my bed of all its coverings, gathered my bath towels and winter coats, I double-up my socks, and cozy up on my couch. I like the rocking chair in my loft, but it won't keep me as warm and comfortable as my velvety couch. I yearn for a cup of hot tea, but I'm not willing to go out in this weather to get it, so I pour myself a glass of brandy—kept here for my father's visits—and hope it helps to warm me on the inside.

It's nearly pitch-black in my house a little while later, and all I can see is my hand in front of me, and only because I have my candle sitting on the end table next to me. I do have my cellphone, but like I'd told Eric, I really do need to save the battery in case the power doesn't come back on for a while. Note to self: go buy a car charger. But I expected this, and that is why everything is right here next to me—my glass of brandy, and the bottle in case I need more, my bag of Pepperidge Farm Goldfish in case I get hungry, and my almost fully-charged Kindle with lots of books already downloaded.

What I am *not* expecting is a car pulling into my driveway. The headlights shining through the window blind me when I push back the curtains, and it's hard to make out what kind of car it is. When the driver turns off the engine, it's too dark to see *anything*. My heart starts racing. I try to remember that every time a situation like this has occurred in my driveway, it's worked out. It will now, as well.

When the knock sounds at my door, the pounding of my heart overtakes me, though, and I forget all rationalization. "My cellphone works and I'm calling nine-one-one right now!" I actually grab the cell *after* I've warned the intruder.

"Haven, it's me. Quest," I hear him shout from outside.

Oh my heavens. It's him again? At least my heart rate slows down. I leave my candle on the end table and keep my phone at my side, but I don't turn on the flashlight app—he doesn't need a close look at my face. Opening the door, I stand in the six-inch space, letting him know under no uncertain terms he's allowed in. "Why are you here?"

"Can I come in?"

"No."

I can barely see him, but I hear him sigh. "You're not going to let me in?" He sounds shocked.

"No."

"I'm standing in the pouring rain, and I'm freezin' my ass off."

Now, I sigh. "No one asked you to come."

"I'm standing here with a gash in my head that I had to stitch myself...all because of you. And I won't even *mention* the beating my balls took. I think the least you can do is let me in."

I don't really give a shit about his nutsack, but I guess I do feel bad about the gash in his head. "You needed stitches?"

"Yes, ma'am," he says formally. "Two of them."

"And you did them yourself?"

"Yup."

"Why didn't you just go to the hospital?"

"Because I have no idea where it is. Haven. Please. Just let me in."

Letting out a really big exaggerated sigh so he knows just how annoyed I am, I open the door and let him in. "Why are you here, Quest?"

After a second, he says, "That's the only candle you have?"

"What do you *want*, Quest?" I ask, walking back to my couch and grabbing a blanket to wrap around my shoulders.

"How long has power been out up here? I noticed the houses get dark about two miles down the mountain."

"You have power?" I ask, surprised that the whole area isn't out.

"We have power in Jersey. 209 has power too. Only the houses that lead up to your development are dark." I feel him move around me, then I see his shadow. He picks up my candle and holds it up.

"It's freezing in here, Haven. Don't you have a fireplace?"

"Oh my god, Quest. Why. Are. You. Here?"

He moves around the coffee table, places the candle down, and sits on the couch, grabbing some of my towels and pulling them over his lap. I abandon my will to make him leave and resign to my spot on the couch. "Please, Quest," I beg. "Tell me why you're here. If it's about the books, I—"

"I wanna know who did this to you," he says while bringing his fingers to my face.

Backing away, I say, "You really don't respect boundaries, do you?"

"What do you mean?"

"Touching me. Pulling off my glasses. People don't *do* that."

"Oh. I guess..." In the candlelight, I see him frown. "I guess I don't. Sorry."

"Well you should. Respecting people's space is important."

"Fine. I'll keep that in mind. Are you gonna tell me what happened to you?"

"Why? Why do you need to know? You barely know me, so why is it so important to know what happened to me?"

He frowns again. "I don't know." He shakes his head and shrugs. "It bothers me to know someone's hurt you."

"Well, it shouldn't."

"It would bother my grandfather, so it bothers me. Who hurt you?"

"No one."

"Haven."

"What do you care? We're not even friends?"

"Haven."

"Did you really need stitches?"

"I really did."

"And you stitched them yourself?"

"It wasn't the first time. Now stop changing the subject. Who did this to you?"

"I don't want to tell you."

"Why not?"

"Because I don't even know you."

"I'm Quest Vescovi. My grandfather left you half a million dollars that was supposed to be mine, but now I have to earn it and it's going to take me five years. In the meantime, I figure I should at least get to know the woman my grandfather thought so highly of that he'd screw over his only grandson. Now you know me."

"Why don't you leave my house, Quest? No one asked you here."

Sighing, he sits back. "I'm not really trying to be fresh, and it does bother me to know someone did this to you. And because my grandfather thought so highly of you, I do feel guilty not being nice to you. So there. You got a confession out of me. Now can you tell me who the hell did this to you?"

"Fine. It was that slasher that's been going around..."

Quest gasps.

"From Stratford."

"Christ. When?"

"July third. About three months ago."

"Oh my god, Haven. That's horrible." He reaches for the candle to pick it up.

"Please don't." The words rush out. "Put the candle down." He does. "I don't want you to see me. Just...please?" I'm not ready for that.

"Okay. I'll respect that...since you say I have no boundaries. Just...I can't believe you were one of them. How? I mean...was someone with you? Were you alone?"

I sit back and rest my head against the couch. I haven't talked about that night with anyone. Besides crying to Marisela, I haven't really discussed the attack. Not since the policemen questioned me in the hospital, and I had to relive the entire night—the fear I felt when I first saw his reflection in the pub's window, the moment my face hit the pavement when he'd knocked me to the ground, the realization that he was going to hurt me and I couldn't get away. The initial stab of pain that ran as deep as my fear when the point of the knife punctured my skin for the first time. My life flashing before my eyes when I thought I was about to die. No, I haven't talked about that night in a while, but maybe the cold dark room, the comfort of my own couch—this practical stranger sitting in front of me—is giving me some sense of courage, because I say, "Yes. I left work about three in the morning and walked down Main Street to my car."

"BY YOURSELF?" he shouts.

"I'm right here. You don't have to yell. And yes, by myself. I know it was wrong, you don't have to scold me...I know I should have waited for my friends, but...but I didn't, okay? I received my punishment, so no need for you to do it." I say all that while forcing the tears away—not that he'd see them anyway. The power outage effectively saves me from that humiliation as well.

"God, Haven, I didn't mean to shout, it's just..." he shuffles closer and reaches for my face. Again with the boundaries. I back away and he sits back. "Must've been painful."

I shrug. "I wasn't laughing."

"How long were you in the hospital?"

"Two weeks."

"July third. That's why you didn't show up to Sam's office."

"Correct."

He brings his fist to his mouth. "Why did you come to my store?"

Swiftly, I blurt, "I visited your *grandfather's* store." Then, softly, fumbling with the fabric of my quilt, I continue with, "I've missed him. And...I wanted to make sure you didn't change anything."

He sighs on a soft laugh. "I don't know enough *about* owning a bookstore to change it. I've never heard of ninety-five percent of those authors. I have no idea what I'm doing."

"I'm sure he kept good records. You'll be fine."

"You know about books and authors. You know anything about running my store?"

"I went to school for broadcast journalism. I know nothing about running a business."

"But you know books. Know what readers are looking for. I can use knowledge like that."

"Have you not heard anything I've said. I don't go where people are."

"Perfect. You can look through my grandfather's inventory and tell me what it's lacking, what I don't need, what I *do* need. I noticed in his records that he did a lot of online searching for books. Maybe you can do something like that for me. I, mean, I'm sure you're going to need a job, right?"

Can I punch him in his private area again? Because I really feel like punching him in the private area again. "Do you have *any* social skills at all? I mean do you know what is and what isn't appropriate to say to people?"

"What? What did I say wrong?"

"You assume because I have an on-camera job that I won't have my job any longer because of the way I look. You're all the same...God. Looks are so damn important. Even the first day we met, you commented on my appearance."

"Holy shit. *You* said you don't go where people are. I assumed you were implying you wouldn't be going on television anymore."

"Well that's an assumption you don't have a right to make."

"Fine. But I really can use your help. Seriously. Whether you're going back to work or not."

I nod in the dark, contemplating his off-the-cuff proposition. I really could use something to do, regardless of the paycheck. I'm bored as hell going from my couch to my rocking chair, reading book after book. I love reading, and though I consider Mr. Daniels and Mr. Darcy swoon-worthy friends, they are fictional after all. At the end of the day, it's still me, myself, and I.

"You have anyone helping you around here?"

"Help doing what?" I say, squeezing my knees up to my chest and trying to keep warm.

"Well, for one, if this power outage lasts long, do you have a place to go?"

"It won't."

"You live up on a mountain. I doubt you get great service with anything even when the power is on. What will you do if it lasts a few days?" He's looking into my eyes, even though it's dark, I can see them trying to read through mine.

So, I avert them and look down at my my fingers picking at the quilt.

"And food. If you don't go where people are, how are you getting your food?"

"The grocery store delivers. When the guy comes, I wear a baseball hat with my hair down around my face, and I put my sunglasses on."

"You don't need to cover up, Haven...you shouldn't be ashamed that you were hurt."

"Well...say that when you have scars all over *you*...for all the world to see."

16.

Quest
    She's right. I don't have scars all over me for all the world to see.

Mine are all on the inside...tucked away for only me to enjoy.

"Haven, it's cold in here," I say, changing the subject. She's been fumbling with that damn blanket on her lap. "Do you have any wood I can throw in the fireplace?"

"No."

"Good Lord. Why don't you just stay with me? I'm sure my grandfather wouldn't want you to stay here. It's twenty degrees outside. You can stay at his house, my house, while I'm at the store, and after I get home, we'll drive up here and see if your power is back on."

She stares at me drop-jawed.

"What? It makes sense."

"No. It doesn't."

"Fine. Your call. Is your cell charged at least?"

"It is." Haven tosses off her blanket, and I can't help but recall the shapely legs hidden under those baggy pajamas she has on. She stands from the couch and turns toward the door.

I take the hint and get up too. "Well...call me if you need anything."

"Thanks." She picks up the candle and walks me to the door.

Before I leave, I say, "Order about a dozen candles next time you do your grocery shopping online. I'm sure the power goes out quite often up here."

As I walk to my car, flipping on my phone light so I don't trip over any rocks in her poorly graveled driveway, it occurs to me that she could benefit from the support group I just joined. I consider going back up to invite her, but I've bothered her enough tonight. I'll ask her another time.

THE FIRST THING I DO when I get to the store the next morning is call Haven's cell, because I cannot get her out of my mind. Images of her thin frame and battered face scroll through my mind as I envision her frozen and alone. Disappointment sets in when the phone rings for the third time, but after the fourth toll, she answers.

"Hello?"

"Glad to see you haven't frozen to death." I joke, though it really isn't a joking matter, and I'm far from laughing.

"I'm fine. Except that I don't have running water, and my toilet won't flush."

"Sounds like your pipes froze. You can't stay there, Haven. Why don't you come down to the store. You don't have to come in, just text me you're here, and I'll bring my keys out to you. I'll give you my address, and you can stay at my house."

"No. No. I don't need to do that. I'm fine." The rise in her voice contradicts her insistence that she is fine.

"Goddammit, Haven. Don't be so obstinate. Just stay at my house. You can't stay home if you don't have heat or running water."

"I'm fine where I am. Why do you even care? It's not like you've known me very long, nor have you even liked me during the time we *have* known each other. You make no sense."

Her question takes me by surprise, but the truth is, I *don't* know why I care. Maybe it's because my grandfather would care; maybe it's not. I can't put a finger on it. "Fine. Have it your way. Try not to freeze to death."

Business is slow throughout the day—maybe because it's still downpouring and cold outside, more likely because the newness of Rainero Vescovi's grandson taking over the shop is dying down. But I use the time to go through the shelves again, and familiarize myself with the inventory and where each book is placed. It's when I come across *The Storm* by Daniel Defoe that I think of Haven up on her little mountain with no heat, no water, and probably no food. It's the first storm of the season, and it's only supposed to get worse. Today's freezing rain is supposed to turn into tonight's wintery mix, and the wind doesn't seem to be dying down. From what the news app on my phone is saying, there are several thousand residents without power now. Both Pennsylvania and New Jersey are affected. It occurs to me that Haven is not going to give in and stay with me, so I make a call to my friend Stephen at the deli and see what he has in stock. The fact that he's also the local general store, helps me to appropriate everything I need, including wood for her fireplace.

Since staying open for the day is futile, I turn the Open sign to Closed and lock up. Then I go to Layton's Goods and Deli and pick up all the essential supplies, short of a generator, I think will carry Haven through the storm. Hopefully, the twelve gallons of water will allow her to use the toilet, and the wood for her fireplace will give her warmth. The cast iron pot Stephen had in the back of the store can be used to make soup and tea.

I pack my grandfather's old Jeep with the supplies and head up to her house. Her CR-Z isn't in the driveway, which ticks me off, because the roads are slick, and if she stays out any longer, they're sure to turn icy when the temperature drops.

I lug the wood up her stairs and lay them on the floor under the eave, then I go back to the truck to look for something that will keep the wood dry until she comes home. In the back of the jeep, I find a black garbage bag filled with books. I'm not surprised. In every corner of my grandfather's house were piles upon piles of books. It's not a stretch to think he'd have them in his car as well. I dump the books into the trunk and take the garbage bag, plus the bag of food, matches, old newspapers, and the pot up to her front deck. Covering all of it with the black bag as best as I can, I take one last look inside her house, knock in vain on the door, and leave, saying out loud to a God I'm not sure exists that He better make sure she's all right.

17.

H AVEN
I wake this morning expecting to return to my new daily routine—get out of bed, put the kettle on for tea, do my business in the bathroom, prepare my tea, take tea to the couch or loft, and read a book or two. Before losing power, that also included browsing the internet. But to my surprise, after sitting down with my tea, the dusty black screen of my television talks to me. *"Haven, just because you declare yourself a hermit, does not mean you need to live in filth."* Not surprisingly, the television has accurately hijacked the voice of Hannah Quinn. I sip my tea and open my Kindle, determined not to listen to this unwelcome opinion, but my eyes betray my resolve when they notice the chalky black screen actually matches the dusty wood of the armoire it sits inside. The side of the coffee table that I don't use for my tea and laptop is a shade or two lighter than the side that gets used. *Filth,* Hannah's voice repeats. *Filth.*

Today, I clean my house.

It's when I'm sweeping my kitchen floor that I hear the beep and hum of my cable box at the same time the ceiling light flickers on. Power is back. Thank God. Thank the person who left me all that firewood and water for that matter. I'd taken a ride to get a chai latte at the Caffé Latte drive-thru two days ago and when I'd gotten home, there were food supplies, water, and chunks of wood covered in plastic on my front porch. At first, knowing that someone was at my house when I wasn't home frightened me, but as I thought about it some more, I realized that it had to be someone who was concerned for my safety, and not some serial slasher, who'd have left me with supplies to get me through the power outage. The more I'd thought about it, the more Quest Vescovi's name came to mind.

I'm in the middle of rinsing down the shower when the doorbell rings. Not now. Please not now. Not only am I concerned about my scars being seen, but my hair is tied up in a rat's nest of a bun and I have on my oldest sweatpants, complete with the huge tear I got when a group of us broke into the high school gym to play volleyball during off-hours—the night I told my mother I'd been nominated for homecoming queen and she dismissed it as swiftly as she does lint from her wool coat.

The doorbell rings again, this time accompanied by a steady knock.

A bit of fear creeps in, but I'm learning that when people knock to be invited in, they aren't here to hurt me. Straightening out a few strands of hair on top of my head, as if that alone will make me presentable, I go to the front window and see Eric and Katie standing at the door. Has anyone ever heard of a phone? Not that I answer it regularly these days.

Eric catches me in the window, and with a smile that reminds me why I connected with him in the first place, he waves. Katie peeks in and does the same.

Dropping my shoulders, but allowing myself to feel the joy in seeing them again, I open the door.

"Oh, Haven," Katie says, tumbling forward to hug me. "Oh, Haven," she repeats, holding me with all the energy she has. I do the same.

I let her break the hold first, then I say, "Hey, guys," as I pat down my hair again.

"Hi, Haven." Eric's embrace is less warm, but every bit as heartfelt when he pats me on the back and says, "It's good to see you."

"God, Haven, we've missed you so much," Katie says when I tell them to take a seat at the kitchen table.

"I miss you guys too. You want something to drink or anything? I have tea, water," I say with my back to them, because I'm doing a quick search of my counter for my sunglasses. Which aren't there.

"No thanks," Katie says.

"I'm good." Eric holds up his hand.

"Hey, be right back," I say over my shoulder as I go into my bedroom, remembering my glasses are on my dresser. I take a look in the mirror, cringe, and pull my hair out of its elastic. With my sunglasses on and my hair falling forward to cover the scars on the side, I return to the kitchen, and Eric's opening the front door to allow Devin in.

Really? Does anyone know how to use a phone anymore?

"What the hell, Randolph? You knew me and Katie were coming today," Eric says.

That's funny, because I didn't.

"What? You have dibs on visiting her? She's my friend too."

"Hi, Devin," I greet my new visitor. It takes effort not to cover my face with my hand. Why call unnecessary attention to it?

"Haven," Devin says, pulling me into a hug.

After Devin refuses my offer of a beverage, he and I join Eric and Katie at the kitchen table.

"So when did your power come back on?" Katie asks. "Ours came back two days ago."

"Early this morning."

"This morning?" Eric bellows. "What the hell, Haven? How have you gotten by?"

"Not easily," I admit. "But two nights ago, someone left me a dozen gallons of water, wood for the fireplace, soup, tea, a cast iron *pot* so I could heat the soup and tea *over* the fireplace, and a whole bunch of candles. Oh, and matches."

"Someone?" Eric asks, his brow knitted in concern. "You don't even know who left it for you?"

"I have an idea who did it. I just haven't confirmed it yet." Or thanked him.

"Are you sure it's not the guy who attacked you?" Eric asks.

I hadn't thought of that, but why would he? "I think it was a friend of mine."

"You better be sure, Haven."

"Eric, geez," Katie says. "Maybe she has a secret admirer."

I snort. "Not likely. No one's admiring me anytime soon...not looking like this."

"Haven. That's so not true," Eric tells me.

"Your friends like you just the way you are," Devin says. "You shouldn't worry about anyone else."

Eric sneers at Devin then adds, "You're so beautiful, Haven."

"If you think Swiss cheese is beautiful."

Eric chuckles, Devin and Katie do not.

"It's okay, guys. I can joke about it."

"So what have you been doing lately?" Eric asks. "Besides hiding up here in your tower."

Now *I* laugh. "Not much I guess. I did clean today though."

"Haven. Why don't we have a movie night this Friday at our house?" Eric suggests. "Invite your friend...Marisol or something?"

"Marisela?"

"Right. Why don't we? You'll get out, and it'll be good for you to be with friends."

I nod. That does sound fun. "Thanks."

"Yeah, that sounds like a good idea," Devin says.

"You're not invited." Eric sideeyes him.

"Eric," Katie says. "Yes, you're invited too, Devin."

"A movie on Friday sounds like a nice idea. Thank you."

"And ask your friend," Katie reminds me.

"I will. So, how's everything else?"

"Good. My cousin Justin sends his best."

The cousin she wanted me to hook up with. "Tell him thanks."

"He's still interested," she says, a little too enthusiastically for my liking.

I push out from the table and shake my head. Not if he saw my face. "I'm going to make tea. Want a cup?"

"No thanks," Eric says.

"I'll take a cup, Haven." Devin waves his hand and simpers. "Even though I'm a coffee drinker."

"I can order instant coffee for next time you come," I suggest.

"Please don't," he says, cringing at the thought.

"Then stop at Caffé Latté before you come," I joke.

"Better. Where's your bathroom, Haven?" Devin asks, pushing back his chair and standing, yanking down his shirt hem in the process.

"Down the hall on your right."

After the door clicks shut, Eric walks over to me at the counter. "You okay, Haven? For real? Devin's out of the room, and I can send Katie upstairs."

"God, Eric," Katie whines.

Keeping busy with filling the sugar bowl, I say, "I'm fine, Eric. Really." I then roll up the top of the sugar bag and put it away. "And thanks for bringing up the movies. I'm looking forward to it." Turning to face him, I smile. "Let's just not watch *Scarface*. Or *Edward Scissorhands* for that matter."

Straining to turn up the corner of his mouth, Eric says softly, "Maybe we should."

18.

Quest

When I moved to Jersey from California, I had no idea that days would go by where I wouldn't think of the incident that led to my being *other-than-honorably* discharged. For me, the events of that night have been branded into my brain—the consistent nightmares the hot iron that won't let the scars heal. But since finding out about Haven's attack, I find myself thinking about her more and more—why was she walking alone in the middle of the night? What was going through her mind when she was so viciously attacked? What is going through her mind now? Was she raped? It isn't part of the slasher's modus operandi to sexually assault his attackers, but he also doesn't carve out whole sections of skin in the faces of his victims. According to reports I've read over and over online since learning of Haven's attack, his approach is to leave two parallel slash marks down the right side of his victims' cheek. From what I could see in the dark, the heft of Haven's lacerations are on the *left* side of her face. It doesn't make sense. The Stratford Slasher has only attacked each of his victims once, but if Haven's wounds weren't inflicted by this same man, could the one that *did* hurt her return to finish the job? I wish she'd take me up on my offer to help me in the store. Then I could keep an eye on her and make sure that doesn't happen. But she barely stays on the phone with me for two minutes when

I call her to ask. And the only time she's ever called *me* was to thank me for the supplies she very much needed during the storm two weeks ago. I know she has a lot to work through since her attack, but I wish she'd let me help her to get through this transition from on-air personality to whatever she needs to do next. Because I know all too well that transitions are difficult. Especially when that transition requires living an entirely different life than before.

With Haven at the forefront of my mind, I can't help but blurt out a question during one of our group sessions. "How can I help a friend who doesn't seem to want my help?"

"You don't," Warren says at the same time Mary asks, "What kind of help does your friend need?"

"She needs help getting her life back. It was pretty much taken from her when some loser used her face as a canvas to do with as he pleased."

"Poor girl," Mary says while the others mumble something similar.

"And now she won't go out in public. She has her food delivered to her. She only goes out in the middle of the night, wearing a getup she thinks hides her face."

"Does she trust you to help her, Quest?" Mary leans forward, crossing her hands over her lap. Mary's name suits her. She's kind, soft-spoken, and nurturing. The Virgin Mary, my mother would say. The mother of all mothers.

I answer honestly. "She hasn't known me long enough."

"Until she can trust you, I don't think she's going to accept your help. Is she getting counseling?"

"I don't think so."

"It sounds like she could use some professional counseling, but would she be open-minded about giving this group a chance? To get her headed in the right direction?"

My eyes go to the fluorescent lights on the ceiling. "I doubt it."

"Then, just be her friend. Don't try to help her overcome this, just be there for her until she finds her way."

So, that's what I resolve to do. Be her friend.

19.

H AVEN
My cell buzzes as Quest's name lights up the screen. He's been calling me on a regular basis for the past two weeks, mostly to try and get me to come work for him at the store. I don't want to work at the store. Let me rephrase that. I *want* to work at the store; I'd love nothing more than to work at the store, but I don't want to work there while the store is open. He won't take no for an answer. When my phone rings for the third time, I answer it. "Hello, Quest," I say, knowing I could have answered more pleasantly.

"Don't sound so thrilled to hear from me."

"I'm sorry. Hi, Quest," I say with little more excitement.

"Are you busy?"

"I'm still not coming to work for you."

"Why not? I need someone who knows books. I found a whole collection of first edition Stephen King hardcovers online and I have no idea if that's even a thing. For all I know, someone's ripping me off. Please, Haven. I can't do this on my own."

"Online? That's all?"

"For now."

"Are you asking me because you need me and not because I need you?"

"Well, I'm flattered that you need me, but yes, it's true, I need you."

"I don't need you," I say quickly.

"I'm teasing. I know you think I'm offering you a job because I feel sorry for you, but I've told you this already—I don't. I barely know you to feel sorry for you. I just know that you know a thing or two about books and my grandfather liked you. To me, that's all the resume I need."

"I don't like being in public."

"That's fine. You can work from home during the day, and come to the store some evenings after I close. I'll shut off as many lights as we can. The only one you'll have to see is me."

But you would have to see me. "Can I think about it?"

"*After* you tell me if these Stephen King books are legit. What's your email, I'll send you the link."

"It's havenlovestoread at gmail.com, " I say after a moment of silence...just before I hang up on him.

"What was that about?" Marisela asks from her spot next to me on the couch. It's our third weekly movie night. I wasn't comfortable at Eric and Katie's, so my friends yielded to my insecurities and changed movie night to my house. Marisela is the first to arrive.

"Quest is still bugging me about working in his store. Only this time, he's telling me I can come in *after* the store is closed. To help with inventory or something like that."

"You *love* that bookstore, Haven. You should do it."

"He just feels sorry for me. I don't need charity." I pull my cardigan tighter around my chest, suddenly feeling chilly.

"You need a job. And you need to get out of this house."

"Why? I got you guys."

Marisela taps my foot with her own. "You have us no matter what, you know that. But you can't stay inside for the rest of your life. You even changed movie night to your house, so you wouldn't have to go out."

"I go to the drive-thru to get my chai lattes."

"How do you intend on paying for your chai lattes?" she asks, turning her head to scan the inside of my house, but too kind to say anything more.

"With my gorgeous good looks?"

WHEN MY FRIDAY NIGHT movie friends leave, I put on water to make some chamomile tea and change into pajamas. I pull up Quest's email on my laptop and click on the Stephen King link he wants me to look at. What I find when I do is the Holy Grail. A set of first edition hardcovers that range from *Carrie* to *Bag of Bones*. The owner is, or was, a true Stephen King fan; every book from 1973 to 1998 is there, including the 1975 *Salem's Lot* version with the original $8.95-stamped dust-cover. I would never sell these books if I owned them. I take another look at all the descriptions before replying to Quest's email.

To: qv1@dingmancornershop.com
Subject: <u>Stephen King Books</u>
Worth every penny if they're in decent condition. If you have the money, and they check out in person, buy them.
Haven

After I send the email, I search for the site I need to claim temporary disability and finally fill out the forms. The rent isn't going to pay for itself.

20.

Quest

"You need to come with me to look at them. I'll pay for your flight."

"No, I can't."

"Why? What's holding you back? You're not working right now. Do you have a doctor's appointment? Are you allowed to travel?"

"I just don't want to."

"Haven, I can't go by myself; I have no idea what to look for. Please. I'm going to pay you. Do I have to beg?"

There's silence on Haven's end of the phone, and I'm hopeful that she's about to say yes to coming with me to look at, and possibly buy, the Stephen King books I would like for the store.

"I'm not comfortable," she says after a while.

"Why not?"

"You know why not. Plus, I hardly know you."

"We're getting to know each other, aren't we? I know you as much as I know anyone."

"You're kidding, right? We talk on the phone. Barely."

"Not kidding. And I have more of a relationship with you than I have with my mother at this point and time."

"That's just sad."

"True story."

"Sad story," she says with a hint of pity behind her words.

"Haven. I'm joking. My relationship with my mom is a healthy one, I just don't speak with her very often. Listen, if I go by myself to look at these King books, will you at least make yourself available over FaceTime or Skype so that I can show you the books as I'm looking at them?"

"You mean you'll FaceTime the books to me and flip through the pages and let me see the binders and all?"

"Yes. Even though I think you look perfectly okay to go *with* me to New Hampshire, I'll settle for video chatting...even though I've never done that before in my life." There's lots of stuff I've been doing lately that I've never done before.

"You only saw me in the dark. You would *not* think I look perfectly okay to be seen with you if you saw me in the light of day."

"Your looks have nothing to do with buying books. Will you please allow me to FaceTime you when I get there?"

"I guess so. When are you going?"

"Since I have to close the store, I'm going to try to get a late flight for next Sunday night and hopefully return on Monday. This way, I'm only closed one day."

"You know, Mr. Vescovi never opened on Monday."

"I saw that. I don't get many customers in on Monday. You think I should make it a regular thing?"

"I do. I also think you should hire a part-time, or even full-time, employee before you burn yourself out. To your grandfather, the bookstore was his life, but you're young and probably need time to go to the gym or the bar or whatever it is you guys from California like to do."

"Guys from California?" I laugh. "I don't think we're that different from guys in New Jersey. Besides, I asked you to come work for me. You said no."

Again, I am met with silence, or rather, a deep sigh followed by silence.

"No pressure, Haven. If you're ever ready, you have a job here *during the day* too."

"Why are you being so nice to me? I thought you hated me."

"Hate's a strong word, Haven. And I never hated you...I just didn't like the idea of you taking what was mine."

"And now you want to give me a job. Essentially, isn't that the same thing?"

"If you wanna look at it that way. But it's a job, not a bazillion dollar book collection."

"So my salary *won't* be a bazillion dollars?"

"Is that a yes?" I ask, again feeling a surge of hope.

"No. I'm not ready."

"But wait...you're still helping me from home, right? That hasn't changed, has it?"

"No, it hasn't. I'll still help you from home...and the occasional after-closing hours when you need me for inventory."

"Thank you, Haven. All kidding aside, that is a huge relief for me. Look, I gotta go. I have to book that flight. Keep looking for books for me, will ya?"

"Got nothing better to do." She hangs up.

My chest constricts. She's got nothing better to do than to hang around at home. Hidden like a battered diamond left in the drawer because it didn't make the cut for the lighted showcase. Why does this bother me?

I WAKE UP HOLDING THE bedroom lamp out in front of me, ready to shoot the goddamn militia commander with it.

But then I realize I'm in my grandfather's bedroom and not running from my tent with my Glock in hand.

After several seconds and with a trembling hand, I set the lamp back down and sit on my bed, reminding myself that I am home now and far from middle-east battle grounds. I'm thousands of miles away from the torturous dehumanization that took place every single day. Right in front of me. Right in front of us all.

Dropping my elbows to my knees, I let my head fall into my hands and attempt to return to the present. The nightmare stays in my head, though, and it constricts my breath. I gasp to collect air, but the image is still there, and I'm unable to let it go. The only way I know how to rid my mind of the horror is by fighting it. By punching the shit out of my bag until I'm convinced I can forget it...at least for the moment. But it's never truly gone. The reality of what happened three years ago sits at the back of my mind like a ticking bomb set to explode at any given moment. But after revisiting that night in my dream, it feels dangerously close to detonating any minute.

I thrust myself off the bed, and with bare feet, I bolt out the door, grabbing the keys to the garage before heading out into the black night.

In the garage, in front of my heavy bag, and with all my anger building in my shoulders, I draw back my arm and swing it forward with all my might, pummeling the canvas so hard the metal hook creaks above me. Two powerful shots with my right hand, one with my left. No gloves. Just my knuckles against the grain. I strike it so fucking hard that drywall dust spills from around the two-by-six I nailed to the ceiling to hang my bag. I hit it again, more white powder landing on my bloodied knuckles. There is suddenly so much anger that begs to escape that I pelt the bag over and over until it's raining drywall all over me. I stop, afraid to rip the mount from the ceiling. Instead, I slip on the muddy work boots that sit by the garage door and go for a run—not giving a shit that the boots are not made for running.

The air is crisp and cold. And the fact that I have on a T-shirt, sweatpants, and no socks worries me none. The weather can freeze my ass off, and I wouldn't give a shit. It'd be that much sweeter, because maybe it would numb my thoughts and get rid of the cutting memory running so rampant in my mind.

Commander Douchebag. Anisa, the little girl who'd hang her family's laundry on the line over the dusty yard. The little girl whose screams I'd hear night after night. Commander Douchebag. The man I'd wished I'd finished off with a bullet to the head.

The little flurries that begin to fall, sometime later, as I'm running up the mountain miles from my house cause me to pause. For how long have I been running? When I realize that it could be well past the time I should be opening the store, I turn around and walk back to my house. My feet are aching, my fingers are blue, and my lungs feel like they have freezer burn, but my anger, along with what put me there, has been pushed back to its corner in the back of my mind. Mission accomplished.

By the time I get home, it's almost eleven, and an hour past opening, but I feel better, so it was well worth it. I defrost in a hot shower, clean off the dried-on blood from my knuckles, then get dressed and head to the store.

AS IS USUAL LATELY, the store is slow, but I still need someone to help with some of my hours. It's difficult to go through the storage room in back when no one is out front minding the store. Plus, it would be nice to have a day or two off. I haven't yet officially announced that I'd be closed on Mondays, so as it stands right now, I am at the store seven days a week, nine hours a day most days. I really need a part-time person to help out. I open up my laptop and look up job search sites to see how to go about posting a help wanted ad. Then, it occurs to me that I should also purchase a help wanted sign to put in the front window of the store. If only I could get Haven to come work for me *at* the store during the day, it would solve both our problems. I'd have efficient help from someone that obviously meant a lot to my grandfather, and she'd have a comfortable job that would not be too stressful for her. Although, I guess if her appearance bothers her, then a job in retail could be more stressful than it would normally be. I shrug it off and continue searching the job search site.

Several minutes later, I'm so engrossed in filling out an application on one of the sites, that I don't bother looking up when the door chimes, signaling I have a customer. When I finally do stop typing, my customer is no longer in the front foyer. In an effort to be helpful, I walk through the aisles to find him or her.

It's a man with a Marine-style High-Top buzz-cut, in his late-twenties or early-thirties, wearing a nylon windbreaker and dark blue jeans.

"Hello," I say to him as he's crouched down in front of my classics shelf. He rises to his navy Converse, and I say, "Is there something I can help you with?"

He shakes his head, and says, "No, thank you."

I remind him that I'm here if he needs me, and then I return to filling out the application. When I'm done with that, I attend to the box I brought with me this morning. A box of books I'd found in my grandfather's garage. Books I remember sitting atop my grandfather's coffee table, and some I remember sitting on his shelf in the small library that connected to his kitchen in the house where he lived with my grandmother. *Charlotte's Web, The Call of the Wild, Oliver Twist* to name a few. It's when I'm in the middle of categorizing them into children's classics and adult classics about fifteen minutes later, when my lone customer approaches the desk and places two books face-down.

"Will that be all, or can I help you with something else?"

His hand twitches as he pulls money from his wallet. "No, I think this is good for now." He sets down three paperback classics—*Nineteen Eighty-Four* by George Orwell, *Crime and Punishment* by Fyodor Dostoyevsky, and *the Catcher in the Rye*.

"Going back to high school?"

"High School? I'm thirty-two years old," he tells me, clearly not getting my joke.

I ring up the sale, bag the books, and wish him a wonderful day. If Mom could see me now.

21.

H AVEN
"Flip the page."

He flips the page.

"Flip another."

He flips another.

"Another."

"Jesus, Haven, they're all the same. Nothing's wrong with any of the pages on any of the books," Quest whisper-shouts over FaceTime, trying not to let the heir to the Stephen King books hear him. Evidently, the original owner died and left them to his ungrateful nephew.

"You want to be sure, don't you? You'll be spending a lot of money."

"Yes, I want to be sure, but I've showed you these six *million* times."

"Well, it's not the same as being there. If I could hold them in my..." Abruptly, I stop talking. I *could* have held the books in my hands if my fear of being seen hadn't kept me from going with Quest in the first place. If I'd gone, I would have been able to look at the books for myself. I would have been with someone other than Marisela, Eric, Katie, and Devin. I would have been *living* instead of sitting here in what's become my prison cell—a cell I can't even afford to pay for anymore. According to the letter I received from my landlord yesterday, if I don't bring my rent payments up to date within thirty days, I'll be evicted by the end of the year.

"Haven, should I buy them or not?" Quest asks impatiently, graciously ignoring my comment by not saying "I told you so."

After a sigh, I say, "Yes. From what I can tell, you're getting a fair price."

I hear Quest sigh in relief before he says, "Thank you, Haven. I'll talk to you tomorrow." He hangs up before I can say another word.

I put my phone down and sag against the couch cushion. I could have been there *with* him. It pains me to suddenly realize I'm letting vanity prevent me from going out in public. It shouldn't bother me what anyone thinks of the gashes on my face. Like Quest had said that night in the dark, I shouldn't be ashamed that I was hurt. I am a victim of assault, and that does not have any reflection on who I am. If anything, it proves that I'm a survivor.

Am I a survivor?

Living in the dark the way I am, hiding from light...and people. I'm not living. I'm barely surviving. But what will it take to get back out there? My mother's ingrained it in my head for my entire life that my appearance matters. How I look, how I act, how I present myself in public—it will all make a difference in how people perceive me and how successful I will be. So, if I take her words at face value, then I'm doomed. There is no amount of makeup that will cover my scars, because they are not just lines cut across my face. The left side of my face, because of the divot the size of a half dollar that was carved out right in the center of my cheek, has thick scar tissue forming from the intense skin grafting I'd needed. The rest of my face looks like a tic-tac-toe board. And while my nose has had reconstruction already, scar tissue makes it look wider and worse than my original, which according to my mother wasn't even that nice. The doctor suggests scar revision once my wounds are completely healed, but honestly, I don't think I could face any more pain.

But I have to change something in my life, because I can't go on this way. I have a decision to make. Do I go out in public and dare to not care what's being said or thought about me—including the judgmental comments from my mother that I know I'll be faced with? Or do I opt for more surgery, so I don't have to worry about the silent stares and conspicuous whispers? The first is the courageous thing to do. The second, the painful one.

I contemplate these choices up until I fall asleep that night, and at four-thirty in the morning, I'm awakened by a phone call from my father.

"Dad? Is everything all right?" I ask, answering the phone without saying hello. My father rarely calls me, so the fact that he's calling before the sun has peeked over the mountain, I know this is not going to be good news.

"Hey, pumpkin, no, it's not. Your mother's had a heart attack. It was a pretty severe one."

"Oh my god, Dad, is she going to be okay?" My mother may be the bane of my confidence, but I still love her, and it scares me to think she could die. *You can do anything you put your mind to*, my mother's voice from somewhere in the past says. I'm wearing my yellow Mary-Janes with my favorite white socks. I see them atop the black plastic pedals as I try to balance on two wheels. *Don't look down*, my mother says. *Always keep your eyes straight ahead of you.* The memory of my mother teaching me to ride without training wheels is a pleasant one. Because of my father's busy workload, it was always my mother and me every day.

"She should be, yes. She's in surgery now," my father says, his voice a mere echo of its usual timbre.

"Oh, Dad," I say on a sigh, right before tears start forming in my eyes. "How are you? Are you okay?" My father is a strong, determined, successful man, but his strength comes from my mother. Like the words of reassurance she'd provided me when she'd taught me how to ride my bike, her support provided my father the fortitude needed to face difficult cases. I can still hear my mother's encouraging words, disguised as criticism, of course, the nights before my father was due in court. *If you have to question the morality of what you do, then you're not the right person for the job. Defending a criminal requires a backbone. If you don't have one, find another way to earn a living.* Yes, my mother's words are harsh, and lately, I haven't had the confidence to listen to them, but they've definitely driven my father's ambition.

"Scared, pumpkin. I'm scared."

At that moment, I realize that I don't have the time to make a decision about whether to be seen in public or not, because my daddy needs me, and I need to be there for him. "What hospital, Dad?"

"Morristown."

"Okay. I'll be there as soon as I can. I just need to get dressed."

"Oh, Haven, thank you so much. I know it means leaving your house, but, but I really don't think I can be alone right now. Your mother's a pretentious, annoying woman who drives me crazy, but I don't want to know a world without her in it," he says in cracked voice.

"I know, Daddy."

I SIT IN THE HOSPITAL parking garage on the top level, the bright winter sun greeting me through the windshield. It could not *be* any more daylight than it is right now. Sliding my sunglasses down to the center of my nose, I say a quick prayer that no one even bothers to look my way. With my baseball cap pulled tight over my head, I finger my long hair and bring it forward to cover as much of my face as possible without looking ridiculous. Then I laugh. I *already* look ridiculous, it doesn't matter if my hair is covering my scars or not. I'm just going to have to suck it up and get out of this car.

Walking to the garage elevator is easy; no one is there. However, getting *off* the elevator is like standing on stage as the curtains slowly draw open to reveal countless heads sitting in front of me. I am scared—the thought of my mother, possibly lying on her deathbed, secondary in my mind. Swarms of people bustle about the floor in front of the open doors. The seconds it takes for me to step out of it feel like a lifetime. The faces staring at me are too many to count. It takes a few beats to recognize that they are boarding the elevator, and the only reason they are looking at me is because they can't get on it with me in their way.

"Sorry," I mumble to no one in particular.

They rush by me without word. Grunts and groans, however, they are *not* without.

I make my way to the reception desk with my head down.

"May I help you?" the receptionist asks pleasantly.

"My mother was just admitted," I say, my head still down, my eyes on the desk in front of me. "Hannah Quinn?"

She searches through her computer, then looks up at me, catching a glimpse of me for the very first time. I know this, because a barely perceptible gasp escapes her mouth, and there's a pause before she looks down—while my hand instinctively goes to my face—and says, "There's no one here by that name. You said she was admitted today?" The woman faces me, but her eyes stay on her computer.

"Um, my dad said she had a heart attack and they brought her here."

Her eyes quickly seek mine before she turns back and says, "She's probably in Emergency still. Sometimes it takes a while for a patient to be admitted." She looks back at me, and I can tell she is forcing herself to keep her eyes on mine, keeping them from drifting down to my face.

My throat closes up, so I nod. I want to ask how to get to the emergency room, but the second I speak, I know I won't be able to hold back a cry. As my chest constricts, I back away and head toward the front doors where a security guard sits. I step outside to cry, but there are people mulling about, and

I don't want to cause a scene. I lift my sunglasses to wipe my eyes and turn around and go back inside.

"May I help you, miss?" the security guard says, and I'm afraid to look at him.

Nodding, I tell him I'm looking for the emergency department.

He steps forward and puts a hand on my shoulder. "Miss, are you okay? Are *you* the one with the emergency?"

His question causes me to laugh and cry at the same time. Of course he would think I'm the emergency. I'm barely holding myself together. Standing taller, and keeping my sunglasses on, I look at the guard, and with a continued mixture of laughter and tears, I say with a pathetic smile, "No, I'm not the emergency. My mother's had a heart attack, and my father's asked me to meet him here." With my fingertips, I wipe the tears sliding down my horrific face. "And I have no idea where to go."

The security guard turns around, pulls out a few tissues from the box on his podium, and hands them to me. "Let me get coverage. I'll bring you there."

I sigh in gratitude. "Thank you."

22.

Quest
The sound of tapping stops me from making a cup of coffee from the new brewer I bought for the bookstore. Walking over to the locked front door, I see Haven striking a finger lightly against the glass, a smile playing on her lips.

A smile forms on my lips as well. "Hey."

"Hey, am I bothering you?"

"Of course not," I say, taking her hand to allow her in. I shut the door behind her and relock the door; the store doesn't open for another half hour. "Is everything all right?" I'm extremely curious as to why she's here, especially because she makes a point of not going out of the house.

She lets go of my hand to adjust her sunglasses, but she doesn't remove them. It occurs to me then that this is the first time I've seen her in daylight since before her attack. Her scars are harsh, but they don't take away from her beauty one bit. "I know we barely know each other—" she says. "—and we're not even sure if we even *like* one another for that matter. And I know you don't—"

"Haven. We're friends. What's up?"

"My mother had a heart attack. She's in CCU."

"Oh, I'm sorry." I'm at a loss for words, except that I'm wondering why the hell she's *here* then.

She lets out a stifled laugh. "You're probably wondering why I'm here."

"The thought crossed my mind."

She chuckles, and the sound is sweet. "I know it's weird. I just wanted to say that if your offer still stands...about working here...during the day...*in* the store...I can really use the job."

"Of course it still stands. Thank you... would you like a cup of coffee?" I gesture toward the new one-cup coffee system on the table in the alcove. "Light, medium, dark, or flavored?" I bought a huge variety box of K-cups.

Shrugging a shoulder, she says, "Tea?"

"Yes, there's that too. Milk or sugar?""

"Yes please, both. Thanks."

I prepare her tea, and, with my back toward her, I say, "So, what changed your mind about working here?"

When I don't hear a response, I finish preparing her tea, turn around and hand it to her.

"Thank you."

Not wanting to make her feel uncomfortable, I don't ask again. Instead, I take a seat on my stool behind the desk. "I hope your mother's going to be okay. Have they said?"

"She should be. It was a pretty severe attack, but they see no reason why she won't recover." Haven sips her tea but doesn't move from her spot by the entrance.

"Good. That's good."

"I was at the hospital yesterday. Headed there now, too."

I nod, and then realize...she went to the hospital. She went out in public. Where there are lights...and people. I'm not sure whether she expects me to acknowledge this fact or not, so I don't. "Which hospital?" I ask instead, not that I am aware of *any* hospitals in the area.

"Morristown Memorial. It's in Morristown."

I smirk. "Good name for it then. You need company?" I ask before I can stop myself.

Her eyebrows peek out from her large glasses. "To the hospital?"

"Yes. If you need moral support. You know, for your mom." But my intentions are really to help her walk through public halls. The night I went to her house, and she was sitting there in the dark with no power, still haunts me. Even through the dim light of her one candle, I could see the fear in her eyes. I've seen that look before. She was frightened by the uncertainty of what was to come. Me seeing her...her scars, her vulnerability. It might not have been the same intensity of fear that knowing your last breath may be a painful and violent one, but she was afraid for her own reasons. And I think about that daily.

"Oh. But your store."

"Right. It's *my* store. I don't have to open it if I don't want to."

I can see she's trying to keep from smiling, when she says, "I wouldn't want you to lose business on my account."

"I won't lose business. They'll come back another day." I lock up the register I'd just opened. "Come on, I insist."

This time, she allows herself to smile. "Thank you. It would be nice to walk through the hospital *with* someone. It may keep people from staring," she adds quietly, reaching for a piece of hair at her neck. "Or from me noticing."

Again, I don't acknowledge her admission. But I do put my hand on her back as I shut off the lights and lead her out. "Would you like me to drive?"

"No, that's okay. My car's parked illegally, so we'll just take mine. I don't mind driving."

"Perfect, because I have no idea where the hell Morristown is."

She laughs. I surprise myself by how much I like that sound.

On the drive over, I decide to broach the subject of her visit to the hospital yesterday. "So, was yesterday the first time you went out in public?"

Her hand grips the steering wheel tighter. "Yes, and the lights at the hospital were *so* bright."

"Were you okay?"

Slowly, she nods. "I almost had a panic attack in the elevator. But I made it out. Kept my eyes on the floor in front of me, mostly."

"That was courageous of you."

Her head snaps in my direction briefly. "Courageous?" Her voice rises an octave. "I didn't save anyone or anything. I'm a coward...I care so much about what people think of me that I hide in the dark. And I'm self-absorbed, because I actually *think* people even *want* to look at me."

"You're courageous, because even though you *are* afraid that people are looking at you and judging you, you still walked through that hospital because your mother needed you. That's a hero."

"No, that's not a hero. Soldiers in war...*those* are heroes."

I scoff. Some soldiers in war are definitely not heroes. "Heroes come in all sizes. To your mother, yesterday, you were a hero."

Haven shrugs and says, "I was there mostly for my dad. I love my mom, but if you'd heard the tears in my father's voice..."

"Then you're your father's hero," I say with a nod of my head.

She turns to me again for a second, before she turns back to the road. "You're not the same person you were when I first met you."

"Come again?"

"You were...angry. Gruff. You're not anymore."

"Sure I am. You caught me on a good day." Not wanting to discuss this any longer, I reach for the radio and turn it on. "Got a good classic rock station up here?"

She plays with the buttons on the steering wheel and puts on a station. We listen to it for the rest of the drive.

To make sure Haven feels at ease, I take her twitching hand and walk with her into the hospital, and I continue to hold it on the elevator, as we get off, as she asks for a pass to room four-thirty-three, and as we approach her mother's room. That's when I pull her close and whisper, "You got this from here?"

She smiles and nods. "Thank you. Sorry I'm so jittery."

"I haven't noticed," I lie.

"I'm *much* better than yesterday, though. So, thank you."

"Anytime. I'll be over there." I shrug my head towards the open waiting room a few feet away and let go of her hand.

"Pumpkin?" A man steps out from the room, puts his arm around Haven, and kisses her atop her head. "I thought I heard you out here."

"Oh Daddy. Are you okay today?" She reaches up and hugs the broad man for a short couple of seconds before she pulls away.

"I am. Your mother's resting more calmly today. Thank you for coming again."

Haven nods. "Is she sleeping?"

"She is, yes." Her father looks my way and holds out his hand. "Hello. I'm Leighton Quinn." Leighton Quinn is a big man. Broad in the shoulders, tall, intimidating. Much like my own late-father.

As I say, "I'm Quest," Haven says, "Oh, Dad, this is Quest Vescovi. A...a friend of mine. The bookstore owner."

"Oh. Nice to meet you." I'm sure he couldn't care less about meeting me while his wife is lying in the coronary care unit, but it is kind of him to tell me so anyway.

"Likewise," I tell him.

"Pumpkin, can I buy you two a cup of coffee or something?" Mr. Quinn asks, resting his hand on her shoulder.

She looks at me, and I shrug while saying, "Whatever you wanna do."

Nodding, she smiles and says, "Okay, Daddy. That sounds good."

"You up for the cafeteria?"

"I think so."

Once again, I take her hand and hold it while her father leads us to the hospital cafeteria. When we get there, Mr. Quinn walks up to the counter first, but I take out my wallet, and say, "Sir, let me. Go take a seat with your daughter. What can I get you both?"

"Thank you. Just black coffee, please," he says.

"Tea for you?" I ask Haven, but she's shaking her head and fidgeting with the glasses on her face. "Just water, please."

I order two coffees, a bottle of water, and three gingerbread cookies. As I approach the table, I notice Mr. Quinn leaning forward and talking quietly with Haven. I falter in my steps, unsure if I should let them be alone for a minute, but the man takes notice and waves me over. "Come, son, it's fine. I'm done."

I place the items down and sit, pushing the cookies in front of Haven. "In case you were hungry."

She opens the bag and pulls out a gingerboy. "My favorite."

"Haven loves this time of year," her father says with a sad smile as she frowns.

It's Thanksgiving in three days. I'm sure this won't be the happiest of holidays this year for the Quinn family. But I've known worse. A Thanksgiving day spent packing up the Jeep Grand Cherokee because your father has just disowned his own father and has now decided to take his family all the way across the country is a Thanksgiving day that goes down as one of my own worst. My grandfather standing in the doorway, tears moistening his leathered face is a memory I'd long since forgotten until now. But I'm sure the Quinn's will get through this. Especially since her mother surviving overnight is a good sign.

"Mom will still be in the hospital on Thursday, right?"

"Yes, but she should be out of CCU by tomorrow. I'll be with her. You should go spend Thanksgiving with Marisela. I'm sure she'd love to have you."

"She's going to Puerto Rico to be with her family. I'll be fine, Dad. I'll come here and sit with you. Maybe Mom will be too weak to talk about my appearance," she laughs, even though what she said is anything but funny.

"She means well, Haven. You know your mother."

"Mmm," she mumbles, looking at her gingerbread man. "I know."

"She doesn't know any differently. Look at her own upbringing." Mr. Quinn reaches for his daughter's hand. "She loves you the only way she knows how."

Haven nods, and her father removes his hand from hers. "I just wish she'd stop with the put-downs. She thinks I'm ugly as sin and wants me to go through all these painful surgeries so I can live the life she thinks I should live. They hurt, Daddy. That was the most painful thing I ever..." she trails off, and I notice tears slipping down her cheek. When she wipes them away, I think it occurs to her that I am sitting on the side of her deepest scar, because she looks at me and gasps, keeping her hand over her cheek.

I don't want her to feel uncomfortable, but I take that hand and hold it between mine. "You're beautiful, Haven. Just as you are."

I hear a tiny gasp from her father, but I don't look his way. Haven is all I want to see at the moment. It's crucial for her self-esteem. She pulls her hand away, and while I let her, I don't take my eyes off of her. More tears cover her face before her hand wipes them away.

"And you're brave," I add, running the back of my fingers against the back of her hand...which, of course, is covering her cheek again.

"He's right, Haven," Mr. Quinn says, cupping his coffee. "You *are* beautiful, and I've been thinking the same thing...how very brave you are for coming here. If you don't want those surgeries, you don't need to get them. Don't let your mother's insecurities become yours."

Listening to their conversation, it occurs to me that Haven's recent attack and facial scars are not the only things she's fighting to overcome. If only I could convince her to come to Group with me. One step at a time, Quest. One step at a time.

23.

H AVEN
    When my mother finally awakes, she appears pale and fragile and so unlike the mighty Hannah Quinn I love and fear.

"Haven," she whispers, and turns to my dad. "Leighton."

"Hannah. How do you feel?" My dad asks, keeping his hands firmly on his chair's padded armrests. An effusive couple, they are not. And I wonder why I am so inhibited?

"Very tired," my mother says to my dad. "You're not working?"

Dad shakes his head and says with a sad smile. "No, I took off for a while."

Even hooked up to machines, my mother finds the strength to reprove my father's decision. "Leighton, you'll lose clients."

"I will not lose clients, Hannah. And if I do, there will always be more."

"Oh, Leighton, I hope you're right. You don't want to—"

"Hannah, please. I'm trying to do something nice here."

My mother tsks and says nothing more. I need to agree with my dad here, though. He *is* doing something nice. He took time off to be with my mother. In all the years I've been alive, I can count on one hand the times my father took a vacation from work to be with us. So, taking time off of work now to be with my mother in the hospital, is a huge gesture, and it pisses me off that she can't be nice to him.

"You know, Mom, Dad cares for you so much that he put *you* before his job. That's pretty awesome, don't you think? Considering neither one of you ever puts anyone or anything above your jobs." My face flushes, and suddenly I regret my words.

"Where did that come from?" my mother says, her voice weak, her tone not.

"It just sucks that you can't be nicer to Daddy."

"Haven, please be respectful," my father says.

"Language, Haven," my mother chides and says, "And don't roll your eyes. Don't think just because you are wearing those hideous sunglasses that I can't see your eyes rolling in your head."

"Ugh," I groan. "I have to get going. I'll be back tomorrow." I stand from my chair and take a step closer to the bed to kiss her goodbye, but she says, "Really, Haven, if you're going to cover your face with your glasses, get a prettier pair."

I look at my father and say, "Even right after a heart attack..."

"Haven," he says, "please don't go yet."

Fine. I sit back down and say, "I'm sorry, Mom," because I am. I *am* sorry for showing her disrespect, especially while she's in the hospital coronary unit. "Can we start over?"

She nods, the thin tubes coming out of her nose yielding to the pressure. "Sure."

"How are you feeling?"

"Tired, Haven."

"Dad said you'll be out of CCU tomorrow?"

"Yes. My heart is getting stronger, they say. But I *will* do what they say, Haven, because the doctors know best. Just like your doctor says that you need that surgery, and *he* knows best."

"Ugh."

"Hannah, stop," my father says. "Haven's an adult, she'll make her own decisions. Let's worry about you right now, okay?"

"There's nothing to worry about. *I'm* going to be fine," she says.

"And so will Haven," my father adds. "Did you know she has a male friend? He drove her here."

"Dad."

"You have a boyfriend!?" my mother asks in disbelief.

I so want to say, "Yes, I do," but I shake my head and tell her, "He's a friend, Mom. Barely that. He's Mr. Vescovi's grandson. The one who took over the bookstore."

"Oh," she says, smirking. "That makes more sense."

"Oh my god. Why couldn't he be my boyfriend, Mother? Because I'm ugly? Loathsome? I don't deserve one?" I look at my father and stand. "This is why I'm always on the defense." Walking toward the door, I turn and add, "I hope you feel better soon, Mother."

I rush toward the elevators, trying to stay composed, and press the down button a couple hundred times until it opens.

"Haven?"

Quest. "Oh my gosh, Quest, I'm sorry. I raced right by the waiting room. I'm sorry."

"No apology necessary," he says, his hands deep in his pockets. "Your mother okay?"

I let out an exaggerated sigh and step onto the elevator. "Yes. She's her normal self, so she is absolutely fine," I say, feigning a smile.

"That's...good?" he says, his eyes questioning.

"For her, yes, it is." Stepping back against the elevator wall, I rest my head against it.

"What happened?"

I raise my head and look at him. "She's weak, right? Her heart is fragile? Well, that didn't stop her from finding the strength to make *me* feel like shit. " I adjust my glasses, reminding myself that they're just as ugly as my face. "Now I need to find sunglasses that aren't as hideous looking as I am," I say out loud, unable to help myself.

"What?" Quest asks, placing his hand on my lower back as we exit the elevator.

"Quote, 'If you're going to cover your face with your glasses, get a prettier pair.'"

"Your mother said that?" He removes his hand from my back to take hold of my hand. Which, incidentally, feels unexpectedly wonderful.

"She did. And my father wonders why I can't be nice to her." I look Quest in the eyes. "Sometimes...sometimes, I *hate* her."

"I'm sorry," Quest says, keeping hold of my hand as we walk to my car. "Has she always been like this, or just since...your attack?"

"She's always had her own unique brand of support and encouragement, but since this—" I wave my hand in front of my face, "—I can't seem to take it. She's embarrassed by me."

"Well, she shouldn't be." Quest squeezes my hand. "Like your father said, this is *her* insecurity. Don't make it yours."

Retrieving the car keys from my purse, I say, "That's just it. How can I not feel insecure looking like this? I'm not comfortable with it."

Quest opens the driver side door for me and shuts it after I get in.

"Thank you," I say when he gets in on his side. "Thanks for being here today, too. It means a lot."

"It means a lot that you let me. Thank you."

I nod, and start thinking about what my mother said about doing what the doctors say—I should continue with surgery. I know I should. I just don't know if I'm ready to take on all that pain again. I liken it to sticking my face in a pot of boiling water. How can I go through that again?

"Haven, can I ask you something?"

"Okay."

"Are you talking to anyone about this whole ordeal?"

"My mother's heart attack?"

"No. *Your* attack."

"Oh." I was supposed to see a psychotherapist when I got out of the hospital, but that meant going outside, so I put off calling the woman that Doctor Begley had referred. "No, I'm not."

"Would you like to come with me to my support group?"

"*You* guide a support group?"

He laughs. "I don't guide it, I attend it. I'm inviting you to come with me."

"Oh. Why do *you* go to a support group?"

"It's not the time to talk about that, but I can tell you, it helps. You wouldn't have to talk in the group. Not unless you want to. But it helps to be in a room with other people who are going through some tough shit too."

"Do any of them look like me?"

"No one looks like you. They don't hold a candle to you. But we won't make them feel bad about that."

I don't know how he does it, but Quest never fails to make me see the lighter side of myself. "Can I think about it?"

"Of course. I go on Monday nights. I'm going tonight if you're up for it, otherwise, just let me know when you're ready."

24.

Quest

   "Quest?" Haven asks, her eyes on the road ahead of us.

   "Yes?"

   "What did you leave behind in California?"

   "What kind of question is that?"

   "One that clues me in on who you are. What did you do when you lived out there? I mean, you must have given up a job or something. A girlfriend? Family? I know you left your mother...but, I know nothing about you." She takes a quick look at me, then at the road.

   Do I want to open up that can of worms? "I didn't give up anything to come out here, except for maybe close proximity to my mother. She and her boyfriend were about all I had in regards to family and friends." Complex question, simple answer.

   "Really?" She sounds surprised.

   "Really. I didn't make many friends out in California." In fact, Derek and Henry were the last real friends I had, unless I include high school teammates.

   "Not even fellow co-workers?"

   "No job."

   "Were you going to college or something?"

   "No, ma'am. Lived in Mom's basement. Like the dutiful citizen I am."

"Your mom needed help?"

"She did not."

"Oh."

Feeling guilty for being ambiguous, I decide it's okay to confide in Haven...a little. "I was discharged from the Army for *other*-than-honorable reasons." A sour taste settles in my throat. I've never uttered those words aloud. Never had any reason to before; those who knew me, knew not to ask, those who didn't know me, didn't exist. Being a self-imposed hermit, allowed me little opportunity to meet anyone new.

"Oh. I'm sorry. I—what's your mother's name?" she asks, conveniently switching the subject to avoid an even more awkward ride home.

"Maria. Her boyfriend's name is Vinnie. My dad was Franco, and my grandparents were Albina and Raniero, Raniero being my middle name."

"Nice. No siblings?"

"No. You?"

"No. Only child. I hated it."

"Me too. It was lonely. Especially after we left New Jersey."

"And your grandfather."

I nod. "Leaving my grandfather was difficult."

"Quest?"

"Yeah?"

"Why were you discharged?"

I don't answer her right away. Instead, I turn my attention back out the window, formulating the words in my head. But before I can expel them, she blurts, "Do you like running the bookstore?"

"It's okay. I'm enjoying the part that bonds me to my grandfather."

"I'm glad you're able to do that. I always loved being in that store."

"I saw something really horrible going on, and I couldn't just sit by any longer and let it happen, so I did something about it."

"What?"

"I'm answering your question from before. Why I got discharged. For interfering with something that should not have been happening."

Her knuckles whiten on the steering wheel. "Oh. Wouldn't that be something good then?"

"Not when the man doing it was the militia commander for the other side."

"Oh." Haven swallows, probably wondering what the hell I'm talking about.

"It's done with. It's over. I did what I had to do, and now I'm living with the consequences."

Haven turns off the highway and onto the street that leads to my bookstore. Without gazing in my direction, she asks, "And what are those consequences?"

"Dishonor. Inability to get a job. No health benefits."

"People won't hire you because of it?" she asks, her pitch rising in surprise.

"Well, in truth, I hadn't really tried. I'm afraid of rejection. I was helping Vinnie with his plumbing business, but that's about it. It is what it is, though, right? It's no worse than what you've gone through."

Haven pulls off the road, parks in the same illegal spot where she was parked this morning, and shuts off the engine. "I'm your friend, Quest. We may not have started out that way, but...I consider you a friend." She nods and says, "I thought you should know that."

"Thank you, Haven. I consider you one, as well."

"That's good, considering I'll be working for you." She attempts to laugh, but it comes out as snort.

Which makes *me* laugh. "Would you like to start work after your mom is home from the hospital?"

"Sooner if you don't mind. I have a lot of bills to pay."

"How about ten tomorrow morning?"

"That works. Thank you, Quest. For everything."

Deciding to leave the store closed for the rest of the day, I stop at the grocery store to pick up some much needed food and head home. After unpacking the bags, I set a pot of water on the stove to boil and pour a can of chopped clams into a smaller pot to heat up. While I'm waiting for the water to boil, I call my mom.

"Quest!" My mother is always excited to hear from me. "How's my boy? I miss you so much."

"I'm good, Ma. Sorry I haven't called in a while. I miss you too. How are things?"

"Good. They're good." I hear a deep voice in the background. "Vinnie says hi."

"Tell him I said the same."

She does. "So, how's the bookstore? Do you think you're going to stay?"

"I think so. I finally got someone to help out. She starts tomorrow."

"All this time you've been working there alone?"

"It's not busy. Truthfully, I'm not sure how Nonno made a living. But I do need some time away from there, and it'll be good to have someone else to help."

"Did you figure out why your grandfather put that condition on you owning the store?"

"No. I stopped trying to figure that out."

"Maybe that girl he left the books to is hiding something."

Yeah, her face. "No, I don't think so, Ma. In fact, she's the one who's coming to work for me."

"What!? Can you trust her?"

"Of course I can trust her. I wouldn't have hired her if I couldn't. Besides, she needs a job. She recently lost hers, so..."

"Are you sure she's not manipulating you in any way?"

"No, Ma, she's not. She's a sweet girl."

"I hope so. I don't want anyone taking advantage of you."

"I think I can take care of myself. So anyway, since I did hire her, I was thinking by Christmas, I'll be able to take the time and come spend a week or two with you."

"Oh, Quest," she pauses. "You just made my day."

"You just did the sign of the cross, didn't you?"

"You know me so well. So will you be able to afford a trip back home?"

"Well, I was thinking of just buying a one-way ticket to save money, and driving my car back here."

"You're going to drive a 1969 Camaro cross-country?"

"That was the plan, yeah."

"Will it make it?"

"I think so. I replaced the engine, so I don't foresee a problem. I'll think about it though."

"Just give it a good tune up when you're here. Oh, baby, it's going to be so nice to see you again. I'm dying for one of your hugs."

"Don't worry, you'll get one."

25.

HAVEN

I slide on my new sunglasses—a purchase I made at the mall when I decided to go a half hour before closing last night—and look in the mirror. Because I opted for a brown lens instead of opaque black, I can see a little better under my bathroom light than I could with the others. But I still can't tell what someone looking at me will see, so I snap a quick selfie and get an instant stomach ache at the thought of looking at it without the filter of a dark lens.

Stepping out of the bright light of the bathroom, I walk over to the kitchen table, sit, and take off my glasses. I slide my thumb over the phone screen and press the multi-colored icon. Acid climbs up my esophagus as I peer at the picture. The larger pink frames cover more of my face than the other pair, but not everything. And I look like I just stepped out of the nineteen-seventies. The annoying sales lady told me that big frames were back in style, but seeing them in this picture...I think she was just trying to make a sale. As I continue to look at myself on the screen, I notice a lot more of my scars than I have before. I never really studied them, since I couldn't stand looking at myself for more than a few seconds. The longer I look, the more repulsive I become.

Because the scar on my left cheek is so deep, I can't even cover it with makeup, but I begin wondering if maybe a little concealer and loose powder will lighten the redness of the other scars, and make me look a little more appealing. If only one surgery would have been enough. I put down the phone and go back into the bathroom, where I search my drawers for my old makeup bag. I retrieve the concealer from my bag and start applying it. As the scar lightens, so does the burning in my chest. Maybe I won't look as bad as I think. But by the time I'm done applying the concealer and the powder, I still look like a miniature golf obstacle course. Maybe the physical pain of one more surgery will outweigh the psychological pain of looking at myself in the mirror every day.

I put on a little mascara, since my eyes are more visible through the brown lenses, and then I run some brow primer and powder over my eyebrows, because wearing my glasses lower on my nose tends to showcase the brow line. I go back into the kitchen to get my glasses, and then take another look at myself in the mirror. Still hideous, but maybe less so.

DINGMAN'S CORNER BOOK Shop is locked.

It's nine-forty-five.

I peer inside to see if maybe Quest is in the back somewhere, like he was the first time I came by after Mr. Vescovi passed away, but there are no lights on and no signs of breathing life inside. Too self-conscious to stand outside on the main street, I return to my car and wait for Quest to show up.

Ten minutes later, there's a knock on my window that causes me to jump.

"What are you doing sitting in your car?" Quest, armed with a big white bakery box, shouts through the passenger side window.

I shake my head, grab my purse, and get out. "Waiting for you to open your store."

He smiles. "Come, humble new employee."

After following him up the sidewalk, I take the bakery box while he unlocks the store. Then he hands me the key. "I had this made for you this morning. Now I can finally sleep in," he says with an evil laugh. *Who* is *this guy?*

"Do you have a multiple personality disorder?" I ask, shaking my head and putting the box on the desk.

He laughs. "What?" He picks up the box and puts it on the table by the coffee.

While I watch him turn on the brewer, I say, "Every time I see you, you're a different person."

Something passes in his expression, but I can't make it out. He opens the box, pulls a napkin out of the basket he has next to the coffee, and hands it to me. "I got one of everything they had. You pick first, then I'll put the rest on a plate for the customers. In celebration of our new manager."

Manager? Quest is nothing like the guy I met that first day. He pleasantly surprises me each time I'm in his company. I pick up the huge blueberry muffin and wrap it in my napkin. "Thank you. I'll eat it later. First, show me what you want me to do. And am I really a manager?" I'll feel stupid if he was joking.

He grins. "If I'm allowing you to open the store on your own, then you're a manager." He touches my arm and says,

"Make yourself a cup of tea and eat your muffin." He takes two paper cups and hands me one. "First things first."

I put down my muffin, and while I'm making my cup of tea, Quest says, "I like your new glasses. I like the fact that I can actually see your eyes through them."

I feel my cheeks blush. "Thanks," I say, keeping my attention on preparing my tea.

When Quest squeezes behind the desk to unlock the register, I follow him and place my muffin on the shelf behind him. "So, what can I do? Show me something."

Nodding once, he says, "Well, since you're so eager to begin the day, how about you mark these books," he pulls a pile of old books off the shelf behind him, "with a price? Someone brought them in yesterday. You know how my grandfather priced things, I'm sure you can figure out what to charge."

"Actually," I say, picking up the first book—*A Knight in Shining Armor* by Jude Deveraux—"Do you charge on consignment? I never brought books in, so I don't know how that works."

"We do, but sometimes, people just donate them and tell us not to bother. These," he says, placing his hands on the books, "were donated." He slides his hand into a space beneath the desk and pulls out a spiral bound book. "This is where I mark the books I get in on consignment and what I owe to the donors. It was my grandfather's system."

I open the book and look at the penciled-in names. It gives me a chill to see Mr. Vescovi's handwriting. I used to love his little notes taped to the shelves beneath the books.

"You didn't take down your grandfather's little notes, did you?"

Quest eyes me sideways. "I wouldn't do that. I've gotten many requests *not* to remove them."

"Good. I also think you should continue with writing your own. Keep the tradition going."

He scoffs. "I don't read, Haven."

"You own a bookstore. You better start."

"I have an idea," he says, as he squeezes himself around me, and pulls out a package of index cards from the top shelf. "*You* can continue my grandfather's tradition. I take it these have been here a while," he says of the yellowed stack of cards.

I take them from him and hold them to my chest. "I just might."

After the first two customers come in, Quest keeps me at the register while he goes through things in the back closet. Being the only one in the store, he hadn't been able to go through some of the books in the back of his grandfather's storage closet, and he'd wondered if there were books that maybe he should put up front. When an hour goes by and no other customers come in, I take the down-time to pull a few books off the shelves—books I've read and am familiar with, of course. I want to begin right away with the notecards. The first book I open up, remembering the plethora of magnificent lines within it, is *The Poetry of Robert Frost: The Collected Poems, Complete and Unabridged*. I search the Table of Contents and as soon as I see it, I know which poem I want to use as my first note card.

When I'm finished with my quote and note, I put the Frost book back on the shelf and tape the card beneath it. In this one act, a piece of my soul is healed. A tiny part of Mr. Vescovi has lived on inside of me. And it makes me smile.

Just as I return to the front foyer and take my seat behind the register to look through the other books I'd picked, a familiar face walks through the door. "Devin, oh my gosh. What are you—"

"Haven?" he asks, surprised. "What are *you* doing here?"

"I told you I was going to be working here, remember?" I ask, walking around the desk to give him a quick hug.

"That was just a temporary job, wasn't it? Aren't you coming back to the station at some point?"

Turning around to take a seat back on the stool, I say, "I don't think so. I don't think Bert is going to want me back."

Devin shakes his head quickly. "No no, that's not true. He still wants you to work for him."

"For behind the scenes stuff, Devin. That's not what I want."

Devin's shoulders drop. "Did he say that? He didn't say that to me. He said makeup can cover any..." He drops his head in embarrassment. "He wants you back."

"He does? I've been ignoring his calls, because I didn't want to hear him tell me I was too ug...that he had other positions in mind for me. Off-camera stuff."

"No. Call him."

I smile at him. "Thanks, Devin. Maybe I will. But even if he wants me back *on*-camera, I couldn't do it. It takes all my strength to be *here*. I don't want my face in front of the entire county."

"I guess I can understand that," he says, pulling on his shirt hem and nodding.

"So, why are you here? Did you come for a specific book, or just to peruse?"

"Just to—"

"Hey, Catcher in the Rye," Quest says, holding a big box as he walks into the foyer. "Nice to see you again."

"Hey," Devin says.

Quest sets down the box and holds out his hand. Devin returns the gesture, and they shake hands.

"Catcher in the Rye?" I ask, curious about Quest's reference.

"Yeah," Quest says. "He came in and bought *the Catcher in the Rye* and a couple other classics we all read in high school, right?"

Devin nods and shifts his eyes to me.

"You *read*, Devin?"

"Of course I can read."

"I mean, you read as a hobby?"

"Not really," he tells me. "Just thought I'd start. You speak so highly of it." He laughs.

"I do. I get to jump into a new life every time I open a book."

"Kinda like Steve and Blue skidooing into those pictures on *Blue's Clues*," Quest jokes.

I shake my head. "No. Not even close."

Quest turns to Devin. "You here to buy more books? *The Great Gatsby*, maybe? *This Side of Paradise*?"

I chuckle, impressed that Quest even knows a Fitzgerald novel besides *The Great Gatsby*.

Quest turns to me with his eyebrows raised. "You're thinking 'how in the world does he even know who Fitzgerald is?' Right, Goldilocks?"

Goldilocks? I pat my hair, realizing that I haven't gotten it bleached since before my attack. I'm half blonde now. Half lifeless brown. "I *was* thinking that as a matter of fact. Yes."

Devin shoots us both a look and then says, "I was just going to look around today. Not sure for what yet."

"So, wait," Quest says, waving his finger between us. "Haven called you by name. You guys know each other?"

"Devin and I are friends. He's part of our movie-night group. We met at the station." I smile at Devin, thinking fondly of my nights there. "He was our cameraman."

Devin nods, then points a finger toward the main section of the store. "I'm going to go take a look."

"Take your time," Quest says. "Got any questions, Haven's here to help." Quest winks at me.

"Are you high?"

"Excuse me?"

I rephrase my question to Quest. "Are you on drugs or something? Either that or you must have multiple personality disorder, because you are never the same person twice. Goldilocks?"

Quest smiles. "I'm happy you're here, Haven." He moves in closer and rests his hands on the desk. Looking straight into my eyes, he says, "You make me forget that I'm broken."

I don't know how to respond to that. My heart certainly does though—it's beating like a bass drum in one of the electronic dance songs I used to run to every morning during college. No one has ever said anything like that to me. I make him forget that he's broken? I'm...at a loss for words.

He lifts his palms off the desk and bends down to pick up the box he put down to greet Devin. "I found some good stuff back there." Quest drops the box behind the desk, effectively blocking me in. "Looks like personal stuff," he says, taking out a stack of old newspapers and laying them in front of me.

Bringing the papers towards me, I read the date on the top one out loud. "March 22, 2014." A Santa Monica newspaper? "Why would your grandfather keep newspapers from Santa Monica?"

"I don't know. I wonder..." Quest's eyes narrow and he grabs the top issue from the stack in front of me. He opens it up and skims each page, stopping a few pages in. "Oh my god..." He looks at one of the articles, then quickly moves the paper to the side to look at the one beneath it. Flipping through it, he gasps and goes to the next paper, and so on, until he's searched through them all, the whole time making throaty sounds and unintelligible words.

"Quest? Are you okay?"

He folds the paper he's reading, then takes each one and folds them back up as well, except for the one on top. He opens it up to the article and hands it to me to read.

LOCAL SOLDIER DISCHARGED

Santa Monica resident, CPL Quest Raniero Vescovi, has been discharged without honors from the United States Army. Caught shooting the opposition's militia

commander in the foot and then beating him within an inch of his life, CPL Vescovi was released from the Army immediately. Though sources within his battalion defend the assertion that CPL Vescovi was coming to the rescue of a young girl being sexually assaulted, Vescovi did indeed go against the Army's policy to not intervene with middle-eastern cultural issues that may or may not involve rape. Both CPL Vescovi and United States Army officials declined to comment.

26.

Q uest

     I watch as Haven walks into the door of the room I call my past. My secret. I could have folded up the papers and taken them home with me. Or ripped them up and tossed them away. Not that all the newspaper articles were implicating. It was only the one. The one I showed her. I could have handed her one of the issues from the bottom of the pile—the picture of me at the eighth grade science fair, the picture of me crossing the end zone during a game-winning play as split-end on the JV football team, the article about the no-hitter I pitched my senior year in high school. There were other small, insignificant articles about me and the kids or teams in my town from years ago. Even my first military photo was in one of the papers. But I chose to invite Haven into my secret hell. No doubt she'll have questions. So why the hell did I let her in?

"Oh, Quest," she murmurs as she finishes reading the short blurb.

"Now you know." I was so happy today. Happy to have Haven to work with daily. Happy to feel something besides utter failure. Today, I was just happy to be. I was all ready to play with Haven after I saw her note on the little card; *Nothing Gold Can Stay* written by Robert Frost was written on top, and her note beneath it read, "Don't fret over a pimple, it will soon disappear. Instead, work on your soul.

For when your beauty's gone, you'll still see the gold." No one else will get the significance of how this relates to her, at least not until they take a closer look, but *I* do. And from that first meeting at the diner, I could see the shimmer through her eyes. I wanted her to know that she was still as bright and beautiful as the sunshine, and calling her Goldilocks was my first step in doing so. But then I found the papers.

"Why would they let you go?" she asks quietly, her eyes still on the article.

I don't get to respond. Haven's friend walks back in.

Brushing off the maudlin, I say, "Find anything you like?"

He hands me *Of Mice and Men* by John Steinbeck.

"Another classic, Devin, I'm impressed," Haven says. To which Devin smiles and says, "Maybe that's my intent."

Well shit, Devin likes Haven.

Devin looks between Haven and me, then says, "See ya soon, Haven. Movie-night Friday?"

"Sure, I just have to check with Eric and Katie."

"Well, I was thinking maybe it could be just the two of us? Just this once?"

"Oh."

I take it Haven's only finding out now that he likes her.

"It's okay," the boy says. "Call Eric, it's fine. I'll call you Friday. Happy Thanksgiving."

"Okay. Um, Happy Thanksgiving to you too." Haven looks sad.

"Sooooo," I start, once Devin's out the door and out of sight. "That was...awkward. Guess the guy wants you."

She groans. "We had been on two dates, but I thought since my whole...never mind."

"You're beautiful, Haven. Regardless of your scars."

Haven gapes, and suddenly pales.

"You're gold, Ponyboy," I joke, trying to bring back some levity.

"What?"

"I may not be much of a reader, but I do like a good movie. I saw your card under the Robert Frost book."

"Oh," she says on a chuckle. "Right. A pimple just doesn't seem like a big deal anymore, you know? And, FYI, in *The Outsiders*, Johnny was talking about Ponyboy's curiosity and innocence. His golden soul. Not his appearance."

"I wasn't talking about *your* appearance either."

"I don't..." she shrugs and shakes her head.

"You're still you. At first, when you came to my reopening, and then the night you punched me in the nuts..." I give her a wink, she cringes. "I thought you'd changed. When I got hint of your face, I figured whatever happened to you had changed you for the worse. And I'm not talking about your appearance either. You seemed...darker. Defeated. I thought you'd lost your sunshine. But then you invited me into your dark, cold home and let me sit for over an hour. Even though I know you wanted nothing more than for me to leave. That's when I knew the sun was inside you there somewhere. Because you're still you. You're still *gold*."

Haven juts her chin and whispers, "Thank you," but her hand goes to the pile of newspapers. "Your grandfather kept these."

I nod. Talk about overwhelming emotions.

"If you did what this article says you did, you're a hero." She shakes her head and holds up her hands as if to say, "So what's the problem?"

The problem is, I went against the Army's unspoken rule.

After a few moments where neither of us says anything, and our eyes don't leave each other's, I say, "I'm no hero. I shot a man, then beat him up. I could have killed him." Taking a breath, I continue. "I guess that counts for something...that I didn't kill him, but because I really *wanted* to kill him, and *still* wish I had, I'm not a hero. I'm just a guy who beat a man to a pulp and didn't even save the girl."

Her eyes have not left mine when she responds with a breathy, "Oh, Quest."

Then my eyes go to the tear that slips out from beneath her glasses. It falls right into the cleft on her left cheek. Before she can wipe it away herself, I step closer and swipe it away with my thumb. Haven doesn't step back, but she does look down, and she does cover her scar with her closed hand. "I don't think it's as bad as you think it is," I tell her quietly.

Her hand moves over the scar, but it never leaves it. "You haven't seen the whole thing." Her voice is only slightly above a whisper.

With both my hands on either side of her glasses, I ask, "Do you mind?"

She flinches, but then drops her hand and shakes her head.

As I slowly lift the glasses off her ears, her trembling hands cover mine. So I set them back atop her ears. "When you're ready."

"I'm ready." She nods. "You shared your story..." Very slowly, she pulls the glasses from her face.

Yes, there are scars. A long one extending from her right ear over her cheekbone and across her nose. The thick part of her nose, part of which was covered by her low-slung sunglasses, looks like it had been stitched together. And though these scars take up most of her face, it's the indentation on her left cheek that makes the most impression. She's right; the cleft where I wiped her tear was not the whole of it. The cleft is certainly the deepest part of the scar, but above it is a quarter-shaped gash where scar tissue has started to form. And though it looks like it was once very painful, it in no way takes away from her beauty. The uncertainty in her eyes when I look at her tells me she believes the opposite.

"I think you're beautiful." I want to say more. So much more. Instead, I run both my thumbs along the tissue that forms her scars.

As, again, we stare into each other's eyes, I get the urge to kiss her, but just before my lips land on hers, she ducks her head and backs away.

"I'm sorry. I shouldn't have done that. I'm sorry," I say, embarrassed that I made the move.

Shrugging her shoulder, she tilts her head. "It's okay."

"Please just forget I did that, Haven. I don't know what came over me. Maybe because we were close, but please don't let this make things awkward. Please don't quit." I sound pathetic, I know, but it scares me to lose her, and I don't want my stupidity to be the reason for quitting.

"Of course not," she forces out. "It's forgotten already."

"Thank God."

She laughs, and I'm relieved. Besides, I'm a complete mess, and kissing Haven would have only invited her *into* my mess...and that wouldn't be fair to my worst enemy.

27.

H AVEN
    I wished I'd kissed him.
I wanted to kiss him.
I regret bowing my head to avoid kissing him.

But with my scars out in the open like that, I couldn't get the thought of how ugly I am out of my head. And that would have ruined the kiss. Because if I'm going to kiss Quest Vescovi, I want all my energy focused on his lips. On his tongue. On the delightful taste of him.

But as we've established, I'm a coward.

I could tell by the way he'd dropped his shoulders that he was disappointed, but I am grateful that he wanted to forget it ever happened, because I do not want there to be any tension between us while I'm working for him.

As I'm driving home after work, I can't help but realize Quest saw my scars. Every single one, yet he still wanted to kiss me. Is it possible he's able to see *beneath* my scars? And like me despite them? A burst of happiness spreads like fire inside of me, giving me a shred of hope in what has been such a hopeless existence these past months. Just as this hope takes form on my face and I smile, a small white church comes into view up ahead. I've driven this road a hundred times and have never noticed the old chapel on the hill. Slowing down, I decide at the last minute to pull into the lot. I sit and stare at the old structure—in need of a good paint job, but charming in its antiquity. An unfamiliar feeling pulls me out of the car and up the steps, where I tug on the door and find it open. It's empty, but not dark. My footsteps carry me through the foyer and into the nave. One aisle separates the dozen or so rows of pews. I sit on the bench in the last row.

Unsure of what drew me into the place, I set my gaze on the pulpit up front. A large crucifix hangs above it. I can't remember the last time I sat inside a church—a wedding or funeral? Going to Sunday services was never on the agenda in the Quinn household, and it never occurred to me to attend on my own. I'm not a stranger to prayer, I include it in my everyday life, but I never thought of entering a church to do so. Tonight, I bow my head and pray. For acceptance of myself, despite my appearance. For forgiveness of my mother's hurtful words—and recognition that her intentions, though misconstrued, are mostly honorable. For guidance on where to go from here.

"Haven?"

My eyes fly open and my head pops up. I'm not alone.

"Haven, are you okay?" A hand settles on my shoulder just as I realize the voice belongs to Quest.

"What are you—"

He sits down next to me and says, "I saw your car parked in the lot. Thought it was odd and wanted to check on you."

"Odd?"

"The lot is empty aside from your car. I was concerned."

"Oh. Well, thanks."

"You okay?" he whispers, as if he's suddenly aware he's inside a church.

"I will be. Thanks. Thanks for worrying, you don't have to. I can take care of myself."

"Never said you couldn't. I have a habit of—"

"Saving girls who need saving," I say without thinking. "I'm sorry. I didn't mean...I wasn't implying about that..." I didn't mean to bring up the girl he tried to save overseas.

"No, you're right. And I didn't mean to imply that you needed my help. It's just how I am."

"It's a nice quality. I'm sorry if I came off offensive."

"No. You didn't. Well, seeing that you're okay, I'll—"

I put my hand on his leg to stop him from getting up. "Thank you for turning out to be such a good friend. We haven't known each other long, but you aren't at all what I first expected. I'm sorry I misjudged you."

A slow tingle spreads up my arm when Quest covers my hand with his. "You didn't misjudge me. I was angry when we first met. I was forced to move across the country and I blamed you. I quickly got over that once I met you. So, it's me who should be apologizing."

Attempting to keep my focus from the flutters that are assaulting my stomach, I remove my hand from Quest's leg and from under his hold. "This is my first time in a church," I admit, feeling the need to share with him.

"Really?" he asks, sounding surprised.

"I take it it's not yours?"

"No. Grew up Roman Catholic. Mass every Sunday. Your parents didn't take you to church?"

"It wasn't on their to-do list I guess. Didn't you say you don't pray?"

"I don't. Doesn't mean my parents didn't drag me with them every Sunday. As soon as I was done making my confirmation, I stopped going."

"Do you miss it?"

"No."

"Is it possible to miss something you've never experienced?" I ask, wondering why I wished my parents did drag me to church on Sundays.

"I imagine it's possible. Especially if you feel something lacking."

I nod and take his words into consideration. Maybe it's time to experience something new. Instead of saying anything, I rise and thank him for stopping in.

When Quest stands, he takes my hand and leads me out of the pew. Before the goosebumps finish begging for attention on my arm, he lets it go. I lead us the rest of the way out. At my car, I again thank Quest and tell him I'll see him in the morning.

ON THE WAY HOME, I call my father to see how my mother is doing.

"Hey, pumpkin," he says, answering on the first ring.

"Hi, Daddy. How's mom?"

"Better. They took her out of CCU. She looks like she didn't even have a massive heart attack."

"Well, you know, Mom...appearance is everything."

"Haven."

"No, I mean it. She's too proud to show any other side but her good side. I mean that in the nicest way." I really don't. *Why* won't my mother show her vulnerable side? It'd make it so much easier on me if she would.

"I don't think you mean that in the *nicest* way, but I'll pretend you did. Are you coming to see her tomorrow? She asked about you today."

"Oh. Well I started my new job. I need to be in at ten and probably won't get out until seven. I'll be there Thursday if that's okay?"

"Of course it's okay."

"Thanks, Dad. I'll see you then."

"Good night, sweetheart."

I end the call and think about the evening. I was inside a church for the first time and I liked the peace it gave me. Quest was so concerned for my safety that he pulled over to check on me. My reaction to his touch made me realize that I just may be falling for him. I'm not sure whether to smile or duck in fear of more change.

28.

Quest

Business on Wednesday is slow. So slow, that at three o'clock in the afternoon, I tell Haven we're closing up shop.

"But what if people come after work? Or after food shopping?" she asks.

"Haven. How many people do you know make a mad dash to the bookstore the day before Thanksgiving?"

She shrugs. "Me."

"Of course you would."

"Some people don't cook the night before Thanksgiving, and so they read."

"I don't cook the night before Thanksgiving, but I definitely do not read." As a child, when my grandparents were part of my story, Thanksgiving was the prelude to the Christmas season. Holiday food smells wafted from the kitchen into the TV room where my father and grandfather watched football all day, breaking in-between games only to eat at the dining room table. I remember sitting with the men because they were men, but wanting to be in the kitchen with Mom and Nonna, where pumpkin and apple pies were cooling on the windowsill, sausage stuffing was frying in the pan on the stove, and a turkey that fed us for days was cooking in the oven. After we'd moved to California, and started a new chapter sans my grandmother and grandfather,

Thanksgiving was just another day where football was on the television, and food was on the stove. Dinner was still eaten at the dining room table, and a turkey still sat center-stage, but other than that, it felt like a Sunday afternoon. Nothing special. Nothing to be thankful for. But there was not one Thanksgiving ever spent reading.

"And as I've said before, being the owner of a bookstore, you really should."

I laugh. "Does watching movies that were *originally* books count?"

She tsks and shakes her head. "No. It does not." But then, she raises a finger, says, "Hold on," and disappears into one of the book aisles.

While she's gone, I switch the OPEN sign to CLOSED, and shut down the register, all the while wondering if I should ask her to stop over tomorrow. I remember her saying her friend was going to Puerto Rico, and I know her mom and dad will be at the hospital, but I'm afraid, since trying to kiss her yesterday, that she'll think I'm asking her as a date kind of thing. And I *don't* want to push that issue with her. All I really want to do is hang out with her.

Haven returns, holding up a book. "Here," she says, placing the paperback book in my hands. "I think you'd enjoy this."

My Grandfather's Blessings by Rachel Naomi Remen. "You think I'd like this?"

She nods. "I do. I have a copy at home. Your grandfather is the one who recommended it to me." She shrugs a shoulder. "He knew I liked to read all kinds of books. Read it. I'm sure you'll enjoy it."

Holding it up, I say, "I'll start on it tonight."

With a satisfied smile, Haven says, "Good."

"So listen, Haven," I start, hoping to God I don't sound pathetic. "I have no plans tomorrow, and I know your mom will still be in the hospital; would you like to come to my house for dinner. I, mean, I don't have a turkey or anything, but..." I trail off, figuring, she knows where I'm going with this, now it's up to her to respond.

She nods as she looks down and bites the side of her lip. "Okay. I'm going to go see my mom for a little bit, but I can come after. Did you have a time in mind?"

"Nope, any time. I can prepare a lasagna ahead of time—" I make a mental note to call my mom and ask her how to make a lasagna "—and throw it in when you get to my house."

"That sounds nice. Thank you."

"What kind of wine do you like? Red? White?"

"Blueberry?"

"Blue...what the hell is blueberry wine?"

"I don't know. Blueberry...wine. Wine made from blueberries."

Shaking my head, I laugh. "Sure. I'll search for blueberry wine then."

"No don't. I have some home. I'll bring it."

"Okay, good." We stare at each other again, but she's the first to look away. "So you're sure about closing this early?"

"Yes. No one's come in the entire day." When I look at her, she's frowning. "Why? You don't want me to close?"

"Oh no, that's not it. My dad wanted me to go see my mother today, but I told him I had to work. But that's all—"

"You don't want to go see your mom?"

She shakes her head. "Not exactly."

"And you don't want to lie."

"No. It's fine, though. I should go see her."

"How 'bout this? Let's go to that diner where we first met, since that's the closest place to sit and eat around here, and you can help me look online for some books worth purchasing? You'll be working, and you won't have to lie."

A broad smiles illuminates her face. "That. Would be. Perfect," she says, splitting up her sentence for effect.

I laugh, and tell her to grab her things.

After a quick drive in the Jeep, we enter the diner, and a waitress sits us at a booth in front of a window. "The apple pie just came out of the oven," she says, placing menus in front of us.

"Oooh, that sounds delicious," Haven says, looking down and fussing with her glasses. "I'll take a slice of that and a cup of hot chocolate."

"I'll need a few minutes," I tell her, opening up the menu.

"Take your time. My name's Lorna."

When Lorna, and her Peggy-Sue style ponytail, walks away, I look at Haven. "Nothing for lunch?"

"Uh, yeees...hot apple pie *is* lunch."

"Oookay. It's not nearly enough for me."

While I'm still searching the menu for hearty lunch choices, Haven hoists her black bag onto her lap and pulls out her laptop. "So," she says as she starts up the computer, "have you ever looked on AbeBooks?"

I place the menu down, ignore her question, and look her in the eyes. "Do you miss your other job?"

"I asked you a question."

"And I asked you one. Did you even try to get your job back?"

The waitress comes back, just as Haven opens her mouth, and sets down the hot chocolate covered in whipped cream. "I'll just have a cheeseburger, fries, and a coke," I say quickly, wanting her to leave before Haven switches the subject.

"Okay," she says, snapping up the menus and walking away.

"Haven. Did you?"

She opens her mouth again and shuts it, right before shaking her head.

"You haven't been in contact with your boss?"

"No. Can we not talk about that?"

"Why?"

"Because we're here to find books."

"Why haven't you called your boss?"

"You're nosy."

"I guess. So why haven't you?"

She closes the laptop and taps the cover. "It's an on-screen position. He's not going to want me as his newscaster."

"How do you know that?"

Pointing all five fingers at her face, she says, "Hello. Look at me. I don't even take my sunglasses off. I can't be broadcasting the news to a bunch of people, even if it is just local late night news."

"I think you're wrong, Haven. I think you should go talk to your boss. You don't know what he's thinking. Or she."

"No, my boss is a he."

"Maybe he's one of those progressive types that encourages distinctiveness, rather than the same old Fox News face. I'd much rather look at you then some made-up Barbie doll."

Her face blushes, but she says, "Stop."

Haven puts so much importance on her appearance. If she could only see herself the way I do—delicate, graceful, magnificent. "You need to talk to him. You can't know what he's thinking if you don't ask. And besides, how is this all working? Your leave of absence and all? You don't need to talk to your boss about that?"

Haven picks up her hot chocolate and extends her tongue to take in the whipped cream. *Holy hell.* It doesn't matter if she has scars, she's still so fucking sexy. I swallow as she sets her chocolate back down. "That's another thing," she whispers.

"So, you may not have a job because you've been irresponsible in handling it?"

She nods.

"And getting fired for being irresponsible is easier to digest than losing your job because of your appearance."

She nods again.

I sigh. "Oh, Haven." Pausing for a moment to grasp her admission, I eventually say, "I guess I understand."

She waves a hand in front of her. "Besides, I like my *current* job."

"I wish I could pay you more."

"It's fine. I was going to ask my father to help me pay my rent."

"You can't pay your rent?"

"Um, well, I'm behind. If I don't make it current by the end of this month, I need to move out by the end of the year."

"Haven. No. Just...you know what? I have an apartment upstairs from the store. Why don't you live there?"

"No. I can't do that. You've already done so much."

"Haven, please just—"

"I'm interrupted by the waitress, who returns with our food.

"Is that caramel?!" she asks the waitress.

"Chef just made it now."

"Awesome." Haven picks up her fork and cuts off a bite of pie.

Since I guess I've pushed the limits already, I eat my burger, and focus on the quiet sounds Haven makes each time she takes a bite. *Reminder: get apple pie recipe from mom too.*

When we finish eating, I take out my laptop and ask Haven to repeat the name of the site she found. She opens up her laptop and turns her screen towards me. As I type the name in my browser, I say, "So, any books in particular strike your fancy?"

She grins and takes her computer back. "Not yet. I don't really know how much your budget is, so I don't want to choose anything until I know you can afford it."

Unfortunately, I tell her the truth. "Right now, there's not much the store can afford. "

"Oh?"

"There's a little there." After a pause, I say, "So let's see what we can find."

Her eyes return to her screen, and a few moments later, I notice her lifting her glasses above her nose. After another two seconds, she slides them up her forward, leaving them sitting on top of her head. I'm not sure she's even conscious of what she's doing, but I watch her anyway. There's nothing more glorious than a woman uninhibited.

29.

Q^{uest}

"You're cooking?!" The blare of my mother's voice fills the car.

"Louder, Ma, I don't think the woman in the car at the other end of the parking lot heard you."

"Where are you?" Her voice doesn't soften.

"I'm in the parking lot of the food store, Ma. I got you on Bluetooth. So can I have the recipe?"

"Do you even know how to turn on the stove?"

"Ma, please."

"You must have a girl coming over if you're going to attempt to make a lasagna," she sings, though still in her loud Italian way.

"Maybe I just want to make it because I'm hungry. Now can you let me know what I need, or should I just look up a recipe online?"

"Oh, Heavens no, Quest. I'll give you mine. Hold on a sec, I have to get down."

"Get down off what?"

"The ladder. I'm hanging shelves up in the garage. It's such a mess." All of a sudden there's rattling and then the sound of a screen door closing.

"Vinnie should be doing that, Ma, not you. You're gonna get hurt."

"God forbid. And why should Vinnie do it? 'Cause he's a man? I'm perfectly capable—"

"I know, Ma. I wasn't implying—"

"Yes you were. You have that whole damsel in distress thing going on. Well I'm not a damsel. And I'm not in distress. Okay. I got a piece of paper. I'll write it down and picture shoot it for you. Is that good?"

"You'll screenshot it you mean? Yes, that's perfect." Then I add, "Can you do that with your apple pie recipe too?"

"Okay, what's her name?"

"Ma. Stop."

"It's that girl from the bookstore. The one that's after your money, isn't it?"

"She's *not* after my money. Her ma's in the hospital, she has nowhere to go. I thought it'd be a good idea to spend Thanksgiving together. That's all."

"Just be careful, Quest, you were the one that was weary of her from the beginning. I don't want her manipulating you out of something you might want."

"She's not manipu...y'know what, Ma? I *can't* be manipulated, so you don't have to worry either way, 'kay?"

"Okay. Give me a few minutes to write up the recipes, and I'll send them to you."

"Thanks. Don't take too long, I'm going into the food store now."

"A few minutes."

"Thanks. Call you tomorrow."

"And take a picture of your lasagna," she laughs. "And the pie."

"Bye, Ma."

As I open the cans of Sclafani tomatoes—after returning from the grocery store—and pour them into the saucepan to prepare the sauce for the lasagna, I start talking out loud to myself. "What the hell have you gotten yourself into, Vescovi? You're cooking for a girl. You're cooking. You never cook. And for a girl. You have no business falling for a girl right now. You're too messed up in the head to bring a girl into your life. Fool."

While I continue to berate myself out loud, I dump a package of ground beef and bread crumbs into a bowl. That's when I notice the picture of my grandmother and grandfather on the windowsill behind the sink. Who better to listen to my grumbles than a man who can't respond. "So, Nonno, what the hell am I doing?" I go in the refrigerator and get the eggs, crack them into the meat and say, "What if I get involved with this girl and I mess her up? Like, what if I have one of my angry meltdowns like I did that day in the bank when they had to sedate me?" The tantrum I took at the bank was six months after I'd been discharged. I went up to a teller to withdraw money, because the ATM said I didn't have enough funds to take out twenty dollars. When the teller told me the same thing, I started shouting, insisting that I had it, and that I needed it to get food for the week. In reality, it was to feed my then-recent alcohol addiction. With my hands on my head, I started pacing the store and talking to myself, raising my voice for most of the conversation. I can't remember much after that, because all of a sudden I was grabbed by both arms and strapped to a stretcher by two paramedics, who proceeded to sedate me before bringing me to the hospital. I went to alcohol rehabilitation after that, but it was determined I was not an alcoholic, just an ex-soldier suffering from PTSD. Just an ex-soldier trying to fit back into civil life. Just an ex-soldier who needed a lot of psychiatric help. That's when I was introduced to Ginny.

Sticking my hands into the meat after I add the minced garlic—I do the sign of the cross asking forgiveness for not using fresh garlic—I roll three inch balls of meat between my palms and toss them one by one into the frying pan. "I don't know, Nonno. I haven't had one of those meltdowns since then, but before moving here, I still had that anger. Maybe I was more in control of it, but deep down, it was there. I haven't felt it lately, but what if, you know? I really like Haven. I'd hate to get involved and then without warning, I show my true colors. Haven's the one *you* introduced me to, by the way. I know you didn't really introduce me to her, but," I look at his picture again, "you kinda did. And I'm so grateful you did...I meet this girl and right away I can't stand her, because she may get what is rightfully mine—and I still wish I knew why you put in that condition." I point to his picture accusingly. "But then, the more I talk to her, and watch her, the more I start liking her...despite her very stubborn personality... then, I invite her to work with me, and suddenly, I realize I think I'm falling in love with her. It's like that quote you have hanging in the store...that Jane Austen one. ' I cannot fix on the hour, or the spot, blah, blah blah.' I get that quote now, Nonno, because I can't even tell you when I fell, but all off a sudden, I found myself down for the count and hopelessly...in love. God, Nonno, I'm in love. I'm in love." I scoff. "But I can't do that right now. Right?

And what if Mom's right, and I do have that whole damsel in distress thing in my head? Haven certainly fits the label; that wouldn't be fair."

I grab a beer out of the refrigerator and pop it open. After I take a sip, I continue chatting up my dead grandfather. "Maybe it *would* be easier if we just remained friends." I set down my beer and tend to the balls in my pan. "Because then I wouldn't have to hurt her if down the line, it is just the damsel thing...or all my anger returns..." Stirring the tomatoes, I remember that I was supposed to add garlic to them as well, so I get my little jar of already chopped up garlic and spoon some into the pot. "But I really do think I love her. I know I do. It can't just be 'cause I wanna save her. Can it?" I look back at my grandfather's picture and say, "You're no help," and laugh. I'm talking to a dead man's picture. I've officially lost my mind.

I finish my beer and go for another, but I don't have anymore. Not wanting to run out to the store again, I go to the hutch where my grandfather keeps his liquor and grab a bottle of Jim Beam off the shelf.

Wiping off the dust with my shirt as I walk back into the kitchen, I grab a glass, fill it with ice, and open the bottle.

It hits me as soon as I take the first swallow. It's gooooood. And despite the coolness of the liquid, it coats my chest with warmth.

"Thanks for the whiskey," I tell my grandfather as I pour my second glass. "It's good."

After turning off the burner beneath my meatballs, I spoon them into the sauce and give it a stir. Then, I finish my glass of whiskey, pour another, and grab my phone off the table. I text Haven.

Me: Looking forward to tomorrow.

While I wait to see if Haven replies, I finish another glass, then consider that I am seriously drunk. Three tumblers of Jim Beam whiskey will do that to a man who hasn't had anything stronger than a beer in the past two and a half years.

But I get excited when my phone dings.

Haven: Me too. Thanks for having me.

Of course I text her right back.

Me: Thanks for coming.

Haven: You don't have to have me. You can still cancel.

Me: No f***ing way!

Haven: Ohhkaay.

God, I really want to tell her how I feel. I want to kiss her. I want to say so many things, but I don't want to ruin what we have building between us. She pulled away from me once, what if she does it again? Maybe I'll start with something small.

~~**Me: I'm glad I decided to keep the store open.**~~ No, that's not right. I delete it before I hit send.

~~**Me: I'm glad you're working at the store.**~~ I delete that too.

Me: I'm glad my grandfather left you those books. That one, I send.

I see the bubbles on my screen and they remind me of ice cubes. I need more ice cubes. I need more drink. I get up and pour myself another glass, and then I hear the phone ding.

Haven: Oh. Yeah? I don't understand

What don't you understand, babe? If he didn't leave you those books, we'd never have met.

Me: Because I got to meet you

Haven: Oh. Me too

She sounds indifferent. Does she sound indifferent to you?

Me: I really really am glad I met you

Haven: Me too. :)

A smiley face? Aww, cute.

~~Me: I want to sleep with you.~~

~~Me: I love you.~~

Me: I want to kiss you

After several seconds, the phone dings again.

Haven: Oh

Oh?

Me: Oh?

She doesn't text back right away.

Me: You don't want me to kiss you?

Again, I wait.

Me: Because I really wish you'd let me kiss you yesterday

Haven: Quest? Are you at a bar or something?

Me: I'm home

Haven: Are you drinking?

Me: Jim Beam

Haven: Are you drunk?

Me: No

Haven: I think you are

Me: I'm not. I just want to taste your lips

Haven: Stop texting me, Quest. You're drunk

Me: I still want to kiss you

Haven: I'm shutting off my phone, Quest. Go to sleep

Me: I wanna kill whoever hurt you. Do you know that? Every day I think about the fucker who hurt you. I wanna kill him.

Haven: Stop.

Me: He's out there somewhere. I don't think he's who you think he is.

Haven: What???

Me: Your scars are different. They're not like the others.

No return text.

30.

H AVEN
In one drunken text, Quest has effectively stripped me of the confidence it has taken me months to rebuild—my feeling of security. I am once again a girl afraid of her own shadow.

My chest constricts and I can't catch my breath. I pace the floor, then go to the sink to get a glass of water. Tap water. Something about the water falling from the faucet into my glass is calming, like an old song. *"Don't cry, Haven, it's just a skinned knee." Mom goes to the sink, fills a glass with water and hands it to me. As I drink the cool water, she says, "You have to get back on that bike right away, or else it'll be that much harder to ride next time. Don't let your fears keep you from doing something you know you enjoy."* The memory washes over me as I stand in front of the sink, the water spilling over the glass and onto my hand. My mother is a tough woman, armed with candid opinions and backhanded encouragement, but I'm beginning to learn that she's rarely wrong in her assessments. I can't be afraid. I enjoy life too much, and I mustn't let my fears consume me.

My phone dings several times before I shut it off. I need to calm down some before I read anything more Quest has to say. The best thing for me to do is go to bed and try to get myself to sleep.

But sometime in the middle of the night, I wake up in bed, drenched in sweat and fear.

His gray eyes stare back at me.

They taunt me.

They torture me all over again.

A nightmare. I try calming myself by restating it. It was just a nightmare. That's all. But as much as I try to go back to sleep, I can't. Quest is right. My scars *are* different from the others. I remember the pictures. I remember Susanna and the others. *Two matching parallel lines.* He never returned to hurt them again. He left his mark and ran. But what if the guy who hurt me wasn't there just to leave his mark? What if he *meant* to kill me? What if he's out there waiting to finish the job?

With my stomach in my hands, I pace the floor and practically jump in fear. Not able to stand still, unable to walk slowly, I'm a dog on the quest to catch his own tail. My body wants to jump out of its skin. I cannot stay put in this house.

I grab my phone and my purse and run to my car without another thought. After turning it on, I peel out of the driveway in reverse, and drive. My only thought to run.

To where? I've nowhere to go.

An hour later, tired of driving route 209 and going nowhere, I turn around and head for Quest's. Since it's only six in the morning when I finally pull into his driveway, I turn off my headlights and keep the engine running, determined to sit here until it's late enough for Quest to wake up. While I sit there, staring at the tiny brown log cabin, I realize my chest is still thumping hard. I turn on my phone, ready to call 911, in case I have a panic attack so bad I end up having my own heart attack, and I see three texts from Quest.

Quest: I'm sorry, Haven. I didn't mean to scare you. I'm just concerned that the pieces don't add up.

Quest: Haven. Please don't be mad. You're my best friend. I need you. Don't be mad.

Best friend? Really?

Quest: I just need to protect you.

Protect me? By drunk texting me?

I put his texts out of my mind and stare back at his cabin, but then my eyes find the surrounding property. Wooded forest. Dark, wooded forest. Scary, wooded forest. What if he's out there right now? What if he's out there just waiting to find me alone again?

That thought is enough to scare me into getting out of my car and running to Quest's front door right now. I pound on the door with both fists so he hears me. Pounding. Pounding. Knuckles against the door, heart against the ribcage. "Open the door, open the door," I shout, manic breaths perforating my words, my fists clobbering the door in frenzied rhythm while my eyes flash across the width of Quest's property. "Open the goddamn door!"

The door swings open. "What the hell?"

Pushing at Quest's chest with both palms, I beg, "Let me in." As I'm about to say the word please, he pulls me inside and closes the door.

"Whaahappened?" he asks, his two words rushed into one, his eyes wide with something unfamiliar.

I let out a huge sigh mixed with a small groan. "He's out there."

Quest takes a few deep breaths, paces the floor, and asks. "Where is he?" His eyes are still wide as he runs from window to window looking for the man who marked up my face.

"No, no. He's not really out there," I say, pointing to the window. "But what if? You're right. It wasn't the same guy."

Quest's shoulders drop and he moves away from the window and toward me. He looks down and catches his breath. "I didn't think so," he says, his demeanor returning to a calmer state. "Something was off."

"So what do I do? Police are looking for one man, but there are two. And what if he finds out I'm still alive? What if he comes back?"

Quest takes my hand and pulls me through the living room into the kitchen. "Sit," he says, pulling out a chair. "Coffee?"

"Uh...I don't know...I..."

"I don't have tea. But I have a fresh pot of coffee on."

"Yeah, yeah. That's fine, that's...sure. Thank you."

While he's pouring my coffee and preparing it, I start rapping my knuckles against the table. "I'm scared now."

"Calm down." He hands me the coffee and takes the seat perpendicular to me. "He hasn't come back for you yet, so I'm sure there's nothing to worry about."

"What if he finds out I'm still alive?"

"Maybe he never meant to kill you, Haven. That Stratford guy never killed. It's probably just a copycat slasher. But I do think you should go to the police. They need to know there may be a second guy. What clued you in?" he asks, genuinely curious and caring, his chin resting on his fist, his eyes intent on searching mine.

"I interviewed four of the victims. Back when I...before. They had two matching parallel lines. I saw pictures of the others, too. Same thing."

Quest sits back and folds his arms. "I saw that on the internet too."

I nod. "What should I do?"

"We go to the police."

"Today?"

"Hell yeah, you should go as soon as possible." He leans forward again and covers my hand with his. "You're supposed to see your mother today, right?"

Again, I nod.

"Let's go to the police station now. I'll take you. When we're done, I'll take you to the hospital and wait for you. This way, you won't have to be alone. Okay?"

Closing my eyes and sighing, I muster a soft, "Okay," and then I sip my coffee. It's not as bad as I thought.

IT TAKES US ABOUT THIRTY minutes to get to the Stratford Police Department. The whole time getting there, I'm in a fog, trying to conjure up the night I was attacked so I'd know what to say to the police, but I'm unable to do so because my brain won't allow the memories to resurface all of a sudden. Of course, when I'm home alone and sleeping, my brain has no problem pressing play on the video of my nightmare.

"You ready," Quest says after turning off his engine.

I nod but say, "No. I don't have anything to tell them."

"Just show them your scars. Make them see that they're not dealing with one suspect." Quest meets me on my side of the car, takes my hand, and gives it a squeeze. "Come on. I got ya."

Inside the police station, I'm met with the same crude officer who asked me out for a drink the day I came in asking questions about the slasher. He narrows his brows, probably trying to place from where he knows me.

Quest speaks first. "I'd like to open a case."

"A case," the officer says with a smirk. "A case about what?"

Quest scans the officer from head to toe, providing his own smirk, and says, "Officer Trent, is it?"

"That's what the name tag says."

Asshole.

"Look, Haven Quinn was attacked last July in your town," Quest says, and Officer Trent throws back his head in recognition. "That's where I know you from," he says, while Quest explains that I was lumped in with the victims of the Stratford Slasher without anyone actually investigating my assault.

"So wait a minute," Officer Asshole says, looking directly at me. I lower my glasses to hide more of my face. "You got attacked in July and you're only coming here now to press charges?"

"We're coming here now to open a case for investigation," Quest says, clearly agitated.

"My scars are different," I add, finally finding my voice. "The Stratford man left two very distinct matching lines on his victims' right cheeks. Mine are not matching, nor are they on one side of my face."

The officer snorts. Jackass.

After the officer finds it within himself to halt his sarcasm, he walks me into an interrogation room, hands me a pen and a piece of paper, and allows me to retell what happened the night of my assault. It takes a little bit of time to finally get to that place in my mind, but once I do, I can't find the words to write fast enough. I feel the adrenaline race toward my pen as it makes its way onto the paper.

My lack of air.

The sudden paralysis.

The thought that I was going to die right there in the alley.

The pain.

After my last words are written, I drop the pen as if it were on fire and run out of the room, straight for the door out of this place.

Quest finds me plastered up against his car.

His hand splays across my back and he says, "Haven. You okay?"

"Can we just leave?"

"Sure." He opens my door, lets me in, and circles back to his side of the car.

Once we're on the road, Quest says, "What an asshole. I just can't understand how a guy like that becomes a cop."

I'm still so distraught from reliving the entire incident to give my statement, that I fail to respond to Quest. Yes, the cop's an ass—I knew that the first time I met him—but I'm sure no one else wanted the Thanksgiving Day shift; they were probably home with their families.

"You okay?" Quest asks, after driving in silence for the past twenty-minutes.

I nod. "I will be," I say, finally calm enough to allow other thoughts to enter my mind. Like the texts Quest sent me last night.

Still, we're at a loss for words, and now I don't know if it's because of how things went at the police station or if his drunken declaration via text has just entered his mind as it has mine. Contemplating whether or not to bring it up, I decide it's best to keep it to myself and let the issue drop. I don't think I could handle any more drama at the moment.

Before my brain registers that we're in the parking garage of Morristown Hospital, Quest is pulling open my car door. "Oh. Oh, geez, I must have..." I must have what? Been sleeping? Daydreaming?

"Come on," he says, not waiting for me to finish. He holds out his hand for me to take, then squeezes it gently as he pulls me through the garage.

"Thank you for bringing me here. I really could have come alone."

"Not from where I stood when you came pounding at my door this morning. *And* the way you ran out of the police station." He tightened his grip on my hand again. "I wouldn't want you alone in that state anyway."

"I overreacted," I tell him, talking about both instances. "This morning, it was so early in the morning, and it was dark, and I'd just had a nightmare, and..." and I just stop talking, because I'm sounding more and more like a lunatic the more I talk.

"Hey, girl," he lets go of my hand to wrap his arm around my shoulder, "I'm a little freaked too. It's okay."

I LEAVE QUEST AT THE café on the first floor, and then proceed on my own up to my mother's room, where I find her sitting in the chair alongside her bed. "Hello, Mom. Happy Thanksgiving."

"Haven. You're here early."

"How are you feeling? You're sitting up I see."

Raising her eyebrows, she says, "Yes. I told you, I'm determined to get out of here,"

"That's good. Do you know when yet?"

"Probably by Saturday."

"That's good news."

"Thank you for coming, Haven. I appreciate it."

Whoa. What? "Thanks. And...you're welcome."

My mother pats the edge of the bed. "Sit."

"Everything okay?" I ask apprehensively.

"Haven, I know I've been hard on you. Actually, I *didn't* know. Your father explained things to me. I guess I always thought I was helping you by being tough on you. I'm not the most sensitive woman, but I don't know any other way." My mother clears her throat and uses her hand to caress it. "Anyway, your father tells me that I should be more compassionate, especially when it comes to you," she pauses, "and your appearance."

I cringe. My mother has etiquette when it comes to snooty stuff, but no filter when it comes to speaking to me.

"Anyway, your father says I should apologize and be nice. What do *you* think?"

"If you *want* to."

My mother purses her lips, but nods.

"I mean, you don't *have* to, but...I don't know, Mom, you just think everyone should be perfect..."

"What's wrong with perfection? I *strive* for it."

I wipe my palms on my sweatpants, and then realize...I'm wearing sweatpants. Shit. I toss the thought and get back to finally opening up to my mother. "Striving for perfection for yourself is one thing, but expecting it of others is a whole other ballgame. It's not fair of you to force your expectations onto me. Especially in regards to *my* appearance. Even before I was assaulted, I was never pretty enough. Or good enough."

"Haven, that is not true. You were, are, perfect in my eyes. It's just that you are in television. If you want to succeed, you need to look perfect. It's an unfortunate reality, but no one wants to look at imperfect looking people. They watch television to escape reality. To forget their own ugliness."

"Mom! I do news. I deliver reality."

"And they want it wrapped up in a pretty bow. Look at Diane..."

"Sawyer," we both say at the same time. I sigh, realizing my mother will never change.

"You're beautiful, Haven, but people are going to judge. It's a sad fact...especially if you're on television."

Jutting my chin, I say, "Well good thing I'm not on television anymore." Then I look down and start pulling on the threads of the hole in my pants.

"But you love being on television. You can't just give up your dreams."

Still fussing with my sweats and averting my mother's eyes, I say, "They're not my dreams anymore, Mom. I like my job at the bookstore." I return my eyes to hers and tell her, "I just started working there, and I love it."

"That little shop?"

"Yes. You used to like it too. And how different is it than working in a library?"

"I'm a librarian, Haven. I received a master's degree to be one. You studied television, and that's beside the point." My mother waves her hand in the air. "My whole point in harping on your appearance, both before and after your...accident."

"Attack."

"Attack...was to help you succeed."

Ok, I'm not so sure if my mother is being genuine or not, but I'm done talking about this. "Okay, well, Mom...I don't want success if it means I have to be beautiful. I don't want to be judged like that."

She nods. "Okay. Fair enough. But aren't you being judged anyway?"

"Mom."

"Why are you covering your face with oversized sunglasses then?"

What? I think, as I take hold of my glasses, leaving them to cover my face.

"Obviously, you know people are judging you by your appearance. I'm not being cruel, honey, but your self-esteem is suffering because of your scars. How can you expect to live a happy life if you're going to always be self-conscious of your face?"

God! I hate when my mother is right.

"I know I hounded you about your nose before, only because I thought it would help your career, but now...*now*, it doesn't only have to do with your career. Your well-being is on the line."

I feel my eyes begin to fill, as I seek the comfort of my runaway thread and realize the rip in my pants has grown.

"I love you enough to tell you the truth, dear. People are cruel. You must know it, or else you wouldn't be wearing the glasses, so either find a way to rise above the stares and silent comments, and not *care* what people think, or finish with the surgeries."

Adjusting the glasses on my face with the hand that's not making the rip in my pants bigger, I consider my mother's suggestion. As much as I dislike the manner in which she imparts the ultimatum, she may have a point. Not that I want to succumb to the pressures of vanity, but my scars *are* the foremost thing on my mind every day. Will they ever *not* be? Constantly, my mind races with questions about my face. My scars. Are they the first thing anyone notices on me? Am I covering them sufficiently? Is the lighting so bright that my scars are causing shadows, making them appear even larger?

Why can't I look like I had before? Will I ever be able to face the world without hiding behind huge lenses?

The longer I think about my mother's words, the deeper I let them sink in, the more clear the answer is.

I don't really have a choice.

31.

Quest

Haven wakes me up by nudging my shoulder. "Quest," she whispers. "Quest."

"Oh. Shit. I must have fallen asleep," I say, straightening my back and sitting upright..

"Sorry I took so long."

Rolling my neck to dissolve the kink, I ask, "What time is it?"

"Eleven. I'm sorry."

"Eleven? It's only been an hour. I thought you were staying longer?"

"I didn't want to keep you waiting."

"Haven, I expected you to be a while, I don't mind."

She nods. "I know. I just...it's fine. I got to talk to my mom, and my dad showed up about forty-five minutes ago. No wonder he said he didn't see you. He came up with coffee from the cafeteria. I asked if he saw you, he said no."

"Yeah. I needed to rest my head against a wall, so I found a good seat here in the lobby."

She laughs. "Sorry. I woke you up early today."

"That's okay." I stand and set my hand on Haven's waist. "You sure you're ready to leave?"

"Yes, definitely. I'm good. I just wanna get out of here."

"Okay," I nod, moving my hand to her back to lead her toward the exit. "You still up for coming to my house to—"

"Yes," she responds before I finish my sentence. "Yes. I don't want to go home."

Nodding once, I say, "Okay then." But I do hide the smile that tries to inch its way across my face.

We're in the car and on the road when I blurt, "So what did your mother say to upset you?"

From my peripheral vision, I see Haven whip her head in my direction. "What?"

"You seem upset. You're somewhere inside that head of yours. I assume it was something your mother said." When I look at her, her head is turned back toward her window again.

"She didn't really upset me," Haven says to the window. "She actually may have been right this time."

"Right? About what?"

I hear her sigh, but no words come out of her mouth. When I look again, her head is propped against the window. I don't ask anymore questions.

"SO, I PREPARED THIS last night," I say as I pull the cold, uncooked lasagna out of the refrigerator. "My mom said to cook it at two fifty for two to three hours." I put the glass pan in the oven, and turn it on. "She said I could cook it at three fifty for an hour, but she said the flavors *meld* better when they cook slowly." I chuckle and look at Haven. "Since it's early, I figure we can let the flavors meld." Then I wink at her.

Her right dimple deepens. "Sounds good."

"I don't have blueberry wine, and I can guess that by the way you're dressed, you probably didn't bring it."

"Ooh," she says, dropping her head and flattening her hand over the hole in her pants. "I never even thought of changing, or brushing my hair," she quickly covers her mouth, "or my teeth."

"Don't worry, I couldn't tell. So..." I turn to the counter and wave the near-empty bottle of Jim Beam in the air. "I can give you a shot's worth of whiskey, or I can make a new pot of coffee."

She laughs. "I never finished the cup you gave me this morning." She picks up her mug from this morning and walks over to the microwave.

"No no no. I'll make a fresh pot," I tell her, and instruct with my finger for her to go back and sit at the kitchen table. When I put the Jim Beam bottle down on the counter I take a second look at it. Shit. Subtly, I pull out the phone from my back pocket and open up my messages.

Shit shit shit.

Setting my phone on the counter, I go about making the coffee. And think about how I'm going to deal with the realization that last night, I not only told Haven I wanted to kiss her, but I also declared her my best friend and told her I needed her. How frigging pathetic. I could always avoid the whole thing and forget I ever texted her. She hasn't brought it up, so maybe she forgot about it. Though, I have a feeling she didn't.

I finish the coffee prep and sit down across from Haven. I'm about to say something—anything—to apologize for my drunk texting when Haven speaks. "I'm thinking about having plastic surgery."

That thought came out of the blue. "What?"

She looks down and then back at me. "Not boobs or anything."

Right away, I claim, with my hands popping up in defense, "I was not thinking that."

Ignoring my comment, she continues. "On my face. I think I may have scar revision done."

"Okay. Okay. How come? I mean, why all of a sudden..."

Haven slides her thumbs beneath her sleeves. "I'm not vain. Not really."

"I never thought you were," I say gently, feeling an unexplained pain in my chest.

Covering her mouth with her hand, she says, "But a little I am, I guess. Why else would I wear these huge things?" she asks, tapping at her glasses. "Obviously, I'm concerned with my appearance if I'm so afraid of people seeing me."

"Did your mother tell you that?"

"My mother's not a bad person."

"I never said she was."

"You probably hate her, because of what I've told you, but she's not bad." Haven pauses. And then she feeds me a line I'm sure her mother's fed her—"She has my best interests at heart."

"Haven. I don't know your mother to hate her. I only know what you've chosen to tell me. So, if you know her intentions are good, then...who am I to say anything?"

"Well, I know she's not the most empathetic person on the planet, but today she surprised me. She, uh, she told me

I either have to accept that people are going to stare and not give a shit that they are, or I need to get the scar surgeries. Otherwise, I'm never going to move on from this."

"What do the surgeries entail? And your mother said *shit*?"

"No, I added the shit part. She despises cursing. And the surgeries entail pain. Lots and lots of pain."

"And the pain will be worth it?"

"You don't know how badly it hurt, Quest. I wanted to die."

"I'm sure. I don't doubt that. That's why I asked if it will be worth it to have them done."

"Look at me, though."

"Take the glasses off."

Dropping her head, she exhales and continues hiding her hands in her sleeves.

"Your mother is right in that you need to accept yourself the way you are. That's a given. I'm your friend, Haven. Take the glasses off and look at me."

She raises her head and looks at me, her concealed hands slowly move to the temples of her frames. It takes her about five seconds, four fingers on each hand peeking out to touch the rims, but she does remove them, and places them on the table. Her bottom lip quivers as she stares at me.

"I think you're beautiful," I say, feeling those words down deep in my gut. Pushing out from the table, I get up and slide into the chair next to her. With my fingertips, I turn her face square in front of me and she lets me run my thumb across her most prominent scar, just as I had the other day. "They're not that bad, you know."

Retreating into the chair's back, she covers her cheek with her hand. "Yes they are. There's a big hole."

"It's not a hole, Haven. It's an indent, and it's not even very deep." Her eyes are cast down again, and she's back to fussing with her sleeves, but I keep talking to her. "I'm sure it looks a lot bigger to you than it is."

"It's the size of a quarter!"

"Okay. Yes. The scar is. But it's not a hole. And I'm sure after a few more months, it's going to be even less noticeable."

She shakes her head. "The doctor said it might need another graphing. The others need work too. I don't know."

Tilting my head, I try to put myself in her place. I've seen so many horrible things in my recent past, but this may be the first horrible thing *she's* encountered. I've seen her before the scars. She was unblemished, self-assured. I can see how looking in the mirror now would affect her confidence. It's easy for her to see the imperfections, when what she was used to was a flawlessly attractive woman. So telling Haven she's beautiful and that she doesn't need any more surgeries may be pointless...because to her, they may be everything.

Since I no longer hear the drip of the coffee pot, I get up and say, "Let me get us some more coffee."

"I'm sorry," she says from the table. "It's Thanksgiving. I shouldn't be bringing you down."

"Are you kidding me? Being with you is the most *up* I've been," I say, before realizing what I'm actually telling her.

"Wait, what?"

I pour the coffee, pour the milk, and decide to pour my heart out when I get back to the table. "I'm not the happiest person in the world. "

"No, really?" Her lip quirks and her dimple stands at attention.

"True story," I joke. "But when I'm with you, I'm *not* unhappy."

"Oh." Her dimple remains, but her lips disappear.

"I enjoy being with you, Haven. Scars or no scars. I like who I am when I'm with you, and without even seeing it coming, you've helped me to heal my *own* scars."

"*Your* scars?"

"We're gonna need something stronger than coffee if I'm going to start telling you about me."

"I'm sorry, no. You don't—"

I laugh. "I'm joking. I mean, yes, we'll need something stronger, but I don't mind talking to you about it." I look around the kitchen and say, "You know what we need? My grandfather's Sambuca. I saw some when I found the whiskey." I get up but continue talking while I retrieve the liquor. "He had an espresso pot on the stove when I first moved in" I come back holding the bottle. "I don't know how to make espresso, but I'm sure it'll taste just fine in our regular coffee."

"Oh my god," she says on a short laugh. "It's still practically morning."

"No judging in my house." I pour the clear liquid into my coffee, then hold the bottle up in silent question to Haven.

"Sure. Why not," she says, holding up her mug.

After flavoring her coffee too, I set the bottle down and pick up my mug. "Cheers."

"Cheers."

After we clink mugs, I chug half my coffee while Haven takes an apprehensive sip.

I pour more Sambuca into my half-empty cup and take another gulp. "So..."

"So." Her hands hug her mug as she waits for me to begin.

"That article you read. About my discharge. Well, that wasn't the first time I knew of stuff like that going on."

Haven's lips make the slightest movement inward.

Remembering too vividly *that* night and many others, I continue. "The man was a sick fuck. No one liked what he was doing; not even his own men. But they couldn't stop him. They wouldn't. None of us would." I get up, take a glass out of the cupboard, and bring it to the table. No words escape my lips until I've poured a full glass of the Sambuca and take a few gulps.

Haven's lips completely disappear while she waits for me to speak again.

"We saw messed up shit all day long. Buildings blowing up, civilians shot, soldiers being blown to pieces. Horrible, horrible stuff. But Christ, nothing was as fucked up as hearing a little girl, *or* a little boy, squealing in pain. Being violated..." I stop talking, needing to compose myself. Tears form in my eyes, but there's nothing I can do to stop them. I don't even wipe them away. When I look at Haven, her eyes are bubbling over as well.

"We were told to stay out of it. Their country, their laws. But after hearing them night after night...after night, I just couldn't. I couldn't stay out of it, Haven; these kids couldn't defend themselves." I look down at my shaking hand cupping my glass. My throat rumbles as I continue. "I couldn't keep quiet one more second. I shot the guy in the foot, originally just wanting him to stop, you know? But when I saw him flinch from the pain, he didn't even scream. He didn't. Even. Scream. It was nothing compared to what he'd done to those kids.So...I...I ran over to him and beat the shit out of him. Punching him and pulverizing him and knocking him in the throat as he lay beneath me." I look at my hands again, the Sambuca sloshing back and forth in the cup, my other hand clenched into a fist, and then I look back at Haven and shake my head. "I heard my name being shouted. 'Corporal. Corporal Vescovi. Corporal Vescovi stand down. Goddammit, Vescovi, get the fuck off him.' I was pulled off of him." My face is now drenched with tears. Haven's is too. "They pulled me off him. But it didn't matter. It didn't matter at all, because the mother fucker lived, but the girl didn't. She was still chained to the bed...and she was already dead." After a long moment of silence, I say, "I never even saved her."

Haven's fingers are no longer wrapped around her mug. They're covering her mouth, and she looks scared to death.

"Oh my God, Haven," I say, setting down my glass. "I'm so sorry. I shouldn't have told you—"

"No. No," she says, setting a tear-covered hand over my hand. "You needed to tell it. Oh my God, though," she whispers.

I nod and grab two napkins out of the holder in the center of the table.

Haven squeezes my hand and we look at each other, the two of us wiping our own tears. "That must have been so hard for you."

"It was hard for all of us. We all wanted to kill him. I was the only one who lost control."

"But that was so brave of you." Haven's thumb runs over mine.

"No, it wasn't. I went against our own policy. He was a commander. We're supposed to turn a blind eye. I just...I was too weak to turn away."

"Well, I think...I think it took more strength to do what you knew in your heart was the *right* thing to do."

"It was in vain anyway. She died. He didn't. I ruined my career." I shrug. "Whaddaya gonna do?" I mutter to myself.

"If you were put in that situation again, would you do anything differently?"

"I would have stopped him the first time I knew what was happening. And I would have shot the fucker right in the heart."

She slides both her hands back and forth over mine. "You're a good man, Quest Vescovi. You're a remarkable human being."

Gliding my hand out from beneath hers, I wipe my face with my fingers and get up, too antsy to stay seated. "Want more coffee? Sorry I don't have teabags. I should have bought some. I was so concerned with buying the stuff for—"

"Quest. Coffee's fine." The screech of the chair sliding across the linoleum causes me to turn. She's standing behind the table one second, and in the next, she's pulled me into a tight hold. I can't remember the last time someone's hugged me like this. And I *let* her. I let her embrace comfort me for so long that I feel the weight lift from my chest. From my shoulders. She's not a big girl, but her hug tells a different story.

My tears are dry by the time she pulls away. "You okay?" she asks, her head cocked, her eyes narrowed.

After one extended blink, I nod. "Yeah. I'm good. Thank you, Haven." We gaze at each other for another few seconds, and then I say, "We missed the Macy's parade, but you care to watch a movie while the lasagna bakes?"

"Sure," she says quietly.

"Follow me," I say, leading us to the living room.

Haven sits on the couch first, taking the seat on the left. Not wanting to overstep my bounds for a change, I take the seat at the other end of the couch.

"So my grandfather didn't have cable, and I haven't bothered getting it, but he has a DVD player, and I bought a few DVDs from Walmart before I opened the store, so you can choose from this huge selection here—" I pull out the six DVDs on the shelf beneath my coffee table and set them on the couch between us. "—or we can watch Netflix on my computer." I lift open the laptop that's sitting on the coffee table in front of us.

Turning my body to face Haven, I wait for her to decide.

"What kind of collection is this?" she asks, thumbing through my six DVDs. "*Pride and Prejudice, The Outsiders, Water for Elephants, Interview with the Vampire, Misery*, and *The Notebook*? An eclectic array, I must say."

"Hey. Don't judge. Besides, they aren't as eclectic as you think."

"Oh no?"

"Nope. They do have *one* thing in common."

She looks through the DVDs again. "Okay, I give up."

"They're all books."

A guttural groan escapes her mouth—as if I'd sucker punched her.

I laugh, shaking my head. "And you say you're a book fanatic."

"Darn, I can't believe I missed that," she says.

Laughing, I add, "I thought since, you know, being the owner of a bookstore, I should at least know the plot of some of the books, right?"

Now it's Haven's turn to laugh. "I think actually reading the books would give you a more accurate depiction. But hey, kudos for trying." She smiles and hands me *Misery*. "Let's watch this. And you should definitely read the book. Stephen King."

"Uh, it says it right here on the back cover. And I do watch Stephen King movies. I just happened to miss this one." I get up and slip the DVD into the player. When I return to the couch, Haven's got her feet tucked under her, looking almost comfortable in my house.

Five minutes into the movie, she also removes her glasses. I realize that this probably has more to do with her not being able to see the screen than her comfort level around me, but I still feel a bit of pride because of it. I try not to let her see that I'm looking at her, but I can't help but stare—not just at her scars...but at her. She really is beautiful. The tilt of her nose, the height of her cheekbones, the fullness of her lips. The huge almond-shaped eyes she sadly hides. I wish she could see her face the way I see it. She thinks her scars make her hideous. I think they make her beautiful.

"Isn't she great?" Haven asks, her focus still on the movie.

"Who?"

"Kathy Bates."

"Oh, yeah. She's good." I'm hardly paying attention to the movie, because all my thoughts are on Haven and how I wish I could be sitting closer to her. Better yet, I wish she could be holding me again—I could smell her hair...and maybe kiss her.

"I think she's perfect for this part. It's like Stephen King wrote the story with Kathy Bates in mind."

Okay, so *Haven's* thoughts are still on the movie.

"Are you not enjoying it?" she asks, finally looking at me.

"Oh, sure. Great movie. I'm enjoying it," I lie, because I haven't paid a lick of attention to it at all.

"Are you still thinking about that girl? When you were in the Army?" Haven frowns, looking sorry.

"No. No. Not at all. Far from it." I wink, so she knows I'm serious.

She picks up the remote and mutes the television. "What's on your mind? Obviously something."

"Nothing bad. I swear."

Haven lifts her glasses off the top of her head and slides them back on her face.

"Don't do that."

"Do what?"

"Don't cover your face. You don't need to wear those in front of me."

Her fingers hover near the frames.

"I don't see your scars, Haven. So, you don't have to hide them when you're with me."

Slowly, she pulls the glasses off and holds them on her lap. While her eyes are cast down, I shift closer to her.

"You really don't need the glasses. Maybe if you start with me," I bring my hand to her neck, "you'll build enough courage to keep them off all the time." I rub her earlobe between my two fingers while my heart pounds with the uncertainty of what I'm about to do. "I'm not just saying it when I tell you you're beautiful, Haven. I mean it."

Her gaze alternates between my face and her lap.

But when I see the corners of her lips swing into a smile, I press my fingers to the back of her neck and pull her toward me. Hoping I'm doing the right thing, I lean in and kiss her lips. They're soft. Warm—a place I'd like to stay for a long while.

I'm not given the opportunity, though, because she withdraws before my lips can make themselves at home.

"I'm sorry," she says, returning her attention to her lap while she fumbles to put her glasses back on.

The drumming in my chest has fizzled into a warble that resonates in the pit of my stomach.

"I'm not ready," she whispers, and again says, "I'm sorry."

"Don't be sorry," I tell her, talking over the part of me that wants to hide under a rock because I'm so embarrassed.

"I shouldn't have done that. I keep...jumping the gun. I'm sorry."

She looks me in the eye this time and says firmly, "Don't be sorry. This is all my problem." She averts her eyes, but then forces herself to look back at me. "I have to work through a lot of things in my head before I can get involved with anyone. Like I said, my scars...they're all I think about. And until they're not, I don't think I can give you...or anyone...any part of me. Especially with us working together...it'd only complicate things. Please don't be mad."

"Mad? At you? Never. Please don't be mad at *me*."

"Not at all." The corner of her bottom lip disappears behind her teeth, but then she grins and says, "And if you're lucky, I won't file a sexual harassment suit against you."

"Haven Quinn, am I sensing a sense of humor?"

"I'm not known for one," she says with a straight face but takes in her bottom lip and announces her dimple.

"It suits you." She attempted humor to deflect the uncomfortable situation I put us in. Color me impressed...and inescapably captivated.

32.

H AVEN
I can't believe I tried to make a joke. I don't think anyone in my immediate family has ever attempted such a task. At least Quest doesn't laugh at my effort. Not sure he's laughing *with* me, but the focus effectively veers from the graceless way I broke our kiss. I didn't want to stop him from kissing me. At the moment, there's nothing I want more. But what happens after? What happens when we return to work tomorrow? Or the next day? Or a week from tomorrow? What happens when Quest takes off his rose-colored glasses and sees my face through disenchanted eyes? The mere thought of touching his lips to mine may make him queasy. Then where would that leave me? Ugly *and* heartbroken. I can't take that risk. I *won't* take that risk.

As part of my silent Thanksgiving prayer, I'm grateful that Quest and I are able to move past our moment of mortification and enjoy a delicious Italian Thanksgiving dinner. Another first for a Quinn. I'm perpetrating all sorts of crimes against Quinn etiquette by not eating the traditional catered turkey dinner.

"What are you smiling about?" Quest asks as he serves me a second helping of lasagna.

"Just enjoying the meal. You're a good cook."

Quest sets the serving spatula down and picks up his fork. "Wanna give my mother a call? I'm sure she'd *love* to hear that."

"Is this the first time you've cooked?" I ask, filling my mouth with another colossal bite.

"First time for this, but I've kept myself fed over the years."

Still savoring the cheesy goodness, I respond with, "Mmm."

To which he responds with a smirk, "Glad you're enjoying it."

I nod with my mouth still full.

As the punch of garlic and cheese and meat and sauce entertains my tongue, my mind again revisits the tang left behind on my lips after Quest's kiss. Oh to jump back in time a few hours. What I wouldn't do to revel in his kiss again. To be uninhibited...what a gift that would be.

"Would you like some more?"

My face burns at his interruption. He's talking about the lasagna. "No. Thank you. I'm stuffed."

"I made an apple pie, too," he says with a jut of his chin.

"Oh my goodness." My hands naturally gravitate to my stomach.

"Mom's recipe," he says, standing and gathering the plates from the table.

I pick up the salad bowl. "*My* mother's passed down her infallible phone reservation decorum."

He laughs as I set the bowl on the counter. "Haven? Do you not really...*like* your mother? You don't have to answer if you don't want," he says, carrying the last of the dishes to the sink.

"I'll wash, you dry," I tell him, walking around him to turn on the water. "You know where everything goes."

He grabs a towel and waits.

"I like my mother," I say, my focus steady on dishwashing. "She's just not your typical warm and fuzzy mom. She lived in different foster homes until she was eleven and my grandmother adopted her."

"Oh." He takes the first plate I hand him.

"My grandmother was a fairly young widow who never had any children. When she was in her mid-fifties, or something, she decided she'd rather not wait for a man, so she adopted.

"They let a single woman adopt?"

"She had money. She was a superior court judge and her husband was a partner at some financial recruiting firm on Wall Street."

"Impressive."

"She wasn't warm and fuzzy either, but I really didn't know her well. She died when I was young."

"You come from some high achievers."

"Unfortunately." I force a smile.

When we're done with the dishes, Quest serves his first ever homemade pie—the guy has some mad skills in the kitchen—and invites me to stay for another movie. I decline. Afraid this time, *I'd* try to kiss him.

BLACK FRIDAY AND SMALL Business Saturday are quite busy, so Quest closes the store on Sunday and Monday, claiming there can't possibly be any more residents left to come in. I take Sunday to push my limits and go shopping at the outlet mall in Tannersville. Why not strengthen my tenacity and face my fears by walking around an outdoor shopping outlet during the height of the Christmas season?

First, I have to get there. The GPS tries sending me via Main Street in Stratford, and I have not been on that road since the night of my assault. My car approaches the upcoming turn, and my stomach begins to burn. I flip up my directional signal, but my brain stops my hands from turning the wheel. A car horn blares behind me. The GPS recalculates. What was so important I had to go shopping? Home is where I should be. Home is safe.

Miles pass before I find myself in unfamiliar territory, unaware how I got here. The screen circles again until it settles on my location. "In three hundred fifty feet, turn left." The robotic voice calms me. I turn left and follow the new route.

Fifteen minutes later, I pull into the parking lot. Instead of fighting the crowd and parking in the main area, I proceed straight and follow the lot around back.

Seated in my car, the engine still running, I talk myself into getting out. Chris Stapleton's *Broken Halos* plays low on my radio.

God, give me a sign.

I clutch my hands on my lap and close my eyes.

Just go home, Haven. This isn't worth it.

Upon opening my eyes, a girl laughs outside, her mother smiling easily behind her as she pushes her wheelchair.

You're a coward, Haven. A coward.

I gather in several seconds of air and reach for my purse as I let it out and step out of the car. My head high, shoulders back, I stroll through the mall, purporting confidence. Inside the Fossil store, a well-dressed saleswoman asks if she can help me. "No thank you. Just here to browse."

After hesitating a second too long, she nods. "If there's anything you need..." she obediently adds.

A floral canvas tote, just the right size to carry a few novels, catches my eye. It's brown leather handles fit perfectly inside my closed hand when I take it off the shelf. I try it on my shoulder, but remember my financial situation. Not today. I set it back from where it came. It's not like I need it anyway.

Just as I make my way out of the store, I see a display of sunglasses. Now these, I may need. A sudden fervor spreads like wildflowers throughout my body. My new obsession. Knowing I need to limit my spendings is not enough to keep me from taking tortoiseshell frames off the rack. The violet temples complement the light-gray lenses, and though the frame size is somewhat smaller than my current glasses, they are elegant. The credit card beckoning from inside my purse agrees. I surrender to its promises, disregarding the financial albatross hovering over me, and buy the extravagant mask.

33.

Quest

Haven has been on my mind non-stop these days.

I drive up to her house, with absolutely no idea what I'm going to say when I get there, bearing two very unconventional sandwiches from some natural market down the road. Who the hell puts basil and hummus on a sandwich?

I'm greeted by a very disheveled but incredibly cute Haven when she answers the door wearing a red bandana tied around her head, her hair up in a messy bun, and ripped sweatpants. "Quest." She wipes her cheek with the back of her hand. "What are you doing here?"

Raising the white bag in my hand, I say, "Lunch."

She pats her temple, then the top of her head. "Oh." Smoothing down her rumpled sweatshirt, she scans her kitchen. "I wasn't expecting you."

"Hope it's a pleasant surprise then."

"Of course...have a seat." She waves her hand toward the kitchen table and disappears down the hall.

"I hope I'm not intruding," I shout. Setting the bag on the table, I go to her cabinets, take out two glasses, and fill them with water. Placing one glass on one side of the table, I sit opposite and put my glass down.

She returns wearing sunglasses with such a light tint of gray they showcase her eyes. "New glasses?"

"Needed a change." She sits in front of the water glass.

"I like them. You can see your eyes." I take the sandwiches out of the bag. "You pick first. *Or*...we can share half of each. I hope you like hummus."

With wide eyes, her mouth breaks into a smile. Such an interesting smile. "You got the roasted red pepper and hummus?"

"You're familiar with the natural market?"

"My favorite."

"I also got some provolone and avocado thing."

Her eyes light up again, and she opens one of the sandwiches. "We can share."

I laugh and open the other. "Napkin?" I hand her one from the bag and we exchange lunches. "So, did I interrupt a cleaning spree?"

She peels pieces of crust off her sandwich and sets them aside. "Kind of. Packing up my books."

"Donating to my store?" I joke, taking a bite of the hummus concoction. Not bad.

"Oh. Uh...I *can*...if you need them."

"No, not necessarily. I was joking. Why are you packing them?" I take another bite and nearly moan out loud, it's so good.

Haven takes her first bite, shakes her head, and points to her working mouth.

"I was only joking. You can donate them wherever you'd like."

"No. No," she mumbles, swallowing her food.

"It's fine. I came here to talk about something...I'd like to talk about *us*."

After a moment's hesitation, she releases her lip from her teeth, "Oh," and takes a sip of her water. With reluctance, she raises her eyes. "I don't think I can be in a relationship with you."

I feel like I've been punched in the gut. Though I planned on reassuring her of our friendship, despite my desire for something more, hearing her say those words..."Why *can't* you?" I blurt before I can stop myself.

Her brow crumples. "Why do you *want* to be?" She scoffs under her breath. "I'm a mess. I have nothing to give." Her fingers return to peeling pieces of crust.

"Nothing to give?"

"Nothing to offer." Her hand rises to her face, fingertips graze the scars. "These are all I *think* about." Her thin fingers fold into fists. "It wouldn't be fair."

As much as I want to fight her on this, I know I can't. She's right. She needs to get to a good place before she can move on in any aspect of her life. Years of therapy, psychiatrists, medications...I'm only now beginning to heal. Haven has only just begun.

Worry grips me in the gut, but I say it anyway. "Come with me to my support group tonight."

"What? Where'd that come from?"

"From what you just said...I think it might help."

"No I don't need it," she says in a rush, picking at her sandwich.

"Okay. It was just a suggestion. I'm sorry." I continue eating my sandwich even though I want to get up and walk out.

Haven continues hacking at her lunch. Several long moments later, she flicks a rolled up piece of bread at me. "What time?"

HAVEN INSISTS ON TAKING separate cars—in case she changes her mind last minute. In the parking lot once we get there, I extend my arm to hold her hand, but she swiftly sticks her hands in the pockets of her camel coat. She says nothing on the walk in.

Mary spots us and meets us before we approach the circle. "Hi, Quest. Hello," she says to Haven and holds out her hand. "I'm Mary."

"Hello." Haven shakes her hand and promptly returns it to her pocket.

"Sit where you'd like, and I'm sure Quest's told you, but you don't have to share anything but your name."

Haven sits crossed-ankle with her fingers folded over each other on her lap the entire meeting, speaking only to tell the group her name. I don't blame her; I still haven't revealed much more than my own name, with the exception of the anger issues I'm trying to take control of. But when Michele acknowledges to the group that her stepfather used to physically abuse her and her mother did nothing to stop it, Haven's skin drains of color and her bottom lip quivers.

I keep my hands on my own lap and ignore the urge to comfort her—even though doing so is like constricting the air to my lungs. With each member's confession, a new horror laces Haven's expression. By the end of session, her shoulders are small, her chin tucked, her jaw tight. She's still white as a ghost. Maybe bringing her here did more harm than not. What the hell made me think this would help? Hearing about other's problems may be of solace for me, but for Haven, it's probably a reminder of all the evil outside her world.

While everyone else gathers near the coffee, I follow Haven out the door. Without conversation, we walk to our cars. She's unzipping her purse when I say, "I'm sorry, Haven."

Slipping her key ring over her knuckle, she strokes the fob between her fingers, her eyes watching the movement. "I can't share. I can't share my story." Without warning, tears fall down her face.

"Oh, Haven, no. You don't have to." I pull her in for a hug and she allows it. "I still haven't shared *mine*."

34.

H AVEN
Quest and I have reached a pretty good place in our friendship and our work relationship over the past week. We've fallen into a quiet and effortless work routine, and we've made strides in reorganizing the store. Quest has been sorting boxes and cleaning up the storage room, while I greet and help the *few* customers that actually come in, and stock the shelves with the books Quest finds in the back. I've also created a spreadsheet and pivot tables to move our inventory into the twenty-first century. I'm in the middle of trying to fix a glitch in one of the tables when Devin walks in carrying a tall white coffee cup.

I save my spreadsheet before greeting him. "Hey, Devin. What brings you by?"

"You were on my mind." He hands me the cup, his fingers brushing mine when I take it. "Chai latte."

"You know me so well. Thank you, this was sweet." The tea is lukewarm, but sweet and foamy when it touches my tongue.

"You didn't come all this way to bring me tea, did you?"

Leaning forward, he rests his elbow on the counter. His breath smells like mint. "You're worth it."

He taps his fingers twice, then reaches for the book on top of my to-be-entered pile. "*Look Out, Cub!*" he reads aloud.

I take the book from his hand and return it to my pile. "Why are you *really* here?"

"You know *me* so well." He alternates tapping his hands three times. *Ba dum bump.*

It must be nice being Devin. Confident, charismatic...comedian.

"Seriously though...I want to take you out Friday night. Eric and his girlfriend have a thing and I know Marisela is still in Puerto Rico, so..."

"Out?" I pick up *Look Out, Cub!* And begin entering it into my spreadsheet. "I don't think so, Dev. I don't really go out unless I have to..."

"You work in retail. Surely you can sit in a dark restaurant."

Sure I can, but do I want to do so with Devin? I don't work with him anymore, so that no longer restricts me, but...Quest. If I'm going to sit in a dark restaurant, or *any* restaurant, I'd rather it be with Quest. "I don't think so," I say, my words weak and vacillating. Why must you be so wishy-washy, Haven?...*Shut up, Mother.*

Devin juts his bottom lip. "I *will* get you to go out with me you know."

I laugh. "Let's just stick to movie nights for now," I say, pleased with myself for standing firm.

With another tap on the counter and the promise of a friendly text, Devin is out the door.

"Was that your friend?" Quest enters the room wiping his hands on the hem of his shirt.

"Yes. We have a sink in the bathroom."

"Shirt's good. Was he here looking for another high school book?"

I hold up my latte. "He came to see *me*."

There is a long silence, his expression ranging from knitted brow to resigned frown, before he turns around and walks out of the room.

Seconds later, the bell above the door rings.

"Mrs. Gannon." Ruth Gannon, Layton's eighth-grade language arts teacher, was another one of Mr. Vescovi's regulars. On more than a handful of occasions, we'd be in the store at the same time.

She removes her sunglasses. Eyebrows are clenched. "Haven? What happened?"

The question stuns me and words take flight along with rational thought.

"Haven, honey." The woman approaches the counter and reaches to take my hand. Curling my fingers under my palm, I succeed in giving her the hint. She withdraws and nodding, she says, "So you work here now."

"Yes." I return my attention to the computer; Mrs. Gannon wanders into the aisles.

The next couple of hours are slow, so I take the time to walk the aisles and choose another couple of books to read and quote for the store. I'm pleasantly surprised when I notice the book I gave Quest to read is back on the shelf, two note cards taped together—loose handwriting scrawled across them—hanging beneath it.

In *My Grandfather's Blessings*, we are invited into one woman's relationship with her Rabbi grandfather to learn the healing power of life's greatest gifts—kindness,

thoughtfulness, generosity. Because of MY grandfather's blessings, I have found the strength to heal and the courage to be grateful. Because of MY grandfather's blessings, I have found a haven, a place I can call home.

He's found a place he can call home.

The joy that spreads like warm syrup across my chest surprises me. I only now realize how much Quest's happiness means to me. I remember talking about this bookstore with him that first day at the diner. He didn't want it. Yet, here he is, calling it his home. I'm sure his grandfather knew what Quest would gain by running the store. His contingency had a purpose, and I'm grateful to be a part of his plan.

AT HOME, I'M CHANGED into my "Nothing's Better than Books and Tea" flannels, my tea is prepared, and the couch is primed with pillows, blankets, and a bowl of popcorn when the doorbell rings. I live in the mountains. My front door should not be getting this much action.

Devin is standing outside my door holding a pizza. "Delivery!" he says with a grin.

I let him in and smile back. "What are you doing here?"

"Movie night."

Movie nights *with* the others, Devin. I really need to start making myself clear.

He sidesteps my kitchen and puts the pizza on the coffee table.

Abandoning my tea, and the idea of a cozy night at home alone, I go to the cabinet to get plates, napkins, and two bottles of water, and set them next to the pizza box. Devin opens the box and centers a slice on each of our plates.

"I didn't think we should skip movie night just because the others couldn't come," he says when he hands me a plate.

So I did make myself clear. He just didn't listen.

"You spend too much time alone. I want you to enjoy the things you've always done."

"Wait what? I enjoy things...and I *don't* spend time alone. I spend all day long with Quest."

"I mean social time." He picks up the remote and aims it at my TV. "What are you into tonight? Scary? Silly? Sad?"

"Suspense."

"Suspense?" He accesses Amazon Prime and scans current titles.

"Alliteration. It was a joke. How 'bout something old?" I take a bit of pizza.

"Fifties? Sixties?"

"Nineties?"

He looks at me amused. "Nineties are not old." Searching nineties movies, he stops a few seconds at each to read descriptions.

"That one?" I ask.

"*Lavi and Ariel*? No," he says, scanning right past the last movie Deanna Emerson ever filmed. Remembering the image of her lying on the floor, her neck slashed straight across, causes my hand to tremble. I place my plate on the table, suddenly sick to my stomach.

"Leo DiCaprio," he announces, stopping at *Titanic*.

I swallow the bad taste in my mouth and say, "Saw it too many times."

He continues flipping through movies until I say, "Stop."

"*Miss Congeniality*?"

"Yes." It's a feel good movie. I'm in the mood to feel good.

We settle on the romantic comedy, and I begin to relax, laughing out loud a time or two.

"Like that'd really work," Devin says when Gracie gives her self-defense presentation S.I.N.G.

"Why wouldn't it?"

"No girl's gonna think that quickly when she's being attacked."

He says it as a matter of fact, but it hits me as hard as Gracie Hart's elbow when it makes contact with her partner's nose. Solar Plexus. Instep. Nose. Groin. She makes it look so easy, but Devin's right. When in the process of being thrown to the ground and bound, the only thing that comes quickly is fear.

Gracie Hart just realizes the crown is the bomb when there's a knock on my door.

"Who the heck can that be at this hour?" I say, silently hoping it's Quest.

Devin pauses the TV and follows me to the door.

"Oh my God," I say.

A backpack slung over his shoulder, his head bowed, Eric is frowning at my front door.

"I left her, Hayv." The backpack slides down his arm when his shoulders droop.

"Oh, Eric." I take his pack, toss it on the floor, and hug him. In the middle of our embrace, Eric groans. "What's he doing here?"

"Nice to see you too," Devin mumbles.

"Anyway, Haven." Eric disregards Devins and continues talking to me. "You mind if I stay with you for a while? 'Til I find something else?"

They follow me to the couch, but Eric sits in Devin's spot, leaving a frowning Devin to sit in my recliner.

"You can stay," I tell Eric, "but I may not be here myself soon if I can't come up with the last three months' rent."

"Perfect," he says slowly, plopping his hands in his lap and sounding sad. "I can give you the money, you can let me stay." He sighs and rests his head back.

"You have a one-bedroom house," Devin points out.

"I can sleep in her loft. All I need is a blanket."

"I have a couch up there. But I don't want to take your money. I can't afford to live here each month but—"

"Let's worry about that next month. So I can stay for now?"

"You can stay." I smile and unpause the TV screen to watch the rest of *Miss Congeniality*.

35.

Quest

"Good morning," Haven sings, a huge smile plastered on her face when she walks into work Saturday morning.

"You're happy this morning."

She puts away her purse and goes straight for the coffee machine. "Want a cup?"

"No thanks. Made one already."

Haven hums while she prepares her tea.

"What song's that?" Haven isn't usually so uninhibited, I'm curious to know what has her in such a good mood.

"I don't even know. *One in a Million* or something. From *Miss Congeniality*." She dumps a creamer into her cup and spins my way, humming wrapped up.

"Movie night?"

"Yeah, just Devin at first. Eric showed up later." She strolls to the desk and sits on the stool.

"Just you and two guys?" Is that why she's so frigging happy?

She blows on her tea, then nestles the cup between her hands. "Devin left right after the movie. But...Eric and Katie broke up, now Eric needs a place to stay."

I close my eyes and crack my neck. "And now he's staying with you?"

Her forehead crinkles. "It'll help me pay the rent." She blows on her cup, takes a sip.

"Oh my God." Dismissing the subject with a wave of my hand, I retreat to the storage room.

She follows me. "What the hell, Quest?" One hand on her hip, with the other, she removes her glasses and sits them on her head. "You're mad at me for giving a friend a place to stay?"

Instead of acknowledging her, I dig through the last few boxes I have left.

"Quest." She waves an arm in front of my face. "Did you hear me? I asked—"

"I heard what you asked. I'm choosing not to respond." Because I'm immature.

She huffs, mutters "Well that's mature," and trots away.

She invites Devin to watch a movie, allows Eric to move in with her, but she isn't ready for a relationship with me? That's bullshit.

I spend the next few hours in the storeroom sulking and going through the rest of my grandfather's boxes. It's during the third hour, with one box left to open, that I come across two clear plastic shoe boxes propped in the corner of the top shelf. I use the foot stool to get them down.

Attached to its faded pink lid is an index card written in my grandfather's handwriting. ***Books to read to Quest when he visits.*** On an index card taped to the other box—a faded blue lid—are the words ***Books Quest may like now that he's a teenager.***

He'd waited for me to come back.

A vital relationship suspended forever, boxed and put away with the books he'd longed to share.

What could have possibly been so bad that my father had to move us thousands of miles away from this little old man who wanted nothing more than to read to his grandson?

In the distance, my phone rings. Instead of letting it go to voicemail, Haven brings it to me. "It's a California number." She hands me the phone and walks away.

"Quest? It's Vinnie," he says before I even say hello.

"Vinnie."

"Your mom had an accident. She's alive," he says quickly, "but she fell off a ladder cleaning a window and now...she's in a coma." I knew this would happen. A loud breath hisses from the other side. "She may not make it."

Dammit. I thump against the door jamb. "When? How long?"

"Two days. I thought she'd wake up. Quest...it doesn't look good. Can you be here?"

My whole body burns. "I'll be there," I say before hanging up.

"Quest?" Her voice is soft. The opposite of how I remember my mother's. "What happened?"

I want to look at her, to answer her, but I can't move. The doorpost holds me upright while I clutch my chest. I can't breathe.

Slim fingers fold over my arm. Press into my skin. Another hand settles on my shoulder, her weight bearing down, guiding me to the floor. "In case you pass out," she whispers before disappearing.

Haven returns with a cup of water. I don't take it, but I do look her in the eyes. "My mother. She fell. Doesn't look good."

"Oh, Quest," she says, and sits down in front of me, holding the water.

"I need to get there."

Squeezing my calf, she says, "You will. I'll help."

Help, she does. By finding me a flight and driving me to the airport. It's a quiet ride into the city, but I'm grateful for the company...and her willingness to help despite my jealous outburst earlier.

At the drop-off lane at JFK Airport, I thank her for her help.

"Try not to think the worst," she says. I won't listen.

"You don't have to keep the store open." I gave her the key because she'd asked, not because it mattered. "We're not profiting anyway," I say at the same time she says, "I want to." I don't have the energy to argue.

We both let it go.

"Thanks for the ride." I get out, but before I close the door, she says, "Text me?"

36.

HAVEN
"Hi, Daddy."

"Haven, what are you doing here?" He's sitting in his leather high back wing chair in the front parlor, a leather-bound book on his lap, a brandy neat on the small round crank table next to him.

I can't get Quest's words off my mind. *We're not profiting anyway*. He has more pressing matters on his mind, but for me, they play like the second hand on a clock. Tick. Tick. Tick. Time is running out.

My father stands, his book dangling at his hip. "Cup of tea?"

"Yes." I sigh. "If you don't mind."

In the kitchen, after filling the kettle with water and turning on the stove, he sets two mugs and the container of tea bags on the table and sits down across from me. "So why are you here at eight o'clock on a Saturday night?"

"I had to bring Quest to the airport. His mom had an accident, he's flying out."

"Car?"

"She fell off a ladder. She's in a coma. Quest says it doesn't look good."

"That's a shame."

I take out a tea bag and place it in my mug. "Is Mom sleeping?"

"Yes." My father drops a tea bag into his mug. "She had a big day. Jeremy came by to do her hair, and Margaret gave her a manicure."

"What?"

"And you know your mother, she felt the need to entertain. Ended up tiring herself out."

"Wait. Mom had her hair and nails done? She's supposed to be recovering."

"It makes her feel good." He flips a hand palm up and shakes his head.

I take the tea bag tag and rub it between my fingers, flicking the staple every so often. It makes her feel good to look good. "Figures."

"Will Quest keep the store closed until he returns?"

"No. He gave me the key so I can open it."

"But?"

"No but."

"Haven, I can hear the but."

I hesitate. "He said I don't have to open it because he's not profiting anyway."

"Does he pay you?"

"Not a lot."

The kettle whistles. Dad gets up to get it. "Are you keeping up with rent?"

He pours the boiling water into our mugs while I contemplate telling my father that in order to avoid being evicted, I let a man move in with me.

He puts the kettle back on the stove and returns with the milk. "I'll take your silence as a no. If you need money..."

I drop my head into my hand.

"You're only twenty-four. It's okay to still come to your father for help."

"Dad," I finally say. "I'm three months behind, and even if you gave me money, I still couldn't keep up the payments. Not without my television job."

"Your bedroom is still in tact."

"Well, see...my friends broke up and now Eric needs a place to stay. He can help with the rent."

"A man is moving in with you? I don't like that at all."

"My only other choice is moving into the apartment above the store, but if Quest has to sell the store..."

My father sits back, sips his tea. "I don't like the idea of you living with a man. Come back home."

That's exactly where I want to be, back home where Hannah Quinn can say—I told you so. "I'd rather not, Daddy."

My father gets up and goes to the refrigerator. "Your mother won't be happy about this either."

"Well that won't be anything new."

Dad returns to the table with the makings for a sandwich. "Hungry?"

"No thanks." I tap out a thought on the table.

"If your mother was up, she'd scold me for eating this late." He opens the deli packages.

"You're a grown man, Dad. You can do what you want."

"All this hostility, Haven. It doesn't suit you." Two slices of bread are slapped on to his plate.

"Dad," I say, still tapping, still thinking. "What if *we* bought the store? Half of it I mean."

"We? As in you and me?" Using a sharp knife, he spreads the mayonnaise. Hummus tastes much better.

I nod. "A partnership...with Quest."

"You want to invest in a failing business?" His sandwich complete, he brings it to his mouth.

"It's a good store, Dad. Mr. Vescovi would be heartbroken if it closed."

"I'm not into the business of throwing money away."

The fate of Dingman's Corner Book Shop is felt in my chest, heavy and thick. My father makes sense, no smart business person would drop a dime into a declining establishment, but my decisions hinge on the emotion of the moment. Any rational idea gets buried beneath my enthusiasm. "What if we make it a book café?" I ask, excited again.

He doesn't look amused.

"We can sell coffee. Lattes. Beverages you can't get at the deli." The ideas start pouring in. "Chai tea. Frozen blended drinks. Smoothies..." I trail off, because my father is more interested in his turkey and cheese on white bread then he is in my proposition. "Dad?"

He swallows the last of his sandwich, then says, "You'd need a license to sell food. And a kitchen. You'd need space for tables...and a handicap bathroom. That store is old, I'm sure it's not up to code. I think what you need to do is figure out where you're going to live before you go and put money you don't have into owning a business."

Emotion effectively plummeted.

"MARI." I EXCLAIM WHEN my best friend opens her front door the next afternoon.

"Haven." She squeezes me. "I missed you, girl."

"I missed you too."

"Great glasses," she tells me as she leads the way to her couch. "So, tell me again why you're not going to work?"

We find our seats at opposite ends of Marisela's oversized sectional and get comfortable by wrapping ourselves in the two fleece blankets she keeps thrown over the back.

"He's in California?"

"His mother fell off a ladder. She's in a coma."

"Oh Lord."

"Doesn't look good either."

"Poor Quest."

"So," I lean forward and tap her fleece-covered knee, "how was Puerto Rico?"

"Not as beautiful as usual, but it was nice seeing abuelito again. I hadn't seen her in two years."

"Right, the hurricanes were vicious this year."

"You're telling me. Fortunately, her neighborhood wasn't hit too hard. But anyway, how's your mom?"

"You know...normal."

"She's recovering okay?" She asks, her tone disapproving of mine.

"Yes. Enough so to get her hair done today."

"Is she still belittling you?"

"You need to ask? She did explain herself for the first time, though. Told me that people are cruel and I either have to get the surgery to fix my face, or stop worrying what everyone thinks—including her—and stop being embarrassed about what I look like."

"Okay, so she kind of makes sense."

"I guess."

Marisela laughs. "What did you decide?"

"I don't want to go through that pain again. It's finally starting to settle down."

"They're not so red anymore either. I'm sure there are some natural remedies you can try."

"That's what I was hoping. I just wish I wasn't so insecure about them."

"In time. You're so beautiful, Haven. Scars or no scars."

I worry my lip and after a moment say, "I want to be confident enough to date."

"Oh." She sits up straighter and tucks her legs inside each other.

"He's across the country anyway, but—"

"You like Quest?"

I nod, shake my head, and wave my hand. "Yes. But before he found out about his mother, he was mad at me for letting Eric stay the night." I hold up my hand when she opens her mouth. "He and Katie broke up. He needs a place to stay, and I said he can stay with me."

"Holy. What will Hannah have to say about that?"

"Nothing nice, but he can help pay the rent if I decide to stay there."

"I guess that works, but how well do you know Eric? You sure his girlfriend's not gonna get all mad?"

"Eric's a good guy, and I don't know if Katie will be mad. His parents live out of state, though."

"As long as you can trust him."

"Definitely. But I wanted to ask you something unrelated...what do you think of my father and I buying half the bookstore?"

"What? Where'd that come from?"

It's going to end the same way it did with my father. I sag against the couch. "He's not making any money and—"

"And buying half of him out will help? That's crazy. It's like—"

"Hear me out," I say, much more confident with Marisela than I was with my father.

She sits back and opens her arms.

"I wanna turn it into a book café. Sell lattes and frozen drinks. Maybe some small snacks. Make it a hotspot."

"Hmm. That may work. It's not like there's anything like it nearby."

"That's what I thought."

"What does Quest say?"

"Well...he doesn't know. I just thought of it last night."

"And your dad's on board?"

"Well...not exactly."

"Haven."

Picking up the blanket's hem, I rub it between my fingers. "He didn't say yes *or* no."

"It's risky. Especially if he gets no business as it is."

"But coffee. That sells."

"It does." She shrugs. "Talk to them both. Come up with a feasible plan that you're dad will feel good about, and make sure Quest is even up for this. He may just wanna cut his loses and sell the whole thing."

At this, I sigh...loudly. "Then he'll stay in California forever."

"Haven? Is this all to keep him here?"

I shrug. "I love that store. I don't wanna see it close." I sigh again and defeat back into the cushion.

37.

Quest

"Haven? It's me. Are you at the store?"

"Oh." I pause. "No. I—"

"It's fine. Listen, my mom is really bad..." I take in a breath to keep my emotions in check.

"Oh, Quest, I'm sorry."

"I just wanted to tell you...don't open the store. I'm closing it indefinitely. I have no idea how long I'm gonna be here...and...it'll cost more to keep it open. I'm sorry though, because I know you need the money. Whatever's in the cash register...just take it. Use it for—"

"No. Quest, I don't want your money. I'll be fine....I'm really sorry about your mother. I hope she gets better."

With the heel of my hand, I relieve the pressure rising in my temple, and I take another deep breath. "It doesn't look that way. Look, Haven, I gotta go. I'm sorry."

I hate hanging up on Haven, but hearing her voice makes me want to cry. I miss her. There are moments when all I want to do is race home and hold her...but I haven't even told her how I feel yet. Now my mother is lying in a hospital bed with little hope of waking up normal...if at all.

I remember our drive from New Jersey to California back when I was in fifth grade. My father in the U-Haul in front of us, my mother and me, somber, in her Volkswagon behind him, neither one of us thrilled to be moving across the country. Not when we'd already built a life in Jersey. My mother was used to not seeing her parents, considering they lived in Illinois, but she had friends in Jersey, and *we* had my grandparents. My parents met at the University of Chicago, and after graduation, they married and moved in with my father's parents until they could afford a house of their own. Mom revealed to me on that trip that Dad's parents were more like a mom and dad to her than her own parents. That was the first time I saw my mother cry. Will she ever cry again?

Like an inarticulate five-year-old whose only channel to anger is using his fists, the urge to hit something comes over me. Because I'm in my mother's hospital room and not near a punching bag, I calmly walk to the window and, instead of getting angry, beg to the God I've denied for the past nine years...to save my mother.

"Maybe I'm too late. Maybe You've given up on me since I've given up on You, but I need your help. I don't ask for help much. Not ever, usually. But I'm humbling myself right now. I need my mother to wake up. She wouldn't have died had I been here. Had I not left. Why? Why did my grandfather call me back to New Jersey only for my mother to get hurt doing something I would have been doing if I were here?"

"Quest?"

I turn and nod to Vinnie, who's now standing at my mother's side.

"You okay?"

My gaze returns to the blacktop roof outside the window. "I should've been here."

"Where?"

"Here. In San Diego. If I was here, I would have been cleaning the windows and then..."

"Have you ever cleaned them before?" Vinnie asks in a tone that says he knows I haven't. "I offered to clean them that day; she wouldn't let me. Said it was like therapy for her. So if you were here, she still would have been on the ladder cleaning the windows, and she still would have fallen." When I don't respond, he says, "It's not your fault, Quest. Not everything is up to you to take care of."

I wipe away the wetness from my eyes, but I still don't respond to Vinnie.

"Sometimes shit happens and there's nothing you can do about it."

"That sucks," I finally say.

"Yeah, it does."

I turn back to face him. "And you're okay with my mom lying here like this?"

"Of course I'm not," he says, raising his voice. "I've been praying every goddamn minute of every goddamn day, going over in my mind what I should've done. I could have insisted I climb that ladder, but I didn't. She's headstrong and likes to do things on her own. Nothing I could have said would have convinced her to change her mind. I can't beat myself up over it, just like you can't. Just like you couldn't save the life of that little girl, Quest. And would her life have been okay if you did? I don't think so. Unless you could have taken her back to America yourself, her life probably would have continued the way it was. Maybe God had it in His mind to take her away from all that..."

"Then why couldn't He take her away from it and kept her alive? Why couldn't *He* have stopped it all from happening? Why couldn't He have stopped me from taking that damn..." I close my eyes and force the thoughts out.

"I'm not sure. Maybe He helped the best way He could? I don't know, I'm not God, and I'm not a real religious guy. Your mother is, though, and she always told me that God has His plans."

"Plans." I scoff. Some great plans I've been a part of.

"That's what she said about your grandfather leaving you that store. 'God has His plans, and my father-in-law probably knows what they are. Something about your grandfather being a real church guy."

"Well what's the plan for my mother then? Is she supposed to lie here indefinitely?"

"I don't know, Quest," Vinnie says, sounding defeated. "I don't know."

38.

H AVEN
Eric has officially moved in. My loft is now his place. At least I don't have to be out of my house by the end of the month. Today, he gets the house to himself. Devin and I are going to my parents' house for dinner. When my mother asked me to come, I asked if I could bring a guest. For moral support.

He picks me up in his black Accord. A gentleman, he comes to the door instead of honking.

"Thank you so much for coming today. With you there, maybe my mom will keep her opinions to herself."

Inside my parents' house, one would never know Hannah Quinn had recently suffered a major heart attack. The dining room table is set with her platinum Royal Limoges collection and the presentation of chilled seafood and lump crab cocktail in the center flaunts an assiduous culinary eye.

"Did you order takeout from Roots again, Mother?" I say as soon as we step foot into the kitchen.

Her flawlessly powdered face falls ever so slightly but rebounds instantly with no one but me the wiser. "You must be Devin. I'm Hannah." My mother's ample smile is followed by her standard two-cheek greeting.

"Nice to meet you, son." My father strides forward and shakes his hand.

When the formal receptions are done, mother directs us to the dining room where we take our assigned seats at the table.

"Devin." Mom starts conversation once we've all filled our plates. "Haven tells me you work at that wonderful little television station up in Pennsylvania."

Oh, Mother, why must you be so catty?

"I do, Mrs. Quinn. It's my first job out of college. I began my higher education later than usual, but I'm learning now what I need to in order to move on to bigger and better. A stepping stone, if you will."

Mother's posture straightens if that's possible. "Very good. It's important to keep looking forward and do what you need to move ahead. Excellent."

"Where did you go to college?" My father asks while cracking open a crab leg.

"University of Southern California, Mr. Quinn. I started when I was twenty-five."

"Very good school. You didn't mind going that far away?"

"I'm *from* California, sir. I only moved out here last year."

"I didn't know that, Devin," I say. "What part of California?"

"Beverly Hills."

"Wait. What?" I'm surprised. He doesn't act like a guy who'd come from such an affluent city.

Devin chuckles. "It's not all it's cracked up to be."

"I looooove Beverly Hills."

Of course you do, Mother.

"Rodeo is my favorite of all shopping experiences. What do your parents do for a living?"

Because that's so important to know.

"My aunt and uncle raised me, ma'am. Aunt Ruth is a neurosurgeon and Uncle John is a plastic surgeon."

"Were they okay with you majoring in television?"

"Dad!" I expect my mother to cavil about the profession, but Dad? "What kind of question is—"

"A natural one. Two professionals—"

"Maybe Devin's stubborn like our Haven, dear," she says, delighted at her quip.

I literally want to sink into the couch cushions and hide behind a pillow.

"They had absolutely no qualms about it," Devin says, unaffected by the interrogation.

"So your uncle is a plastic surgeon?" Mom raises her brow. "How about that, Haven? Maybe Devin can take you to..."

Oh, shut the hell up, Mother. "No. Just stop—"

"I think Haven is beautiful just the way she is." Devin's interruption catches me by surprise. "There is no need for surgery on her face, she's perfect the way she is."

Devin. "Oh my gosh, thank you." I sit up straighter and say, "Did you hear that mother? I'm perfect the way I am."

"If you're thinking of getting back on television—" My mother carries on as if the conversation isn't causing my skin to catch fire. "—you can't have those scars. And since you are still wearing sunglasses, even though they're a different pair, obviously, you still feel uncomfortable walking around in your own skin. We talked about this."

After a slow, deliberate breath, I respond to my merciless mother. "I am not going back into television, Mother."

"But that's all you wanted to do before," she says, as if she supported my career choice from the beginning.

"I changed my mind." I look down at my untouched plate of food.

"Why did you change your mind? If it was the accident, a good surgeon—" She looks at Devin for emphasis. "—can make being on television possible again."

"I don't want that. My dreams changed."

"Your dreams? What are your dreams now?" She doesn't bother to hide the condescension, but I ignore it.

"I want to buy half of Mr. Vescovi's bookstore. I want to turn it into a book café."

Devin turns to me and whispers, "Really?"

I nod.

My mother sets down her silverware, removes her hands from the table, and sets them on her lap. I know her hands are clenched beneath the table. "A book cafe?" she asks calmly, her anger seething quietly inside her. "Surely...you are not serious."

"She is, Hannah," my dad says. "I even decided to offer to help her with a loan."

"Really, Dad?" I ask, surprised, right before my mom says, "Absolutely not. We did not send you to college so that you could run a coffee shop."

My dad sighs as he drops his head.

"It's not just a coffee shop, Mom. It's a bookstore too. How the hell is it any different than what you do as a librarian?"

"Language, Haven. And as a librarian, I do not sell coffee. I need a Master of Library and Information Science degree to do my job. You don't even need a high school diploma to serve coffee. And what happened to your dreams of becoming the next Diane Sawyer?"

"You mean my dreams of being held in the same high esteem that you held Ms. Sawyer? You met her *once*, Mother." I hold up one finger in exaggeration. "At some fundraiser. She doesn't even know who you are, yet you worship the ground she walks on."

"I don't know what you're talking about, Haven" she says with an eye roll. Children roll their eyes, Mother.

"I came home with my Homecoming Queen ticket, Mother, and all I got was a 'that's nice, dear' while you continued to watch some Diane Sawyer 20/20 episode. You didn't even turn your attention away from the damn television. Not even to glance at me! You didn't even know that on *that* night, I broke into the high school."

My parents' eyes widen, but not as much as Devin's.

"Yup. My friends and I had an impromptu game of volleyball after the school was closed. I'd have never done it had I gotten the loving response I'd hoped to get when I got home. Nope. I got a 'that's nice, dear' because Diane was on."

"Can we not do this now, please," my father says.

"Diane Sawyer was so important to you. All because she told you she loved your *salmon* dress." Using my fingers for air quotes, I carry on with my tirade. "'Diane is such a kind woman. She's so humble and down-to-earth.' 'Look how refined and dignified Diane is, Haven. Even in real life, she is the epitome of class.'" I continue my melodramatics, air-quoting and waving my arms above my place setting. 'There is no better journalist than Diane Sawyer, Haven—"

"Haven—" My mother tries to interrupt.

I don't allow it. "Just listen to how intelligent she is, Haven. It's so important to come across as smart, Haven.' And when it wasn't about Diane Sawyer, it was something else. 'Wear a prettier dress, Haven, you need to look like you belong.' 'Sit up straight, Haven, ladies don't slouch.' 'Study harder, Haven, you'll never marry a doctor or a lawyer unless you're intelligent. God knows, you'll need to.' God, Mom...I never even knew what you meant. Did you mean I'd need to marry a doctor, or I'd need to study harder to be smarter? And it doesn't even matter," I say, continuing with an exaggerated wave of my arm. "Because I don't need your attention *or* your respect anymore. Because I respect myself, Mother...and I don't need your approval to do so."

"Haven?" Devin says, confused by my behavior.

"That's enough, Haven," my father says in that tone that tells me I'm skating on thin ice.

I don't care. This breakdown has been a long time coming. "This assault. My accident. It may have left me horribly scarred on the outside, but you know what? It helped to heal the scars that *you* gave me, Mother. The ones no one else saw. I'm not afraid of you anymore. And I don't care what you think."

"Okay, Haven," my father scolds. "This has gone on long enough. I get you and your mother have had your problems, but you can't explode at her like that. Especially not in front of company."

I drop my hands to my lap and find Devin's hand is already there. How long as his hand been on my leg? Leaning into him, I whisper, "I'm sorry."

His response is a gentle squeeze to my thigh.

"Have you finished your *harangue*?" my mother asks, picking up her utensils and returning to her appetizer, my rant ineffectual.

I consider pushing away from the table and leaving, pulling Devin along with me, but I wonder which will serve to salvage my dignity more—staying? Or leaving?

I look to my father, whose eyes impel me to behave. I swallow the dregs left over from my outburst as remorse settles in my stomach. I resolve to stay. Picking up my fork, I pick at the shrimp on my plate. The next hour goes by painfully slow, but after I help my father clear the dinner plates, I'm preparing a pot of coffee to have with dessert when my mother enters the kitchen. She's transferring individual cheesecakes and tortes from the bakery box to the dessert platter when she says quietly, "I was proud of you for being nominated for Homecoming Queen. I was disappointed you didn't win." She finishes arranging the eight cakes and closes the bakery box. "Maybe you can sell desserts like these at your new little coffee place."

I look at my mother, surprised she's not coming down on me like a ton of *War and Peace* books. "That's a good idea."

Sitting around the table eating dessert is a lot less awkward, and mom is even closed-lipped when Dad offers to lend me the money to buy the *entire* store from Quest.

In Devin's car on the ride back to my place, I say, "I'm so sorry about my behavior tonight. I shouldn't have exploded like that."

"I never realized you had a dark side." He laughs. "That was nice of your dad, though, to offer you a loan."

"I know. I wasn't expecting that. I just need to find out if that's what Quest wants to do."

"Why do you want to buy half of the store? Why not the whole thing? Why does Quest have to be involved at all?"

"I don't know," I say quickly. "It's his store."

"His family's in California. Didn't you say he didn't even want the store to begin with? He was just going through with it so you wouldn't get the Hemingway deal?"

"Right. But if he doesn't keep it—"

"Give him back the collection."

"What?"

Devin glances at me. "Tell him if he sells the store, he can have the collection. Just because the lawyer gives it to you, doesn't mean you can't give it back. I don't know why you guys didn't discuss that to begin with. It's kind of an easy provision to get around."

It *is* an easy provision to get around. Why *didn't* we discuss it?

"Haven?"

I blink out of my thoughts and respond to Devin. "I don't think I can afford to buy him out completely. Only half."

"That's not what your father said."

"I'll lend you the money to buy the entire store, honey, if this is what you really want to do," were his actual words.

"I think you should take him up on the offer. Half percent interest is a good deal, and he makes a little money off of it."

Devin's right, my father did offer me a nice deal, but *my* deal was to keep Quest here in New Jersey. Considering he hasn't called in three weeks, that may not even be an option.

I don't respond.

A half hour later, Devin says quietly, "I know you still have a thing for that bookstore owner."

I do. I do still have a thing for that bookstore owner.

39.

Quest

"Give her the Hemingway shit. I'm selling the store."

"It's been three months."

"Right. That's why I said give her the shit."

Sam Hart is silent on the other end of the phone.

"Do I have to sign anything? I'm in California and I'm not going back to Jersey."

"California? For how long?"

I squeeze my temples to alleviate the pain. "I've been here for three weeks. My mother just woke up from a twenty-one day coma, and she's going to need assistance for the rest of her life, so I'd say I'm here indefinitely. If there's paperwork, can you scan it and email it or something so I can sign them?" A beep indicates an incoming call.

"Yes, certainly. I'm sorry to hear about your mother."

"Thanks."

"Are you sure you want to do this, Quest? Maybe you can take some time to think—"

"I've thought about it long enough," I say quickly, ignoring another indication of the incoming call. "I don't want the store, and I don't care about the collection. And you can sell the house, too."

"The house? Are you sure?"

"Yeah. I'm gonna need the money."

"Okay. I can contact a realtor about both places. I'll forward you the paperwork, and I'll get the books out to Ms. Quinn this week...that's some Christmas present you're giving her."

"Yeah, well, that's the least I can do."

After I end my call with Sam, I delete the notification that I missed Haven's call. Again. I leave the hospital and decide to take a drive out to the beach in La Jolla. If I don't get in my car and go somewhere, I'll punch something. When my mother opened her eyes yesterday, I nearly dropped to my knees in gratitude, but an hour later, when all she could do was blink, I stepped outside and cursed the sky with every expletive in my vocabulary. My mother is in a vegetative state. She may never use her words again. She may never walk again. She may never fucking feed herself again, and there is nothing I can do to change that. My mother will always need someone to take care of her. That is why I made the decision to sell my grandfather's properties. How can I go back to New Jersey and leave Vinnie to care for her without my help?

My only company at Windansea Beach is the angry surf that takes its temper out on the large rocks that protect the land. Its ability to hit and run makes me envious. The sweet release of a powerful pummel without concern for consequence. Strike the shore, surrender into the sea.

I take a seat on the martyred sand, zip my jacket up past my neck, and contemplate my world right now. It sucks. My mother lays half dead in a hospital bed, and I am cutting ties with the woman I could see myself growing old with. Why am I severing that relationship? Because three thousand miles is too great a distance to work on a connection that was struggling when no stretch of land came between us. Haven once told me that *she* had little to offer because of her preoccupation with her scars. Truth is, with the future of my mother unclear, and my time devoted to her care, *I* have even less to give. Do I miss Haven? More than I'm missing my own mother right now. Yes, I feel guilty about that, but I'm being honest. I want nothing more than to get on a plane and fly back to her, but my mother needs me. If the doctors are right, her recovery will be very slow, and she won't be able to fend for herself. Vinnie has a business that he can't let fail, not if he wants to help pay my mother's bills. And what if he doesn't? They're not married. He's under no obligation to stick around. What if he doesn't? I am all my mother has...and so I must surrender any hope for a future with Haven.

Even though it breaks me to do so.

40.

H AVEN
On the afternoon of the twenty-fourth, a Federal Express delivery man asks me to sign for a large box sent from the law offices of Hart and Foster. The Fedex guy leaves the heavy box inside next to my front door. Blood rushes to my chest as I use a scissor to split open the strip of packing tape that secures the box.

It can't be.

My trembling hand lifts the first flap as I silently pray that I am wrong. Please, God, no.

With my opposite hand, I raise the second flap. Brown paper filler conceals the contents, but my heart sinks nonetheless. I know what's underneath. The final goodbye.

Removing the filler exposes more than a dozen hardcover Ernest Hemingway books. The first one I hold, *The Sun Also Rises*, is signed by Hemingway himself. As well, *A Farewell to Arms, Men Without Women,* and *Death in the Afternoon*—all autographed by Papa Hemingway.

And then I see it.

The book I held in my own hands the last time I saw Mr. Vescovi. A copy printed in 1924, in excellent condition, and now a reminder of everything past.

Mr. Vescovi.

An unmarred complexion.

An unsullied soul.

Quest.

I place *in our time* back in the box and allow myself a moment to grieve. Had I not refused to discuss a potential relationship with Quest when he'd asked, would he be giving up the store? If we'd agreed to date each other, would I be in California with him right now? Would he be answering my phone calls?

Because I need answers, I search my phone for Sam Hart's number and call him. His secretary says he's behind closed doors.

"Hey, what's all that?" Eric says when he lopes down the stairs.

I don't bother to respond. I grab my purse and my keys and take a ride to Mr. Hart's office.

"It's Christmas Eve, Ms. Quinn," his secretary tells me when I ask to speak to the lawyer. She sets down her mug and says, "Mr. Hart is scheduled to leave as soon as he is done with his conference call."

I sit down on the black leather couch against the wall and say, "I'll wait. I'll only take a minute of his time."

"Ms. Quinn," she says, irritated by my insistence. "I will have him call you on Wednesday when he returns." She types something in her computer and says, "I'm entering your name into his calendar now. You will be the first one he calls Wednesday morning."

"Wednesday is too late." My hands are crossed over my lap, I'm sitting up tall at the edge of the couch, and I am determined not to leave until I speak with Sam Hart.

She shakes her head and returns her attention to her computer. It sounds like she's typing a thousand words a minute. I get a whiff of chocolate and mint and realize it's the day before Christmas. I knew it was Christmas Eve when I got up this morning, but it just hits me now how pathetic I am to be sitting here waiting for a lawyer to tell me the status of my relationship with the boy I like. Essentially, that is why I am here. I don't want the books. I don't really want to know what Quest is doing with his grandfather's store. I just want to know what he said when he told the lawyer to send me the collection. I just want to know where I stand. How pathetic am I?

At the thought, I stand my pitiful self up and apologize to the secretary for barging in. "Wednesday will be fine."

The door behind her opens and out walks Sam Hart. "Hello," he says when he sees me.

"Mr. Hart," his secretary begins, "this is Haven Quinn."

"Miss Quinn, I take it you received the books," he says, gesturing for me to come into his office.

I abide. "I'm sorry I'm bothering you today...I...it could have waited." I regret not waiting, not giving myself a chance to cool down."

Sam Hart closes his office door. "Please, sit, Miss Quinn."

I don't.

"You're wondering *why* you received the books."

"Yes."

He holds up a manila folder and says, "Quest Vescovi signed over his rights, and he's selling his grandfather's home and business." He places the folder down.

My heart sinks for the second time today. Quest really isn't coming back. If I open my mouth to respond, I won't be able to hold back my tears, so I nod, raising my brow to make it look like I agree with Quest's decision to sell. Maybe it is the right decision for him. Maybe it didn't make sense for him to uproot his life after all, especially if his mother needs him. Hopefully, his mother does need him, because it would mean she's still alive.

"Miss Quinn? Do you have any questions?"

I widen my eyes and will myself not to cry. "Would he consider selling the store to me?"

41.

Q UEST
Christmas dinner at my mother's new temporary home is dry turkey, saltless mashed potatoes, and cold creamed corn. Nursing home food sucks. But my mother needs to be here, and if I want to spend Christmas with her, then Vinnie and I need to be here too.

The head of mom's bed is raised so that she is sitting up. She is out of the vegetative state and responsive, but still unable to speak. We're hoping that changes soon. If she isn't able to say anything in the next couple of days, she may never. My flavorless meal barely gets touched. It's hard to build an appetite watching my mother struggle to keep her head up.

"It'll be okay," Vinnie says, *lying* to reassure me.

"If only there was something I could do."

"Sometimes, the only thing you *can* do is love them."

"Too bad loving someone isn't enough to save them," I murmur.

Vinnie sets his food tray aside, leans forward, and holds his girlfriend's hand—*is* girlfriend the term used when a couple is in their late forties? "Don't underestimate the power of love, Quest."

On the way home that afternoon, I stop at the cemetery. It's been too long. Franco Salvatore Vescovi, September 2, 1970 to May 7, 2008.

"Oh, Dad. I'm sorry it's been so long." I drop to my knees in front of his stone. "Oh my God, Dad." I cry.

I cry for a long time. I cry for my father for the first time since I've been discharged. My reason for enlisting. My punishment.

When I finish sobbing like a three-year-old, still on my knees, I tell him about his father's last wish of which I am the sole beneficiary. "I'm not sure what happened between the two of you, but I guess there's no point in trying to figure that out now."

I sit back on my heels. "I hope you're not upset with me for forgiving him for whatever it is that came between you." Sighing, I attempt to find courage to say more. "More importantly…" Oh my God, this is so hard. "I'm so sorry, Dad. I'm so sorry. I still haven't forgiven myself. Ma thinks I did. She thinks I'm just struggling with my discharge. Oh God, Dad, it's so much more than that."

I close my eyes and drop my head. Clasping my hands together, I pray for the words to come.

A sudden chill trickles through me, a warm sensation. A peaceful sense of calm.

"I should have taken the back roads. You said I wasn't ready for the 101." The tears return in swift rapids. A decade's worth.

I'd had my driver's license a total of thirty minutes and insisted I drive home from the test. Dad told me to take the long way, declaring I'd never driven the freeway and I needed more experience before attempting it. Being the obstinate teenager I was, I didn't listen. I got on Route 101 with my father scolding me from the passenger seat. An SUV with a family of five, driving somewhere in the vicinity of seventy-five miles per hour, minding their own business in the right lane, plowed into my father's sedan as it merged onto the highway. Three more cars followed, causing our car to spin and flip, my father taking the brunt of the force as the car tumbled twice before landing on his side of the car.

"I've never forgiven myself, Dad. If I'd listened to you, you'd be here right now. And maybe Mom would be okay. Maybe that one event...sealed all our fates. Maybe I ruined us all."

TWO DAYS LATER, MY mother says, "Hi," when I walk into her room.

"Holy shit...Ma..." I rush to her. "You can talk."

She nods and smiles. "Quest." It doesn't come out exactly right, but I know she's saying my name. She's saying my name.

Vinnie walks in behind me and sets his hand on my shoulder. "She's going to recover. Maybe not a hundred percent, but enough. It's going to be slow...but it's going to happen." Vinnie's voice cracks.

Thank God.

A half hour into my visit with mom, I receive a call from an unknown number. I put the phone back in my pocket to deal with later.

When I do check my voicemail later, there's a message from an Annabelle Wick, a real estate agent. Someone put in an offer on the store, books and all.

I call her back and accept it...and try not to think about the sadness that washes over me.

42.

H AVEN
"...and, well...I ended up buying the bookstore," I tell the group. I've been attending Quest's support group each Monday night since he left, but tonight, I finally shared my story. All of it. Including my fondness for and irritation *with* him. He didn't even call after we closed on the sale. I thought for sure I'd hear from him then.

"I'm proud of you," Michele says. "In a short time, you not only overcame the assault, you also gained enough confidence to stand up to your mother *and* find a career that makes *you* happy...not because you think it's something that would please someone else, but because it's something you truly want. You should be proud, Haven."

A cold chill travels up my spine, and warmth spreads through my chest. I should be proud? Pride is the last thing I'd associate with myself. Most days I feel like a disgrace. My badge of shame carved into my face for all the world to see. Yet, Michele is right. I have been standing up to my mother. I did buy the bookstore because it's what *I* want. I didn't ask permission, nor did I worry what my mother would think. I wanted it, I asked Dad for a loan, and I bought it. *My* choice. Though I don't have a choice about wearing my scars every day—even more surgery wouldn't leave me scarless—maybe I shouldn't be *ashamed* of them. Instead of wearing my flaws as some scarlet letter meant to remind me of my weaknesses,

I can wear them proudly, as someone who not only survived a terrible attack but thrived in spite of it. Maybe. Old habits do die hard. "Thank you," I say to Michele, grateful to her for recognizing something I didn't.

"She's right, Haven," Mary says. "You should be proud. Proud, too, that you were able to share your story. It's a huge step toward your recovery. Revel in it."

Revel. It *is* time I celebrate something, isn't it?

WILL PAY IN BOOKS AND Coffee. That's what the sign outside my store window reads. My father loaned me the money to buy the store and renovate it, but I still need help with rearranging shelves, painting, and anything else the big contractors charge too much for.

My sign works...that and the pleading phone calls I make to everyone I know. Fortunately for me, it's the middle of February and there's not much going on, which leaves my friends plenty of time to get their hands dirty and help me turn Mr. Vescovi's wonderful bookstore into a quaint book *café*. Even Mrs. Gannon and Layton's local author James Meadows are here helping to revive the store, and Mrs. Gannon promises to have her class come in and help after she receives all parent permission slips. Small towns have wonderful benefits, and I'm looking forward to not only serving the community but living within it as well. I'm in the process of moving out of my house and into the apartment above the store. Eric is taking over the lease.

Though it's come to my attention that Katie is not thrilled with the idea.

I find this out this morning when a mix of staccato-strikes against my window and echoed shrieks into the breaking dawn startle me awake. I turn on the lights, and go to my front door.

Katie. Eye sockets black as raccoons, scleras bloodshot and wet, lips purple from single-digit temperatures. Katie is mad.

"What the heck, Katie? Come in." I pull her in by her frozen hands. "Come on, sit down. There are blankets on the couch," I tell her on my way to the stove.

I'm filling the kettle when, with chattering teeth, she says, "You're sleeping with him, aren't you? I knew this would happen," she shouts, wrapping a blanket around her shoulders before she marches through my house. "Where is he?"

"Upstairs." I turn on the stove and don't bother giving truth to her accusation. She'll figure it out.

Eric is clueless. From the groggy sound of his voice, it sounds like he thinks he's dreaming. "Whoa, Kate?" he asks, baffled. "What...why are you...what *time* is it?"

"You planned this, didn't you?" Katie continues in a shrill tone I didn't think she was capable of.

"I did not plan this; I was sick of all your accusations..."

Leaving them to work this out on their own, I go back to bed.

I don't wake up until well past daybreak. It's quiet in the loft, but I don't attempt to see if they're still up there. Instead, I take a shower and leave the house with my hair wet. Eric's car is in the driveway, Katie's is not. Either one of them can fill me in later.

Before going to the store, I stop at a salon three miles down the road and smile at their WALK-INS WELCOME sign. I'm in need of a change.

A big change.

I walk out of the salon forty-five minutes later, hair twelve inches shorter.

AT THE STORE, DEVIN is already standing out front.

"Don't you have to work today?" He's wearing old jeans and a sweatshirt.

"I called in sick. You cut your hair," he says with a frown.

Naturally, I bring my hand to my bare neck. "I needed a change." A big change. This morning I had the hairstylist cut twelve inches off. She donated it, and I got a choppy bob.

"It's short." He unzips his hoodie and tosses it on the small metal ladder I have pushed up against the window.

"Short was the point. It wouldn't be a change if it wasn't. So how can you call in sick when you're the station's only cameraman?"

"I can and I did. What do you need me to do next?"

I shrug off his mood and hand him an empty box and tell him to take the books off the bookshelves in the center aisles. "There are more empty boxes piled against the back wall. And thank you for helping."

He nods and gets right to work.

I'm in the middle of removing books from the shelves as well when James Meadows walks through the door. "Hey, Haven," he says, unzipping his jacket and tossing it on top of Devin's. "I like your hair."

"Thank you," I say, smiling, relieved *some*body likes it.

"I'll continue with the front?" James asks, referring to removing everything from the front foyer so the contractors can start on construction. The foyer is where most of the work will be done. It will encompass most of the cafe, where only a few couches and chairs will be added to the actual bookstore.

"Yes, please. Thank you so much for the help."

"Like I told you yesterday...whatever you need me to do, I'm here. That's the beauty of working from home...my schedule is flexible."

Behind me, something lands with a crash.

"My books!" The bookcase Devin was working on is laying on top of the case next to it.

"Sorry, Haven, guess I should have started from the top down."

I step around Devin to get another empty box and start piling them in. "Let me get them," I tell him, worried he won't stack them in proper order.

"How the hell did that happen?" James asks Devin. "You were working from the other side."

"*I* was working from this side," I tell him. "I started from the bottom up too."

"Still..." James says, not finishing his sentence.

"I'm sorry, Haven." Devin crouches down next to me, and hands me a fallen book, the corner of its cover bent in half. "I'll be more careful."

I sigh, sorry for the ruined book. "Don't worry about it, Dev. I'm sure this is the first of many small casualties to come."

Devin helps me pick up the rest of the books only after promising to keep them in mostly alphabetical order. When we finish, the two of us bring the filled boxes and the empty bookcase into the storage pod parked outside and begin again on the next—this time working from the top shelf down and keeping all books safe.

When we're all three finished, and Devin and James have left the store, I lock the door from the inside and take my cell from my purse. Quest hasn't responded to any of my calls, but I still want to reach him. In the corner of the storage room, nestled behind another box of books, I found a small shoebox full of pictures I thought he would want. Old pictures. Pictures of a young Mr. Vescovi and what looked to be Quest as a child. A boy whose face seems familiar. The box of pictures might not be the real reason I searched online for his mother's home phone number, but it gives me a good excuse to call without looking *too* pathetic. And maybe she won't have caller ID and he'll actually answer the phone.

43.

Q UEST
      Vinnie and I return home from another day at the
nursing home with Mom. Vinnie goes every day after work, I
do not. Being there makes me feel powerless. Nothing I do
will help her get better. Progress has flatlined, but she's being
released this Friday. Physical therapy will be done at an
outpatient facility. She can speak, not as fluently as she used
to, and she can walk, not as effortlessly as she used to, but her
speech and her gait are slow. It's clear by the pained
expressions on her face that she is frustrated. Which makes
me want to punch a goddamned brick wall. As of yet, I
haven't, but I fear the bags in the basement won't be enough.
Running twice a day is helping my endorphins stay balanced
at least, but it hasn't slipped by me that I'm back at square
one, living in my mother's basement and doing nothing
productive with my time.

      I *am* looking into buying another beat-up car to restore
though, and using the money I got from the bookstore sale,
I'm thinking of starting my own restoration garage. Mom
has a good-sized detached garage I can use, and I'll be able to
keep a close eye on her as well.

      "Can you play the messages?" Vinnie asks as he sags
against the chair. "I'd get up, but you're right there."

"Sure." I press PLAY on the answering machine and return to making a cup of espresso from Mom's espresso machine.

"Probably just more of your mother's friends..." Vinnie stops talking because he doesn't recognize the voice coming through. It's younger than the usual get-well wishers, and the message is not to wish anyone well.

"...and I thought you might have called...at least after we closed on the store. I wish you had. I don't know how your mother's doing...or if she...well, just know, that I've been praying for her. But that's not why I'm calling. I found a small box in the storeroom. You probably overlooked it. Quest, it's filled with pictures of your family. You as a boy. You and your granddad! Probably your mom and dad too. I'm sure you'd want them. Anyway, I found your mother's phone number online. I think this is it anyway, and I can mail these to you, but I can't be sure the address I found online is actually hers. Maybe you can call me just to give me the right one. I'm sure you'd want these, and I know...I, well, I don't..." There's a long pause, and then, "I miss you. I wish you'd call me." Another pause. "Anyway, in case you don't have my phone number anymore, well, you can always call me at the store. I'm not changing the number...bye."

"Haven bought the store?" I say mostly to myself. I can't believe she bought the store.

"You don't know who you sold it to? Isn't that something you *needed* to know in order to sell it?"

I rush to the desk in the living room and grab my laptop. I play Haven's message again and sit down to open my email. Her voice soothes me. Oh, how I've missed her. I feel a tear escape but I brush it away and open the final PDF. There it is...Haven's name. Bringing my hand to my mouth, I close my eyes.

"You really didn't know who bought your store?" Vinnie asks again.

I open my eyes and look at him. "I just wanted to get the thing out of my hands and put it behind me. I signed by the red X's and sent it back." I shake my head. "I can't believe she bought the store," I mutter again.

Vinnie gets up, leaves the room, and returns with a Fedex box. "Is that why you never opened this?" He slides the package across the table. The package I received on Christmas Eve and still haven't opened. "Because you wanted to put it all behind you?"

"Pretty much." I drop my face in my hands. How could I have just cut her out of my life the way I did? Who did it benefit?

"Quest?"

I raise my head and rest it on my thumbs.

"Did you want to put *her* behind you too?" Vinnie goes to the counter and continues with the espresso that I never finished making.

No. I drop my shoulders and sigh, leaving a long stretch of silence. "I thought I was doing her a favor."

"How's that?"

Sighing again, I drop my hands onto the table. "I'm *here* now. I can't be with her. She's been through a lot and she needs someone who can be there with her...not someone who's three thousand miles away."

"Did you ask her how *she* felt about that?"

"No. She would have said something to make me feel okay about it and all. She's too kind."

"So instead you do something *un*kind?"

I turn to look at him. He's leaning against the counter, his eyes questioning.

"I wasn't doing it to be unkind," I tell him. "I'm a mess." I never even got over killing my father, and then I let a little girl die. Haven doesn't need someone who's on the verge of exploding at any given moment. Proving my point, I unintentionally start ringing my hands, my precursor to throwing a punch.. "She's broken herself...she doesn't need someone else who needs fixing."

"Maybe she wasn't in it to fix you. Maybe she just wanted to love you."

Love me? "I'm not so sure it went that deep for her."

Vinnie pours the espresso into little cups and then adds a splash of Sambuca to each. He hands me one. After he sits back down, he says, "She could have just mailed the box to the address she found online."

I look at my little cup of coffee. She could have.

"Why are you still here, Quest?"

"Well that's a stupid question."

"Is it? Your mother's been living in a home where other people are taking care of her. She's coming home in two days because she's well enough to take care of herself. Plus, I'm here. So why are you?"

I sit back and say, "Who's gonna take care of her when you're at work? You need to keep working to help pay her bills...and..." I hesitate saying this, but it needs to be said.

"What if you decide you don't *want* to take care of her anymore? Where's that leave her?"

"Kid, did you fall on *your* head? I've been with your mother since you were overseas. Been living with her for the past two years. Where do you think I'm going?"

"Well...you're not married, you can just—"

"I *asked* your mother to marry me. Two years ago. But you were in such a bad way, she didn't want to upset you anymore."

I sag onto my elbows, dropping my head back into my hand. "Well I've messed up *every*one's life, haven't I?"

"No, kid, you didn't. But I do think you're messing with your own life. You've been in limbo for three and a half years. It's time you pick a side."

It's time I pick a side. Left or Right? Crazy or sane? California or New Jersey?

"And it's okay to be scared." He knocks back the rest of his espresso in one gulp.

"I'm not scared," I say instinctively, too defensive to be believed.

"And it doesn't mean you love someone any less just 'cause you're three thousand miles away." Vinnie pushes back on his chair, gets up, and brings his cup to the sink. "Catch you in the morning, kid."

I stare at the Fedex box in front of me. What *am* I afraid of? Why did I run away so fast? And why the hell am I finding it so hard to go back home?

44.

H AVEN
Dingman's Corner Book Café is ready for reconstruction. Mrs. Gannon's fifth grade class was a big help in sweeping floors, wiping down walls, and alphabetizing the pile of children's books we never got around to listing.

"Well it looks like you're one step closer," says James, after the kids leave and it's just James, Devin, and me left in the store.

"I know. I think I'm getting scared now."

On a short laugh, James says, "Listen, Haven, while Devin's in the back, I'd just like to ask you...well, can I take you out for a drink? I bet you can use one, and well, I've been wanting to ask you out for a while now."

"Really?" I ask, surprised anyone would want to voluntarily be seen in public with me.

"Really." His smile is warm and genuine.

I don't know what to say. I like James, he's a sweet man. But he's not Quest. Then again, Quest isn't here, and it doesn't look like he's coming back. "Sure," I say before I chicken out. "That sounds nice. And you're right, I *can* use a drink."

"Great. I'll go get out of these dusty clothes and come back and pick you up."

I'm all moved in upstairs and have been living there for the past week. I agree to James coming back to get me. "And...thanks," I add, grateful that he's even interested in me.

I turn around and bump into Devin.

"Oh my gosh, I'm sorry."

"Careful, pretty girl," he says, his hands firm on my shoulders.

I pat his chest and apologize again. "And we're done for the night, so you don't have to hang around. I'm just going to return my father's call and go upstairs."

"Okay," he says, bending to kiss my cheek. "I'll call you tomorrow."

After I lock myself inside, I call my father back. When he'd called before, I was on top of a ladder nailing in a piece of crown molding that had come loose. On the third ring, he answers. "Hey, Pumpkin."

"Hi, Dad. Sorry I missed your call, I was on a ladder, and...anyway, so what's up? Is Mom okay?"

"Yes, yes, she's fine. I just wanted to tell you I heard from my friend Roger. The judge in Pennsylvania."

"Oh?"

"They caught the Stratford Slasher."

"Really?"

"Really. His name is Nevil Nukpana. And he admitted to all the slashings in Stratford, claiming a vengeance against his girlfriend who slighted him."

"He admitted to mine?" My knees go weak, but I look around and there's no place to sit. I walk to the wall and slide my back against it, stopping when my rear-end hits the floor.

"Roger doesn't have all the details, but I think so, yes."

I can't get excited. Not yet. Not until I know for sure he's the one who did it. I wipe the dust off my backside and lock up the store.

I brush any negative thoughts aside and stick the key into the door that leads to my apartment. I turn the key, turn the knob, open the door...and then...

I'm shoved into my dark hallway, my knees and hands breaking my fall against the stairs, but only for a moment, because in the next second, my face is jammed into the edge of a carpet-covered step. Ouch. I push myself up, but I'm quickly driven back into the stairs with the weight of a couple hundred pounds. The weight...of a man.

I press my forehead into the carpet. Shit shit shit. But then I hear the crack of a pocket knife as it snaps into place. No. No. Not again. I will not...I close my eyes, and try to remember what Sandra Bullock demonstrated on *Miss Congeniality*. What was it?

The man behind me grunts and twists my arm behind my back. His other hand holds the knife. I know this, because the blade's point is now situated at my eye. He groans again.

S-I-N-G. Sing. What did it stand for?

The blade skims the corner of my eye.

S-I-N-G. Come on, Sandra...S-I-N-G. So...Solar Plexus. I elbow him in the gut.

S-I-N-G. Instep. I can't reach his instep, but I throw my foot back and stick my heel into his shin. He drops his hand. No more knife by my eye.

"Stop!" he shouts in a deep voice. A voice that sounds forced.

N. Nose. I turn my head. He's wearing the same black ski mask. Same gray eyes. *Wasn't he caught?* I use my free hand and backwards-punch him in his mask-covered nose. His head jerks.

"Hayv..." In that same really deep voice, he starts to say my name but stops.

S-I-N-G. G. Groin. With all my might, I push up from the stairs. Push back into him. Sandra, don't fail me now. I ball up my hand. Tighten it. With the memory of all the pain and fear I suffered this past year, I crush my fist into his nuts.

"Ohhhh." He releases his grasp from the hold he has of my hand behind my back and he clutches where I punched him.

I use the opportunity to kick him while he's down, so I turn to face him and shove my boot heel into his face. His head cracks against the door and he yells, "Shit, Haven," in an unmasked voice.

I freeze in fear.

And shock.

I'm about to vomit.

"Devin?"

He jerks his head to look at me, and his eyes fill with fear.

"Why?" I mouth, a tiny breath of air expels.

Still holding his crotch, he shifts toward me.

I back up and trip on the bottom step. Phone. I need my phone.

My eyes watch his gray eyes. How had I never noticed the color of Devin's eyes?

I turn and run up my stairs.

"Haven, wait," he yells, but I don't turn to him. I open my apartment door and bolt it from the inside. Then I call 911 and pray the police get here before he breaks in.

The woman on the other end asks me detailed questions, while Devin continuously knocks on my door.

"I'm so sorry, Haven. I'm so sorry," he cries from the other side of my door.

"Ma'am," the operator says, "I have men on my way. Stay on the phone with me. Is your deadbolt secure?"

"I think so, I don't know."

"Haven, I love you. I just wanted you to love me too." The knocking has stopped, but he's still crying against the door.

"Ma'am, I can hear him. Go into another room so he's..."

"Haven. You were just too beautiful. They all wanted you. Can't you see, if I don't make you ugly, I'll never have a chance. C'mon, Haven, we're friends...don't..."

Friends? This is what he calls friendship? I can't even open my mouth to speak to him.

"Go into another room, Miss Quinn." I hear the operator, but I can't pay attention to her. All I hear is Devin's pleas.

"All I wanted was for you to be with me. Haven, everyone wanted you. Katie's cousin, the bookstore guy." The operator is still talking into the phone, but Devin...he's crying. But he hurt me, I shouldn't care if he's crying. "I thought that if I took away your beauty, then they wouldn't want you. Haven, are you even listening to me? Dammit. If that stupid bookstore owner didn't get in the way."

He stops talking when he hears the sirens outside.

"Miss Quinn. The officers are on your street, they'll be there any min..."

I hear commotion in the stairwell.

"Put your hands up," someone shouts.

"They're up. They're up," Devin says. "I'm not gonna hurt her anymore. I just loved her."

"Miss Quinn," a deep voice says. "We have him, Miss Quinn. It's Officer McLoughlin. Can you open the door?"

When I open the door, I see two other officers leading Devin outside. He turns and looks up at me. "You're too pure to be ugly," he says as he disappears from my sight.

At the police station later that night, I give my statement of events and ask if Devin has said anything more. Officer McLoughlin tells me that Detective Page will be in to see me in a few minutes.

All this time.

All that fear.

All that trust I put into his friendship.

My heart is not accepting that it was Devin who hurt me. Why? My attacker was right in front of me this whole time. Oh my God! He's been in my house. On my couch. I let him hold me. What the hell is wrong with me that I can't even see evil when it's right in front of me?

"Miss Quinn," a shorter, darker officer walks into the room and hands me a can of soda. "I'm Detective Page." We shake hands before he takes the seat across from me. "So Devin Randolph was a friend. I'm so sorry."

I shrug. "Why? Why would he do this? Twice. I don't get it."

"He's mentally ill, Miss Quinn. He has a warped sense of reality."

"The Stratford Slasher? My father said they caught him."

"They did. It looks like your friend—"

"He's not my friend," I interrupt quickly.

"Right. He's definitely not. But he was trying to make it look like a copycat to redirect the blame." Officer Page sighs.

"Did he say why he did it?"

"Classic jealousy case. We've seen it before. They can't have you, so they don't want anyone else to have you. In Devin's mind, though, he thought if he made you 'ugly' enough—" Officer Page uses finger quotes, "—then no one would want you, and *he* would have a chance. You're lucky, though."

"I am? How so?" If this cop thinks I'm lucky, *he* has a screw or two loose too.

"If you didn't fight back, he probably would have killed you tonight. He confessed as much."

I cover my mouth and my stomach, because the urge to vomit has reappeared.

The detective gets up and retrieves the wastebasket sitting by the door. "Just in case," he says when he sets it on the floor next to me. After he returns to his seat, he pushes a box of tissues in front of me.

"Devin Randolph also confessed to the murder of his own father."

"Oh my God."

"He was eight...said it was self-defense. He watched his father slice his mother's neck right in front of him."

Oh my God. This time, I do throw up. Three times.

"It's the reason his aunt and uncle adopted him and changed his last name. He was cleared, but they didn't want the case following him all his life. Plus, his parents were celebrities."

"Celebrities?" I ask, wiping my mouth with the tissue.

"Lars and Deanna Emerson. Lars was in the eighties metal band Hatchet and Deanna was in—"

"*Lavi and Ariel.* Yes, I'm familiar with the story." How the hell? I hold my head in my hands and wonder what the heck my mother's going to say when she finds out I befriended a psychopath.

45.

H AVEN
The morning after...

I raise the blankets over my head and turn onto my stomach, the sheen off the snow-covered branches outside my bedroom window is way too bright this morning. I might as well have gotten blasted drunk with James Meadows last night. I can't imagine it being any worse than the reality hangover I have right now. Devin Randolph, no, Emerson put these scars on my face. How could I not have known this? Is my perception of people that far-off? Am I that gullible that I cannot see the truth when it's right in front of me?

My cell phone rings, interrupting my thoughts. My mother.

I sit up in bed and answer my phone. "Hi, Mom," I say, ready to play defense. I left a message on their landline when I got home last night.

"Haven. We just woke up and got your message. You should have called our cells. You know the battery's always dying on our Freedom Phone." Mom still calls their cordless phone by the name of the first cordless they ever bought. "What happened? Are you all right?"

"I'm all right, Mom. I swear. I'm just..." Embarrassed.

"Daddy said they caught the Stratford man. Did someone *else* attack you?"

"Oh, mom. I can't even begin to tell you..." I stop talking to ready myself for the affront.

"Haven, please. I'm so upset. What happened?"

"It was Devin, Mom. Devin is the one who slashed my face, *and* he's the one that attacked me last night."

"Devin? Your friend, Devin? He was the Stratford Slasher?"

"No, he wasn't the Stratford Slasher, he was *my* slasher. My own personal slasher. I'm sorry. I'm sorry I didn't know. I'm so stupid—"

"Stupid? How are you stupid, Haven?"

"Because I let him into my life. I thought he was a friend, and—"

"And you trusted him? Because that's who you are? You're apologizing for that?"

"Wait...what?"

"He had *me* fooled too. I'm sorry this happened to you again. Were you hurt? Did he...did he cut your...your face again?"

I lay back down and sink into my pillow. "Not really. Just a tiny scrape at the corner of my eye."

"How'd you get away?"

Thinking about it for the first time since, I chuckle. "I fought back, Mom. Using something I saw on some Rom-Com."

"You fought back?" she asks, surprised. "I'm impressed."

Wait. Impressed? "I impressed Hannah Quinn?" I allow the sarcasm to drip into the receiver.

"Yes, Haven. You impressed your mother. My tongue can contend with the best of them, but put me in a physical altercation and I'm toast."

"Toast?"

She laughs. "Haven, did you find out why Devin did this? I still can't wrap my head around it. He seemed so nice."

I think about this some more. It's all I've been thinking about since last night. "He *is* nice, Mom. I think he's just demented or something. His father killed his mother, and *he* killed his father."

"What!?"

"When I finally stopped puking up my guts last—"

"Language, Haven."

Oh, Mother. "When I finally stopped expelling the contents of my stomach into the wastepaper basket at the police station, the detective told me that Devin not only confessed to hurting me, he confessed to killing his father with a baseball bat after he witnessed him murder his mother."

"Oh my goodness. What kind of people do you deal with?" Before I can say anything, she says, "I mean," her sigh is so loud I can hear it. "But I still don't understand why he needed to hurt you."

"The same reason his father killed his mother...possession. Jealousy."

"That's sick."

"It is, Mother. Very sick."

There's a stretch of silence, and then, "I'm sorry all this happened to you, Haven. You have such an innocent heart.

And I hate that there's someone out there that tried to break your spirit."

Who is this? And what did you do to my mother?

"I know I'm not the easiest person to take, but...well, your father keeps reminding me that I need to *show* my compassion. I do have compassion, Haven. I just have a hard time expressing it the way...one normally expresses...compassion and empathy."

"Thank you, Mom. That means a lot. Especially coming from you. Thank you."

I hang up with my mother feeling so much better than I did before she called. A smile splays on my face, and I can't stop it from spreading. My mother apologized...*and* she complimented. Talk about a mother's healing touch...

After I take a shower and sip some chamomile tea, I decide I need to take a ride and get something out of my system once and for all. First, I stop at the little chapel down the road. A prayer of thanks is definitely in order.

46.

H AVEN
Even the sun is smiling today. Spreading its joy on glistening shop awnings and snow-covered curbsides. Car windshields echoing the sentiment impel the need for darker sunglasses, so I swap my blue ones for the large black ones Marisela first got me. Despite last night's snowfall, I need to unzip my ski jacket to cool off.

Main Street in Stratford is eager this morning with bustling businesses, coffee-clutching mothers chasing spirited children, and local policeman keeping an eye out for expiring parking meters. If I weren't on a quest to put the past year behind me, I'd let the energy infect me. Alas, I need to overcome my fears, lest I drown in them.

I take my first steps past the bar and grill, black duck boots meeting pavement at an unhurried pace. The only unlit store window on the block, I'm reminded of the streetlight that stands across the street...currently off guard-duty. My footsteps slow to a stop when I reach the alley, and my heart rate picks up. Ground zero in front of me, I steel myself to move forward into the alley. One step, two steps, three steps, four...I place a palm on red brick and come to another standstill, memories flashing before me as I stare at the grungy ground...amidst the aggression, a lone firefly hovers above. I remember it now. My sole witness. A sign of hope on my darkest of nights.

Hand unmoving on the brick, I'm unwilling to submerge totally into the anamnesis. There is no need. Intentions are to face fears, not relive them. Set the event in the past and keep it there. I can't help, though, to picture his face. Those steel-gray eyes behind the mask. The eyes of a friend. One of my best. How had I not noticed? Was I that grateful to have accepting friends that I ignored the clues? Was I that desperate to have someone take my mind off of Quest that I didn't recognize the signs of a killer? *Were* there signs? Besides the two most obvious, displayed front and above center on his face, I can't recall any tell-tale traits that might have suggested I watch out for Devin. He was gently there for everything.

"Haven?"

I drop my hand from the brick wall. I know that voice.

"Are you okay?" His voice is soft, close.

My already swift heart rate picks up its pace, and a soft chill dances up my spine. Doubt prevents me from turning around. All this time, not a word. A sudden chest pang reminds me of the many tears that comforted me during his absence. The many desperate voicemail messages I'd left in the middle of a lonely night. The box of books that broke my heart...proof he wasn't coming back.

"Haven," he says again, his breath warm on my ear. His hand lands on my shoulder and I want to cover it with mine, bring it to my face, and disappear into it. Face him, lean into him, and rest against his chest and never let him let me go.

But I can't.

I step away from Quest, hear his hand thump against his thigh, and turn to face him. "How'd you know I was here?" Not the question I intended to ask.

"I followed you. Saw you getting into your car, called your name, but you didn't hear me."

There's a pause because he's waiting for me to respond. I don't. I'm mad. He abandoned our friendship. I thought I'd meant more to him than that.

"This is where..." He doesn't complete his sentence, he changes it. "Is this your first time back?"

"Why are you here?" I want to say his name. Feel the word on my tongue, hear it said aloud. But I know it will accompany tears, and I can't afford to cry in front of him. Not when it was so easy for him to cut me out of his life.

"I miss you. Too much. You're all I think about, Haven." He stands there, his hands still at his thighs, his shoulders hung low. "And I'm so sorry I never answered your calls."

I don't respond. I'm not sure how. Hug him? Punch him? Curse him?

"I didn't know what to say to you. I didn't know how to tell you I wasn't coming back."

"It's because of my face, isn't it?" The repressed thought appears unexpectedly, and I can't help but divulge it out loud.

"Your face?" He steps forward, lifts his arms, but drops them before his fingers touch my arms. "Not even close. You gotta know me better than that."

"I don't know you at all. The person I thought I knew would never just stop calling. I don't even know if your mother's dead or alive. I thought I meant more to you than that."

"You do, Haven. You mean everything. That's—"

"Everything? I haven't heard from you in three months. The only excuse I can think of is that you no longer wanted to be in my life. So how can I mean everything to you? You don't make sense."

"No. It doesn't make sense. Not really. I thought I was doing you a favor." He makes a fist with one hand and runs the other through his hair. "I'm fucked up, Haven. Not just what happened in Afghanistan." After a long pause, he says, "I killed my father. Not intentionally. Nothing like that." His hands dip into his front pockets. "I was driving the car that killed him. Took the highway he told me not to." He frowns. His eyes tear. "And then my mother..."

"Did she..."

"No, but she's got a long road ahead of her."

"Thank God."

"Thanks," he whispers. "Oh, Haven. I wanted to pick up the phone and call you. So many times. I listened to your voicemails just to hear your voice, but I...I didn't know if my mother was going to live or die, and if she lived, they told me she'd never be able to take care of herself again. They weren't entirely wrong." He reaches for my arm again, but then just as quickly drops it and sticks it back into his pocket. "I thought I needed to stay and take care of her. If I was there in the first place...I don't know, but my heart was here with here. I just couldn't leave my mother, Haven. That's not who I am."

I nod, not expecting anything less from Quest. "I know."

"Vinnie heard your message. The one you left on my mom's phone. He watched me listen to it. That's when he told me that I didn't need to stay. If I'd only talked to him earlier, Hav...I thought the two of us were just too fragile to survive a long-distance relationship. You with your...scars. Me with mine." He pulls a hand from his pocket and holds it up again. "Not your scars in the way you think I mean...I mean, the scars inside. The ones that take forever to heal. We're two really damaged individuals...and I was wrong to think that together we would break." He slips his other hand from his pocket and this time, when he reaches for me, he doesn't think twice. His cold hands are wrapped around mine when he tugs me close and says, "Together, I think we could be at our most whole."

47.

Quest

She doesn't pull out of my grasp. I relax in relief.

"Not one word," she says, her voice cracking, causing her to pause. "You were my friend. Friends don't do that." She lets go my hands and quickly brushes one across her cheek. "Though lately, I'm not sure what friends are capable of anymore."

"I am so sorry. There's nothing I wanted more than to hear your voice, see your face." I bring a hand to her cheek and use my thumb to catch a tear. "I felt unworthy, Haven. You needed someone who could be there for you. You were still dealing with your own self-esteem issues, and with all *mine*? I couldn't be there the way you needed me. And I was in a really bad place. I was embarrassed for you to see me like that."

She covers my hand with hers. "I get it. I'd be a hypocrite if I didn't."

We drop our hands and pull each other in for a hug. The scent of vanilla hits my nose and sends warm chills down my back. "I've missed you so much, Goldilocks," I breathe into her hair, which now falls only to the nape of her neck. "I like your hair."

"I needed to cut out all the blond."

"I'm still calling you Goldilocks," I tell her, closing my eyes and melting into our embrace.

When she sighs into my neck, I ask, "Why are you here, Haven? Why are you torturing yourself?"

I feel her head move slightly and she lets out a long breath before she steps back and slides her hands down my arms. I twist my hands to clasp hers. I don't want her letting go. "I'm not here to torture myself, I'm here to free myself. All this time, you know, it's been lingering..." she lets go my hand to gesture near her shoulders. I take her hand again and she says, "I don't want to hold onto it anymore."

I pull her back into my arms and say, "I don't blame you."

"It was Devin," she whispers into my neck.

"What was Devin?"

She drops her head and buries it against my collarbone. "He did this to me." Her words are muffled, but unmistakable.

Blood rises from my gut, heat burning my chest, as rage washes over me and all I can see is red. Behind her back, my fists clench. I break our embrace and back away. "I'll kill him." My temples pound, my forehead sweats, and I bring my fists to my head before I turn and strike the brick building with the flat of my knuckles.

"Quest" Her panicked voice is thin. Sharp.

The same hand, I punch it again.

"Your hand, Quest, stop there's blood." Her words are rushed.

I hear her, but I can't stop. Again, the brick stands up to my fist and I scream. "Where the fuck is he? I'm gonna kill the mother fucker." One more time I abuse my hand, then look Haven in the eyes. "Where is he, Haven?"

"Jail." She lifts my hand then pulls a sleeve from beneath her jacket and wipes the blood from knuckles. "I think you broke it."

"Don't care. He's in jail? For good?"

She's still dabbing at my hand. "I hope. We should go to the hospital, Quest. This really looks broken."

"Haven." I touch her face with my good hand. "I don't care about my hand."

"Then let me at least clean it up?"

I follow Haven back to the bookstore, all the while trying to calm the hell down. Devin fucking hurt her and has the balls to stick around and embed himself in her life? I could literally kill him...if I ever see him again, God help me.

I park my car in front of the bookstore. It's odd being back. It hasn't been all that long, but it seems like a lifetime ago. From outside, the store looks dark. Empty. I'm reminded of my first day here. Though my grandfather had books displayed in the window, the feeling is the same. This isn't my store. This store isn't my life. But the two people who do belong in that store? They are. I may not have known my grandfather long, but he had more to do with who I am than anyone, aside from my mother. And Haven? With any luck, she'll have everything to do with the man I become.

"Why is the store empty?" I ask her when she gets out of her car.

As she fumbles with her keys, she says, "I'm remodeling it." Instead of walking towards the entrance of the store, Haven stops in front of the door to the apartment upstairs and unlocks it.

"You live here now?"

"I do." She opens the door and I follow her up the stairs.

"Guess that makes sense since you bought the building."

Inside, she tosses her purse and keys in the large basket by the door. "Sit. I'll go get some peroxide and washcloths."

When she disappears from the room, I gather it in. It's cute. The appliances are old and the wallpaper is stained, but the few pieces of furniture she has gives it warmth. "I like your apartment," I tell her when she returns. "It's cozy."

"It's horrendous. But I need to focus on the store right now. The rest'll come later." She sets the peroxide, a washcloth, and white first-aid tape on the table and grabs a bowl from the cabinet. "Give me your hand."

While she mends my bloody knuckles, I ask for answers, trying to keep my blood at a low boil. "When did you find out it was Devin?"

Watching the pain stretch across her face as she prepares to answer infuriates me more. "Stop," she says, talking about the sudden clench of my fist. Gently, she uncurls my fingers. "Last night. He attacked me right out front."

I push my chair back and slam both fists on the edge of her table. "Goddammit. I'm gonna—"

"You can't kill him," she says quietly, placing her hands, along with the bloody washrag, on her lap. "He's in jail, and he confessed. Had no choice actually. Hopefully, he'll get a few years. Now let me work on your hand."

I scooch forward, give her my hand, and search her face for any new slash marks. "Did he hurt you again?"

"No, he didn't." Her dimple deepens when she grins. "Actually, I hurt *him*."

"You did?"

"Using a technique I learned from a movie I'd watched with him. You ever see *Miss Congeniality*?"

"You *sang* him?"

"I did."

Boy, she's cute when she smirks. "But why? I don't get it. I thought he liked you."

"He did. But he didn't want anyone else to."

"Jesus. He's sick."

She wraps the white tape around my hand. "Evidently, he watched his father kill his mother for similar reasons." Her voice cracks and she shivers. "I actually researched his mother's death for a story I was doing."

"Did he know you were researching his mother?"

"No. I didn't even know she was his mother. Deanna Emerson...remember her?"

"You're kidding?"

Haven continues filling me in on the story while she cleans up the table, but I don't want to hear anymore. It's making me mad. I approach her at the sink and take her hand. On the couch I ask, "How did you buy the store, Haven? I thought you were broke."

"I am." She raises a shoulder. "My father gave me a loan. I couldn't let you sell it, Quest. I loved that store. Your grandfather loved it. I was so surprised you were letting it go."

My chest stings. I hear the sorrow in her tone. "I couldn't see another way. I really thought I'd have to take care of my mother forever. She still could use my help, but...Vinnie insists he can do it. With the help of a nurse. I really needed to be here too, though" I rest my bad hand on her bent knee.

"Please forgive me for ignoring your calls. It was honestly because of *my* shortcomings that kept me from calling, not yours. I'm so sorry."

"I'm not gonna lie, it hurt. And I did take it personally. But, after you explained...I can definitely relate. Scars are a fickle thing. You never know when they're going to flare up and infect every damn part of you. I get it. But...I still think you should have trusted me."

I reach over with my good hand and cup the side of her neck. "Oh, baby, it was more about that fact that we both needed to heal. I was wrong though. I should have trusted our friendship."

She smiles and I know it's time to tell her.

I slide my hand down her shoulder, her arm, her hand. "Haven, the fact that I didn't reach out to you has nothing to do with my feelings about you. And I never did tell you, but...I fell in love with you all those months ago. And being away from you has only made me fall harder. I know I don't deserve it, but I don't want to be just your friend. I want to be more. A lot more."

Her soft skin feels like satin beneath my fingers. "Quest..."

"I love you, Goldilocks. With every broken part of me."

She comes at me quick and covers my cheeks with her hands. "I love you too," she says, leaning in and kissing my lips with one short peck. "I always regret breaking our kiss on Thanksgiving. I wish I had just let you. I think about it all the..."

"How 'bout you shut up and kiss me now?"

She shuts up and kisses me. And I don't let her go.

48.

F*OUR MONTHS LATER*
    HAVEN

Today, I will be re-opening the doors to the store that has captivated me since I was a child...and Quest will be by my side. He can do so, because he sets his own hours at the auto body shop he opened two months ago. Using the money from the sale of the bookstore, he turned his grandfather's garage into a pristine shop for restoring vintage vehicles.

It's been a year since Devin attacked me in the alley on Main Street. As devastating as it was to be assaulted like that and learn it was a close friend who'd hurt me, it also led me to this wonderful place I am right now. A place where I can be free to be me. If I hadn't been shaken to my core, and ripped to shreds, I'd still be attempting to reach a goal I never even wanted to achieve. I'd still be succumbing to the expectations that my dear mother put on me, or...dare I say I put on myself because of my perceptions of her expectations? Regardless the reasons, the assault on my face was my reawakening, and in a lot of ways, my coming of age. I am grateful.

I start the day much earlier than I am accustomed, but since I can't sleep anyway, I'm up well before my alarm goes off. Today is my grand opening. Dingman's Corner Book Café will open its doors to the public for the first time at six this morning. My heart is trying to climb its way up and out, because I can feel it pulsating in my throat. Instead of pacing the floors of my apartment, I hasten my morning routine and spend the anxious moments before opening downstairs in the shop. I leave a sleeping Quest in my bed. Considering he was up until after midnight making sure everything in the store was in its place, it's the least I can do.

Inside the store, I lock the door behind me and turn on the lights over the coffee bar. My stomach joins my heart in my throat, because now I feel like I am going to be sick. I prepare a cup of chamomile tea to help assuage the sudden onset of nausea, and I sit behind the bar and sip it as I look around the store. Most of Mr. Vescovi's bookshelves remain intact, as do his original index card quotes. Instead of a wall separating the main section from the foyer in front, I decided to knock through that wall and make it one big shop. We removed the center shelves completely to accommodate a few vintage sofas. And of course, Mr. Vescovi's oversize desk and short stool display prominently in the back center of the reading area, where I sit and compile my inventory on the new computer that Quest bought me. The front of the store houses the tables and chairs and my antique dark-wood coffee bar that matches the dark wood of the desk and original bookshelves.

Behind the bar, the walls are painted with black chalkboard paint so I can handwrite our beverages and snacks, and along the other faux-white-brick wallpapered walls, I hung framed printed quotes from books of every type and genre. Hanging on the wall behind the antique cash register sitting on the corner of the bar is a framed picture of a younger Mr. Vescovi reading to his grandson in this bookstore. It was one of the photos in the box I found. I had to hang it up.

I'm sipping my tea and still scanning the new layout when a gold frame sitting on a bookshelf catches my eye. At first, I wonder if I forgot to hang it up, but as I hop off my stool to examine it, I realize that I didn't buy any gold frames for the store. As I near the shelf, I realize it's a framed quote—one that I did not print. "I went to war, and I met with the devil. I nearly killed him, and got myself discharged. And, because my grandfather died and I had no life, I came to New Jersey, seeking my inheritance. So, I love you because something bigger than the both of us conspired to help me find you." A smile washes over my face as a wave of euphoria surges through me. I take the frame and turn it over in my hands. In Quest's handwriting, my name is scrawled across a small envelope taped to the back of the frame. Carefully, I untape the envelope and place the frame back on the shelf where it was—in front of Paulo Coelho's *The Alchemist*. I open the envelope and retrieve the paper inside. In Quest's penmanship, he writes—*in case the composition looks odd, I replaced Paulo Coelho's prose with my own...to make it authentic. Don't be too impressed.*

"Oh my gosh," I whisper to myself right before my bluetooth speaker starts playing Savage Garden's "I Knew I Loved You." Turning toward the speaker, which is situated behind the bar, I see Quest down on one knee in front of the bar and he's holding open a blue velvet box. Of course my hand flies to my mouth in disbelief. "Oh my god," I breathe into my hand.

"Pretty lady, will you marry me?" he asks, his dimple deepening as his lips form a slightly crooked smile. A smile that melts me every time.

My free hand joins the other as they meet in prayer position in front of my mouth. We've been going together for almost ten months, much of that time spent at one or the other's home, but he and I have never talked of marriage. Not even in the hypothetical sense. So seeing him on his knee in front of me comes as a huge surprise. Yet it's the most natural thing in the world, because *of course I want to marry him*. Of course I want to share the rest of my life with this deeply sensitive and caring man. Maybe something bigger than us conspire to bring us together, because standing here right now, I can't think of anything more perfect than the coupling of us.

"You know, beautiful, I want you to be sure and all, but if you can answer me soon, my knee would be very grateful."

"Oh my gosh, Quest," I say, taking his hand and lifting him up. "Yes. Yes yes, I would love to marry you!" I exclaim, wrapping my arms around him and kissing his ear. "Yes," I murmur again.

Quest returns a kiss to my ear and disconnects our embrace. "Would you like to wear the ring?" he asks, holding out the box that holds a sparkling bright pink stone.

I'm still in awe when I say, "Of course!"

He removes the ring and slips it on my waiting hand. "It was my grandmother's engagement ring. It's a pink ruby," he says with a mixture of pride and reservation. As if I'd prefer a diamond over this exquisite heirloom.

"It's beautiful." My eyes are drawn to the large round gem. "I'm honored that you want me to wear it." Returning my attention to Quest, I ask, "Is this Mr. Vescovi's wife's ring or your mother's mother?"

"Grandma Vescovi's. My grandfather left it for me in an envelope with a letter addressed to me. Sam mailed it to me when we closed on the store. It was totally meant for you, Goldilocks. Even my grandfather knew it."

49.

MY DEAREST GRANDSON Quest RANIERO VESCOVI,

By now, I am sure you are wondering why in the Lord's name I left my favorite book collection to a girl you barely know. I will get to that in a minute.

Hopefully, you aren't reading this letter before the five years are up, because there is so much I want you to learn that I don't think you will if you leave this store behind. My wish for you keeping this store open is threefold.

Number One: I want you to remember me and the time we used to spend together. You and I spent a lot of time here at this store when you were young, and I still draw upon those memories every single day I'm alive. Your mother would drop you off at my house in the morning, and we'd drive to the store together in my Jeep. You used to call it, "Poppy's Jalope," and you'd want me to drive on this rocky path to get to the store so that your bum would fly off the seat. They've since paved that road, but thinking about it now,

I can see it clear as day. And if I close my eyes, sometimes I can hear your little voice pleading, "Go faster, Poppy, go faster." But I digress.

When we were in the store, while I was helping customers, you'd walk through the aisles looking for a book for me to read to you during the slow times. Sometimes you'd vary on which book, but mostly, you'd choose your favorite—*The Nick Adams Stories*. You loved those short stories, and I have to admit, I liked them much better than the *Captain Underpants* books you'd sometimes pick out. Bonding with you at this store is one of my favorite memories to fall back on, Quest. When your father took you away from me, it was one of the saddest times of my life, second only to the day your grandmother passed away. I know your father had his reasons for leaving, but I also had mine for doing what I did to cause him to leave. You see, your grandmother was sick. Very sick. She'd had cancer, and the doctors had her on chemotherapy and radiation for so long that she just wasn't living anymore. So your grandmother and I discussed it, and she asked me not to make her get anymore treatments that the doctor said could possibly cure her. Possibly. There was a ten percent chance, son, and though I'd do anything to keep her alive even for a little while longer, it was her wish to not have to go through that pain and nausea anymore. So, I'd abided by her wishes, and let her live her last days sick-free. Your father didn't agree with me letting her forego all that nasty treatment. He said if there was a chance she could survive another five years, then I should be making her do whatever the hell that was to keep her here. But your Mimi, she wasn't having it. Her thinking was that if she had a ninety percent chance of dying, then she wanted to live those last days sitting on the front porch drinking lemonade with me and you. Your Mimi loved you with all her strong and loving heart. She was weak for a lot of the time you spent with us, but her heart was always strong, and she loved you with every part of it. Fortunately for her, your father didn't take you away until after her funeral. And deep in my heart, I know your father still loved me. He just needed someone to blame, and he wasn't going to blame his sick mother.

Anyway, I want you to remember those early days of your life, and I think being in this store will help jog your memories.

I also want you to know that I never lost sight of what you were doing even though you were in California. Back then, there wasn't the whole World Wide Web thing where I could just type in your name and find out in a flash where you lived and all, but one day, a customer came into the store holding that day's copy of the Santa Monica

Mirror. She'd said her son had brought it home with him from college and she'd recognized my name on the front page. Well, it wasn't my name, son, but yours. "Quest Raniero Vescovi Wins First Place in Santa Monica Middle School Science Fair". Now I knew where you lived. Maybe I should have caught a train out to find you, some days I regret it with all I have, but I didn't, and I'm sorry. But after that, I had my friend Stephen from the deli down the street order me the Santa Monica *Mirror* every week, so that I could see if you showed up in the news again.

Which brings me to Number Two: I saw the article, my dear boy, about your discharge. If I were to come out at any time to see you, THEN should have been the time. But my health was failing, I'd already had several heart attacks, and the doc didn't think it was a good idea. Maybe I shouldn't have listened to him. Maybe I should have figured out how to contact you—the whole big web existed now, hadn't it? But I didn't. I was a coward. I'd heard my son died (something else I'd read in that newspaper of yours), and there was no excuse for me not coming out to you. So I am forever sorry.

I did worry about you coming home. I'm afraid of how you probably lived your life after that. I, what do you young ones call it? Googled? I Googled you after that. I read how brave you were to stand up for that poor girl, and I understand why you almost killed the man who hurt her. I also know there are rules that soldiers have to follow, so I know why you had to be discharged. But, son, your heart was pure and in the right place, so never forget that. You did what you did out of love, and that is the most important thing.

I also know what it's like to have to start over and find your place in the world. I came here with your grandmother and her pregnant belly and we had no money at all. I worked all the odd jobs I could, and when I came home at night, I'd use my new library card and read to settle down from the physical work I did all day. That's how I learned my English, as broken as it is. I love to read. And one day, your grandmother said to me that I should live in a bookstore, not in a factory or working on some rich man's farm. So, with her help selling her very good pies and scrimping every penny, we bought this bookstore, and all of a sudden, I had a place in the world.

I don't know if you remember those Nick Adams stories, but in one of them called Big Two-Hearted River, Nick comes back from war and finds himself in a devastated place. He must learn to live again. I'm not going to get into the whole of the story here, but I think you should read it again, if you haven't already. Because in the end, Nick does find his place in the world, and he is able to put behind him the trauma of the war he'd returned from.

Which brings me to Number Three:

Quest, sometimes, it's a woman who helps us find our place in the world.

Miss Haven, Mia Bella (my little name for her), is a fine woman who frequents my bookstore every time she gets paid.

The first time she came into the store, she was about nine-years-old. You were sitting on my desk listening to me read *Indian Camp* and she waved at you. It was the first time I ever used the phrase, "Did the cat bite your tongue?" It irritated you that I got the expression wrong. "It's cat GOT your tongue, Poppy," you said before hopping off the table and leaving the store in a huff. I knew then that you were smitten.

Anyway, my wish is that, if you keep my store open, you will have no choice but to get to know the adult Mia Bella. And I think you will fall in love with her just like you did when you were ten.

So, Quest, my grandson, if you are reading this letter before giving my store a chance, please re-think it. It deserves a chance, because YOU deserve a chance to be whole again.

And if you're reading this letter after the five years are over, then I hope you've enjoyed your time at the store. I hope you got to know Miss Haven, and I hope you have plans to marry her.

I love you, my boy. I'm sorry I missed getting to know you as an adult, but I hope through this store, you've gotten to know me.

From Heaven above, I'll be looking down on you and smiling.

Love, Poppy

EPILOGUE

QUEST

I take my place upon the stool at the vintage bar in the back corner of the store. Haven bought it off of Craigslist; she thought it'd add charm to the café at minimal cost. It's her grand opening. She calls it a *re*-opening, but considering the store looks completely different, and the fact that it's now a café as well as a bookstore, I deem it an opening. No matter what we call it, I revel in watching my fiancée shine in the place where she belongs.

As expected, her book café is teeming with customers—some here for coffee, some here for books, all here to wish my woman well. Since Layton, as well as the surrounding New Jersey and Pennsylvania towns, isn't the biggest of towns, it didn't take long for the townspeople to find out that Haven was the victim of two vicious attacks, consequently inciting both their sympathy *and* affection toward her. Which resulted in Haven meeting a lot of new people over the last several months. With every nail hammered into the renovation of the store, Haven received encouragement and good wishes from folks who'd stopped in to see her progress. It seemed that Layton was just waiting for someone to give them a nice place to hang out. Judging by the enthusiasm in the house today, Layton and its friends have been granted their wish.

"Oh, Quest, isn't this just fabulous?"

I grin wide and nod my head. "Yes, Mrs. Quinn, it certainly is."

With graceful form, Haven's mother steps up and sits on the stool next to me. "I'm so proud of her," she confides. "She's really made something of herself hasn't she?"

"She really has. It's not everyone who figures out their calling and actually achieves it. I'm proud of her myself," I tell her.

"I know you are," she says, tapping a manicured finger against my cheek. "I see it every time you look at her."

"I do love looking at her," I admit, taking a sip of my double espresso.

"You know, I haven't told her this, but I'm not only proud of her for opening this store, but..." Mrs. Quinn hesitates and looks around to find her daughter in the crowd. She swallows, then says, "I'm proud of her for not following up with more surgeries."

"You are?" I ask, surprised by her admission.

She nods. "I wouldn't have had the courage to *not* get them if I were her. That says a lot for the type of person my daughter is, doesn't it?"

"It certainly does," I say, feeling the swell in my chest.

"Hi, Mrs. Quinn, hey, Quest," Eric says, walking up to us with his on-again girlfriend, Katie and Mr. Quinn in step behind him. "Isn't this great? She's so happy."

We all agree as huge grins wash over our faces.

"Thank God that creep Devin is out of the picture. I knew there was something off with him the first time I introduced him to Kate and he told me, 'No girlfriend of his would be caught dead with a shirt cut as low she was wearing. Not unless she was *looking* for a beating.' Creep."

"And you didn't warn Haven?" I stand, feeling the urge to clench a fist, but mentally talking myself out of it.

"W-well s-she didn't even like him. I didn't think it was relevant."

"Not relevant?" I ask, my ears burning as my blood rises.

Mr. Quinn steps forward, places a hand on my arm. "It's over. He's been put away."

On my thigh, Mrs. Quinn lays her smaller hand.

"Quest, Quest." Haven dashes over, oblivious to the tension, and thrusts her laptop into my hand. "Look what Marisela did." Before even giving me a chance to look, she continues. "I think I have the best website in the world. She's a genius."

Sitting back on my stool, determined to quiet my nerves for her sake, I glance at the screen. Haven's best friend created a kick-ass website for the store. The background of the homepage is an enlarged image of my grandfather's note cards hung on the newly varnished wooden shelves. My grandfather's handwriting lingers in the background as I scroll down the page. Colorful photos of books old and new are interspersed with vintage teacups and coffee mugs, all adorned with quotes from famous books. And centered at the bottom of the page, emerging from a steaming cup of coffee, a Phoenix symbol emblazoned on the front of the white mug, reads a quote from J.K. Rowling about light and dark breathing inside all of us, but the side we decide to act on is what makes us who we are.

My once closed and angry heart has expanded so much in the past year, that seeing Haven fulfill her dreams, an actual extension of my grandfather's own dreams, may actually cause it to explode. I'm content with my little shop and recovering the magic of a classic car, but seeing a renewed Haven thrive while restoring the dream my grandfather worked so hard at achieving brings me to another level of happiness. An elation so strong, that I find myself crying just looking at the sight of her.

"Haven." I pass the laptop to Mrs. Quinn and turn back to my beautiful bride-to-be. "Have I told you lately how beautiful you are?"

She narrows her eyes and says, "What the hell you talking about, Vescovi?"

"I'm talking about you, Quinn. From head to toe, from heart to soul, you are the most beautiful being in the entire world. Thank you for sharing your beauty and goodness with me."

"You're corny, Vescovi. What happened to the angry oaf I met last summer?"

I silently thank God and my grandfather before I say, "You happened, Goldilocks. You happened."

The End